"Linda sets a breathless mystery p... ...vide what all great stories do—new information, connection, and a contribution to life's meaning. With this latest investigation of Teri, P.I., you'll want to read straight to the finish. *Chat Room* speaks to the value of staying connected to the Server that really matters."

—Jane Kirkpatrick, bestselling author of *A Name of Her Own*

"In *Chat Room*, Linda Hall does it again. Mysteries within mysteries and a story about a real love—touching and compelling. You won't put it down."

—Lyn Cote, author of *Summer's End*

"*Chat Room* is a taut, well-crafted thriller, full of the twists and turns relished by any reader of whodunits. But it's much more than that—it's a story about real people, folks you come to know in the pages of Linda's book. Step into the world of *Chat Room*—but beware! You never know for certain whom you're talking to..."

—Thom Lemmons
author of *Jabez: A Novel* and the Daughters of Faith series

"*Chat Room* grabbed me in the first sentence and kept me hooked till the very end. Linda Hall explores the complex symbiosis between predator and victim. Sharp dialogue and a strong sense of place made this book a real pleasure to read. Highly recommended!"

—Randall Ingermanson
Christy Award–winning author of *Oxygen* and *Premonition*

"Once again Hall peels away the layers to expose a deftly written mystery. A glorious read from start to finish, *Chat Room* is detective fiction at its best. A must for fans of the genre."

—Janet Benrey
coauthor of *Little White Lies* and *The Second Mile*

CHAT ROOM

CHAT ROOM

TERI BLAKE—ADDISON, P.I., MYSTERY SERIES
BOOK TWO

LINDA HALL

Multnomah®Publishers *Sisters, Oregon*

CHAT ROOM
published by Multnomah Publishers, Inc.
© 2003 by Linda Hall
International Standard Book Number: 1-59052-200-1

Cover image by Getty Images/Anthony Marsland

Multnomah is a trademark of Multnomah Publishers, Inc.,
and is registered in the U.S. Patent and Trademark Office.
The colophon is a trademark of Multnomah Publishers, Inc.

Printed in the United States of America

For information:
MULTNOMAH PUBLISHERS, INC.
POST OFFICE BOX 1720
SISTERS, OREGON 97759

Library of Congress Cataloging-in-Publication Data

Hall, Linda, 1950–
    Chat room / by Linda Hall.
        p. cm.
    ISBN 1-59052-200-1 (pbk.)
    1. Missing persons--Fiction. 2. Loneliness--Fiction. 3. Friendship--Fiction.
4. Maine--Fiction. 5. Texas--Fiction. I. Title.
    PS3558.A3698C47 2003
    813'.54--dc21
                                                              2003012652

03 04 05 06 07 08 09—10 9 8 7 6 5 4 3 2 1 0

For Rik, always

Acknowledgments

I have two individuals to thank for their valuable assistance in providing information about chat rooms, computer hookups, and the like. The first is Adam Baker of the University of New Brunswick, and the second is my son, Ian Hall, who's been playing around on computers since he was two. Thanks for answering all my frantic e-mail questions.

A special thanks to Rod Morris, my editor, for years of help and encouragement. I have become a better writer because of Rod's masterful editing.

And last, my parents for their continual support and for always loving everything I write, no matter what.

Prologue

An hour earlier and I would have been dead. An hour earlier and I wouldn't have been standing there with my plastic shopping bag from Wal-Mart at my feet where I'd dropped it, the bottle of conditioner rolling across the wooden floor and into the blood. I left it there.

That morning I'd gone to town. I was the only one who ever left. But I wasn't like the others. I even wore jeans. I wasn't really part of the group anyway. It was just my friendship with Coach that allowed me to hang out at the farm in the first place.

Still, Coach frowned on my going. "He won't like it," he told me.

"Do I look like I care?"

"I'm just telling you. I'm the one who gets in trouble when you leave."

I needed shampoo, conditioner, Pop-Tarts, Oreos, whole wheat bread, and peanut butter. So I rode my bike, like I always did, to the end of the road, laid it in some bushes, and then hitched the rest of the way. I'd been late getting back. Which saved me.

After cruising through Wal-Mart, I had caught the bus to where my friend works, and we went to Starbucks and talked and talked. I had a lot on my mind, a lot she needed to know. By the time I was riding my bike down the road toward the farm, the light was fading.

Closer, I knew something was wrong. Too quiet. It's never this quiet. And no lights. I would have expected one of the girls to be on the porch reading out loud, arms in motion, practicing in the half-light. But nothing.

"Hey!" I called. "Coach? Anybody here? Breanne? Jo?" My sneakers crunched on the gravel as I made my way toward the darkened farmhouse.

And that's how I happened to be standing there watching my bottle of Pantene conditioner roll as if it were a living thing toward

Deidre's leg. There was so much blood that it actually flowed, little rivers of it like after it rained.

I picked up my bag, swallowed hard, and backed away. I pedaled crazily down the path, zigzagging, losing my balance and getting up again. I forced myself not to throw up, swallowing, swallowing. I rode all the way into the city, but when I got there, I didn't call the police. I didn't call my friend. I didn't call anyone. I rode my bike up and down unfamiliar streets, not thinking, not breathing. Every once in a while a little sound would escape my mouth that was somewhere between a groan and a cry.

I ended up in a neighborhood of square houses with windows lit like eyes in the night. A house at the end of the street was dark, and I made for it. I pushed my bike up the driveway and around the back where I huddled inside my jacket against a metal garden shed. I shivered and cried and hugged my knees. I was cold, so cold.

I slept fitfully, a night full of dreams and images and the taste and smell of blood. I woke once, my mouth sour, so thirsty, my stomach hurting. I chewed on half an Oreo and went back to sleep.

I came awake fully in the predawn, and by the time most people were up and at work, I was at Georgina's. Georgina runs a sort of rooming house in the city. She's a tough lady, and her rules are worse than any of the foster places I've ever lived in, but she doesn't ask questions. I liked it there. I slept all day that first day.

A few days later I found out what happened. It was all over the news by then. Every channel. Every night. In all the papers. Coach had shot and killed the four of them, and then turned the gun on himself. It was all a part of some sort of religious commune cult group and this was a group suicide.

I got to wondering about the money. I read all the papers, and there was nothing about the money. So on a warm afternoon, I got on my bike and rode all the way out of town and back to the farmhouse.

There were no police cars there, although the house was still strung around with yellow tape. But I wasn't going in there. There was a path out back that led half a mile up the hill to an old well. I hid my bike behind some trees and hiked up. I pulled the moss away, moved the rock, pulled out the brick. And there it was. No one had been here. I pulled out the backpack and unzipped it. It was all there. I zipped it back up, dusted it off, folded the flap over the top, and took it with me.

I rode all the way back to the city. It took an hour each way, and by the time I got back to Georgina's I was so exhausted I fell onto my bed and slept, clutching the backpack like a teddy bear.

So His Highness hadn't found this. That was good and bad. Good because now it was mine, but bad because His Highness was known for his tempers. He would not stop until he found it. Or me. Or both.

I would have to disappear. I'm good at that.

1

"I can sort of understand why the police aren't doing anything," Teri
said to the tall, nervous woman who sat across from her in
Governor's restaurant. They were having lunch, and while Teri
was eating a double burger and a heap of fries and wondering whether
her diet could accommodate a turnover spilling with Maine blue-
berries for dessert, the woman across from her had only succeeded in
moving food around on her plate with her fork.

"I used to be a cop," Teri said, spearing a fry. "With children,
they get right on it, but with adults, well, she might be on vacation
somewhere. She could be anywhere. It wouldn't be top priority."

"But she *isn't* anywhere." The woman raised her fingers, splaying
them out like pointed sticks. "That's what I'm trying to tell you. Her
phone is disconnected and even her e-mails are bouncing. Last week I
called the police but they aren't doing anything. And then I heard
someone at church say you were a private detective, so I decided to
give you a call." She put a thin hand to her throat.

"I'm sorry," Teri said putting her fork down. "I know this is difficult. And I don't mean to come across as hard. But couldn't she just be
away somewhere? With her boyfriend, maybe?"

The noise level in Governor's had risen exponentially with the
arrival of a bunch of kids to an adjacent booth. The woman's "no" was
barely audible. Two little girls were arguing loudly about the fairness
or unfairness of something, while two whined that they didn't ever get
to go to McDonald's.

The woman smoothed her wiry hair away from her forehead and
looked around her. She closed her eyes briefly, then looked down at
her white, veined hands.

Teri knew a little bit about her. Her name was Glynis Pigott and
she was thirty-two, yet today looked older somehow, with her under-
sized silver granny glasses, her narrow shoulders, and her mop of

frizzy brown hair ribboned already with gray. Behind her glasses, her eyes were dark and deep-set, her brows bushy and wild, like her hair. She looked vulnerable, lost inside the cave of her face, somehow, and Teri resisted an impulse to reach across and put an arm on her shoulder and say, "There, there."

Glynis and her missing friend Kim went to the same church that Teri and her husband Jack had started attending. She also knew that Glynis Pigott worked as a receptionist in a law office. There was a blank space in her work history for about a year before she came to work at Smith and Egan eight years ago. Teri was a good PI. She made it her business to know all she could about a client. She had been burned more than once by not researching a potential client well enough.

Across the table from her, the woman was sighing, the bones of her shoulders rising and falling through her pink sweater set, which looked cashmere. You could watch her breathe, the tiny pearl buttons rising and falling.

"I'm sorry," she said. "You must think I'm off my rocker. It's just that everything is bothering me now." Her fingers moved from her throat to her forehead.

"We could move," Teri said. "I could ask the waitress to get us another table."

Glynis waved her hand. "No, we've got our food already. I don't want to be a bother. We're half finished."

Teri looked doubtfully at Glynis's plate. She had eaten so little that all they would have to do was straighten up her food a bit and hand it to the next customer.

As gently as she could, Teri said, "I know what it's like to lose someone. I know what that does to a person. You've told me that your friend..." Teri looked down at her notes, "your best friend went away with Gil Williamson, a man she met on the Internet, but what I would like from you is the whole story, right from the beginning, how she met him plus what you can tell me about him."

Glynis looked up. "Does that mean you'll take the case?"

"Let me hear your story first." Teri wrote something in her notebook with her favorite thick-line mechanical pencil. "Just start at the beginning."

Glynis took a deep breath and began. "Okay. I've told you some already, but, well, Kim and I go a long way back. We've been best friends our whole life." Teri tried to get the high points down in her notebook as Glynis told her story.

The two girls were seven when Kim and her noisy family of brothers and sisters and their eccentric mother and loud father moved into the house directly behind Glynis's.

"All those kids," Glynis's aunt would say, putting her hand to her chest. "All those kids" became a kind of mantra for her aunt who would stand by the kitchen window, one hand on her hip, the other on the edge of the sink, and shake her head.

"Would you look at what all those kids are doing now?" or "I've a good mind to report all those kids to the police."

In time Glynis and her aunt and mother came to understand that most of those kids were foster children that the Shocks took in.

"Did you say Shocks?" Teri asked.

"That's Kim's last name. Shock."

Teri held her pencil in midscribble. The name Shock was familiar, and she wondered over this as Glynis went on.

"Kim and I were like sisters." Glynis was picking at the edges of a cuticle while she talked. "I remember the first time we met. I was out in the backyard and just standing there looking at all those kids..." She smiled. "I'm an only child so I wasn't used to so much noise. And then Kim came over and asked me my name. When I said Glynis, she said, 'That's a nice name.'"

Teri wrote that down in her shorthand, although she wasn't quite sure why.

"Do Kim's parents still live behind you?" Teri asked.

Glynis shook her head. "Glen Shock died. And then Susan, Kim's mother, moved away. Especially after Kim's brother..."

And then Teri remembered. She leaned forward. "Are you talking about Barry Shock? Is he Kim's brother?"

Glynis nodded, took off her glasses, and cleaned them with one of those black antistatic cloths fetched from her purse. "Kim's father died then. Just dropped dead one day. There's been so much tragedy in that family."

A number of years ago. Five? Teri couldn't remember. A young man named Barry Shock was involved in a murder–suicide that made headlines all over the country. Teri chose her words carefully. "Do you think that Kim's disappearance has something to do with what happened to her brother?"

Glynis shook her head. "I don't think so. No."

"Would she have been depressed in any way?"

"Kim? Never."

Teri took another bite of her hamburger and said, "Okay then, go back a bit. Tell me about you and her."

Kim and Glynis both studied law at the University of Maine in Portland, Teri learned, but Glynis "never quite graduated," is how she put it. Her mother was sick, and Glynis was needed at home. Teri knew that Glynis had gone to university for only a little more than a year, and had failed a number of key courses which would allow her to be accepted into law school. Kim, on the other hand, graduated with honors from high school and got a scholarship to university and law school. After law school, she became an associate with the small law firm where Glynis still worked as a receptionist.

"You two were roommates?"

"At college we were. We got an apartment together. Even when she was engaged she lived with me. And just about that time, I had to move back home with my mother and my aunt. My mother was very ill and my aunt needed my help. That's where I live now. After my mother died, I offered Kim a place in my mother's house with me. I've got such a big place now all by myself. But Kim wanted to be closer to work."

"You said when Kim was engaged...she and Gil are engaged?"

Glynis was moving coleslaw around her plate with the side of her fork. "No. She was engaged to someone else for a while. It didn't work out." She played with her fork, twirling it on her plate. Teri had to strain to hear over the noise of the children beside them.

"When was this?"

"A few years ago. Maybe three. It was after her father and her brother died."

"If you can get me her former fiancé's name and address, I'd appreciate it."

"His name is Martin Monday. He lives somewhere on Mount Desert now, I think."

"Have you checked with him?"

"She wouldn't go there. That's not what she would do. Kim has to have all this adventure in her life, and Martin is quiet and stable."

"Still, I'd like that address and phone."

Their waitress poured more coffee for her. When she left Teri asked, "Tell me how she met this Gil Williamson."

"Kim is very fun loving and energetic, but she's been through a lot. With her family, and then with Martin. After Martin, I suggested that we try a few of those dating services on the web. We stuck to the Christian ones, of course."

"Of course."

Glynis was twisting her paper napkin into little corkscrews. "We had fun watching all those videos."

"Videos?"

"Internet dating videos. When you join these Internet dating services, you send in a video. Kim found Gil's video."

"Can I see this video? Did you download it anyplace?"

Glynis shook her head. "I didn't, and a few weeks ago I went looking for it on the web and it was gone." She told Teri the name of the dating website, and Teri wrote it down.

"Kim thought this guy looked nice. I remember she was so excited about finding him. The next thing I know they're e-mailing every day. She met a couple of guys on the Internet, but no one seemed to inspire her as much as Gil. They really seemed to connect, if you know what I mean. I figured all she needed was a new love in her life. I was happy for her."

"And he came to Maine for a visit?" Teri looked at her notes. "Four months ago?"

Plates of food arrived for the crew at the next table, which made the noise level drop suddenly and dramatically.

"Didn't you meet him when he was here?" Glynis asked her. "He came to church, and Kim was introducing him to practically everybody."

"We're still pretty new in church," Teri said. "I don't think we were here then." Teri and her husband Jack were building a log house on a parcel of land thirty miles from the place near the university where they presently lived and where Jack and his first wife had lived all of their married life. Married just a year, Jack and Teri wanted a new start. And that included a new house and a new church.

But getting this house built, getting contractors and subcontractors lined up, was turning into a nightmare. Taking on a case at this point would be a diversion.

"...the nicest guy. He truly was..."

With a start Teri realized that her mind had drifted. She took a long drink of her coffee and said, "Tell me again what Gil was like. Let me get it down."

"He's from Texas." Bits of torn napkin like confetti were all over Glynis's food. "Texas men," Glynis said and shook her head. "Maybe all Texas men are like that, but he was so charming. He was supposed to be in love with Kim, yet I would find him looking at me in this way I can't explain."

"How did he look at you?"

"I don't know. I would look up and I'd find him looking at me. Staring at me."

"Did you tell Kim about this?"

"Of course not. Kim was so happy with him. And, of course, then I thought it must've been me."

"What does Gil do for a living?"

"He's a civil engineer. He's also an ordained minister."

A waitress hovered over them. She took Teri's empty plate, but looked quizzically at Glynis, who folded what was left of her napkin on top of the uneaten food and nodded. Then she asked for a cup of Earl Grey tea. Black. Teri decided to go for it and ordered the blueberry turnover.

"Then what happened?" Teri asked.

"He went back home. And then the first thing you know, Kim's talking about going out there for a visit. About a month after Gil left, he had told Kim about a job opening in a law firm down there which would be quite a step up from Smith and Egan. Kim was interested. But the clincher was that she had to come right away for an interview. It was the cousin of a friend of Gil's who was with the firm. They had a lot of people lined up for the job from all over North America. So, the next thing I know, I'm driving her to the airport," Glynis said.

"She wanted to move there?"

"I don't really know. She kept a lot to herself during the time between when Gil came to Maine and when she left. She didn't talk to me much then. I kept thinking something was wrong. I would go to her and ask her what was wrong, and the only thing she said was that she knew what she was doing and that one day we would have a good talk about it all."

"Do you have any idea what that meant? That she knew what she was doing?"

Glynis shook her head.

"Had Kim ever acted like this before?"

"When Kim's working on a project or defending someone, she becomes really focused. She puts all her energy into everything she does."

"So then she left for Texas and that job interview and you never heard from her again?"

"No."

The waitress set Teri's turnover down in front of her, poured more coffee, and placed a little metal pot of tea in front of Glynis, who waited until the waitress left before she continued.

"About a week after she got there she e-mailed me saying that she and Gil were thinking about getting married. I was so shocked. I thought she was coming home in a week, and then I get this e-mail. I e-mailed back right away and said, 'Are you sure?' and she said, 'I've never been so sure about anything in my life.' I thought maybe she's really in love with the guy. She also said she'd decided to stay down there and not come home at all. She was going to get someone to pack up her apartment and send everything to her. Then a few weeks later, she's e-mailing me asking for my help in planning a wedding. I said, of course, anything she needed. Even though I was so shocked. It was so sudden. We were doing a lot of the planning of the wedding over the Internet. I'm good with fashion, that sort of thing, which is probably why she asked me. She was in this new job, she told me, and it was quite demanding. Then her e-mails began to be fewer and further between. She seemed quite distracted. Once she even wrote asking me for money."

Teri looked up. "She asked you for money?"

"She needed it to pay a bill and her first paycheck was a long time in coming. Sometimes they are. I sent her a check for five hundred dollars."

"Did she ever pay you back?"

Glynis sighed. "No. She's my friend. I would never ask for it back. As far as I'm concerned it's a gift."

"When's the last time you heard from her?"

"August 2. And she went to Texas June 28."

"What happened to the stuff in her apartment?"

"I went to her apartment, and all of her stuff was gone. All of it. The landlady said that Kim had called with instructions to pack everything up and ship it out to her and then send her the bill, and to sell all the furniture. Everything's gone. It's so strange. Someone else lives there now."

"I'll need that address. How about where she works now? You said they went to El Paso?"

Glynis put her hand to her mouth. "I never found that out. Exactly where she works, I mean. I know that sounds stupid because she's my best friend, but she never gave me a name. Just said that it was a big place with lots of lawyers and a very high learning curve, and that she was very busy."

"How about Gil's number?"

"I tried it, but it just rings and rings and rings."

"How about where Gil works, do you have that?"

She shook her head again. "I have no idea where he works at all. Some engineering firm. He builds bridges." She fished in her purse. "I have a picture of them. Would you like it?"

"Of the bridges?"

"No, of Gil and Kim."

"I would, very much."

It was a grainy three-by-five of a tall, good-looking, fair-haired man with his arm around a tall, slender woman. The picture was taken at such a distance that it showed more of the scenery than the two people, and their faces were indistinct. There were palm trees in the picture.

"Who took this?" Teri asked.

"Kim sent it to me. She sent it over the Internet and I printed it."

"Do you have any others?"

"I have lots of Kim."

"Good. I'll need some good, clear face shots. How about Gil?"

"Only this one. I'm not much of a camera person. When he was here I didn't think to take pictures."

"Can I have this?"

"Go ahead. I can print off another if I want one. I keep thinking this has something to do with his work. He travels quite a bit. Once Kim e-mailed me that Gil was gone, and I e-mailed her back, 'So, where is he?' and she said he was off in Barbados building bridges." She looked up at Teri. "I have money, Teri. I inherited all my mother's, plus her house is paid for and there's just me. My father made wise investments, and I have all of that. I could afford whatever you charge. Whatever it is, I could pay it. I just want to know where Kim is."

Teri fished in her leather satchel. "I brought along my standard contract. Take this home, read it, and if you're interested in these terms, I'll be on the job. A couple of things I would like though. Can you print out or e-mail me all of your e-mails to Kim, any she wrote to you, plus any information or e-mails you have from Gil? Plus, if you happen to know any of her numbers, that would be a plus— Social Security, bank accounts, credit cards, plus any contacts in El

Paso you may have heard about, the church they went to, anything. Bundle all these things together with the advance check, and I'll be on the job. And here's my card. The mailing address is new. We're not at that address for a few more weeks, but the e-mail, phone, and fax are the same."

"There's just one thing," Glynis said.

"Yes?"

"If you could find Kim without talking to the people at my work, at Kim's old work, I'd really appreciate it. I don't want them to know I've hired you."

"Why's that?"

She looked away. "It's a personal thing."

Teri said she'd exhaust all other possibilities first, and if she found she needed to talk to Kim's work colleagues, she'd let Glynis know.

2

On Teri's way home she took a small detour. At the public library she waved at the librarian, grabbed the first available computer, and started searching the Internet. Barry Shock. Her pursuit led her to a *Bangor Daily News* five years ago. Bless you, thorough reporter, Teri thought as she scanned through the archives.

It was five years ago and Teri, still a police officer at the time, had been there. It was a brutal crime, the ritualistic torture and eventual murder of four girls who were held hostage at a farmhouse twenty miles west of here by a religious extremist and cult leader. Their bodies were found by a neighboring farmer who investigated after he began to notice a vile odor emanating from the place.

It was dubbed the King James Murders because of the proliferation of King James Bibles throughout the farmhouse. Neighbors told reporters that they often heard loud reading of the Bible each afternoon and evening. In the mornings the young women in long skirts worked in the gardens. Barry Shock, the young cult leader who turned the gun on himself after shooting four girls, was Kim Shock's little brother.

It was determined that he had found his victims, all young women, on the Internet. He frequented chat lines asking names, finding out where they lived, where they went to school. He posed as a basketball coach, a teacher, a YMCA youth worker, a med student, a drama coach, a nice teenage boy, whatever would get him in the door. Shock was only twenty-two when he died, not much older than the girls he had lured away. Barry had been adopted by the Shocks when he was two, and it was determined that he suffered from a kind of posttraumatic stress syndrome common to adopted kids. In very rare cases children who've been adopted out of abusive situations appear normal and loving. But then somewhere along the line, usually in puberty, they snap.

Teri had seen what this snap had done. It wasn't long after that that she quit the force. She was supposed to be tough, but she couldn't shake the nightmares. She had seen the seamier side of life for five years, and it was time for a change. It was time to leave. She went on stress leave, and when it was over, she never went back to police work.

She hadn't thought about that case in a long time, yet as she took her printed copies from the archives, commented on the weather to the librarian, and drove toward their property, the memories flooded back.

Ahead of her, sunshine hit the road in finger-painted smears of gold and red. God had created this color on the highway. He had created the woods, the squirrels, and the red weeds that crunched under their feet as she and Jack walked around their property. But if God was in this beauty, where was He on that rainy day in May five years ago when four girls were enslaved and finally killed in a farmhouse in central Maine. Oddly, it was asking that question that, rather than taking her further away from God, drew her back to Him.

After quitting the police force, she ambled a bit, then got a job searching for people on a PeopleFind website. After that she worked in the English faculty at the university, and finally landed a research job at the university assisting in a genealogy research project, another love of hers. When that job ended, she got her private investigator's license and put an ad in several major newspapers, *Looking for someone? I can help*. She had worked as a people-finding private investigator ever since.

She pulled off the highway and onto the lane that wound down to their property. The electrician was supposed to be here today, and she wanted to ask him to wire the bathroom and kitchen first.

She shouldn't take this case. Really, honestly, she shouldn't. They had just sold their house. She had moved out of her office in downtown Bangor and disconnected her phone lines. In her office she had had an unlisted land line, a separate line for her high speed modem, plus her cell phone. At home they still had their regular home phone number, but could she work from home with just one phone line, her cell, and a dial-up modem connection?

Seeing their log house come into view ahead of her, snug in the trees surrounded by piles of boards and dirt, always filled her with a kind of anticipation she couldn't explain. This would be hers. Hers and Jack's. Theirs.

Six months ago she and Jack had purchased this piece of land from a colleague of Jack's. That was the easy part. Then came the poring over of house plans. It didn't take them long to agree on a cedar log house with two offices and a guest room and a master bedroom loft.

The main structure was up, but the inside work was being delayed. The contractor they had hired all of a sudden got a big government job, and so had put their house on hold. Unfair, but Jack in his kindly, gentlemanly way had said that was okay. Jack didn't know how to be mean to anyone, and that sometimes infuriated Teri. Meanwhile, their house had sold, and the buyers were taking possession in less than a month, which was why she was going to persuade the electrician today to do the bathroom and kitchen first. Worst-case scenario, if they had to live here while it was being finished, they'd have indoor plumbing, hot water, and a place to make coffee.

"You like camping, right?" Jack had said.

"I hate camping."

Maybe taking the case would be a good thing, she thought. Maybe it's good that I don't have to be there while Jack packs up and gets rid of a quarter of a century's worth of memories of his first wife. The house he and Jenny had shared and that Teri had recently moved into was filled with Jenny: cardboard boxes stacked with photo albums, old cards, her journals. There were even boxes of Jenny's clothing in the basement. Childhood sweethearts, Jack and Jenny had married at eighteen. They had two children: Cooper, who was twenty-three and living with an aunt in Pennsylvania and going to school, and Lily, who was twenty-six and living on her own in Boston. Kids that Teri hardly even knew. Six years ago Jenny had died of a virulent and fast growing ovarian cancer. It was sudden and shocking to everyone.

Teri got out of her car. No vans with electrical company logos on the side. The place was empty, everybody off working for the government. And this after the guy promised he would be there today. Without fail. Absolutely. You can count on me.

Teri unlocked the front door and walked inside. Nothing had changed since the weekend when she and Jack had stood on this spot and decided where their new couch would go, where the CD player would be, and how best to install a cat door. She had run her hands over the fragrant log walls and wondered aloud about hanging pictures, about nooks for her houseplants, about drapes and curtains.

Despite the warmth of the sun in the yard, it was cold in here today, and she hugged her arms around her. Most of the interior walls weren't up yet, and sturdy studs marked the places where they would go. Their large front window looked out on a wooded space, spruce and pine trees with a bed of needles for their front yard, and down below, the Penobscot River. Jack wanted to eventually put in grass, but Teri said why? We'll just have to mow it. Kelly, their springer spaniel, would love it here, she thought. Their cats would, too. Gilligan, the grumpy old man of the two, would, she was sure, take up residence in this front window and never leave, while Tiger, the rebellious teenager, would regularly leave offerings of mice and other critters on the front steps.

She turned around and faced the place where the kitchen would be. There were holes in the bare floor, and thick strands of twisted wire stood up like the broken-off hands of a robot. There's where the fridge will go, she thought, the stove over there, the dishwasher there, the sink under the window.

She walked between the studs into what would be the downstairs bathroom with holes in the floor and pipes for the various fixtures. And then back into the front hallway where Sheetrock was stacked four feet high.

She ascended the rickety makeshift steps to the loft. Large, spacious with a generous skylight, she tried to imagine it with the new knotty pine bedroom suite they had ordered, and a hanging plant under the skylight. Nice, she thought, twirling around. This will be nice. Their en suite bathroom hadn't even been started. She could tell that they'd be tromping up and down stairs for quite a while yet.

On her way back to the car, Teri saw Elizabeth, her new neighbor, trot toward her with her dogs at her heels, long gray hair flying. Elizabeth and her husband Irving were their closest neighbors. Their house with its pink vinyl siding was a monstrosity, according to both Teri and Jack, who commented on it every time they drove down their road.

Early on, when the foundation of their log house was being dug, Irving and Elizabeth, carrying a tin pie plate of muffins, had walked over with their two huge dogs.

"Welcome, welcome," the woman had said. "We finally get to meet. I'm Elizabeth. We brought you something."

Elizabeth wore the largest glasses that Teri had ever seen on a human face. Pink, huge and square-framed, they also had the grimiest lenses she had ever seen. It instinctively made Teri want to take off her own and clean them on the bottom of her T-shirt.

"I'm Irving," the man had said, extending a rough hand.

"And these are our children, William and Harry." Elizabeth indicated the dogs.

"They're huge," Teri had said.

"They're Newfoundlands. Gentle as lambs, the most wonderful dogs you'll ever want to meet."

Today, Teri waved and yelled, "Hi!"

"Hello there!" called Elizabeth.

"Has anybody been by here today? Have you seen anyone?"

"Not a soul, dearie. Sorry."

Teri sighed. "There's still so much left to be done."

"It looks like you already have a good house there," Elizabeth said. "Look at us. We've been in our place for forty years and still haven't gotten around to putting siding up on the back. When is it you move in?"

"About a month. And now this electrician hasn't come. He was supposed to be here today."

"You want me to talk to him?"

Teri looked at her with surprise. "Pardon?"

"No, really. If I see him, I'll give him what for, and don't think I won't."

Teri didn't.

When Elizabeth and the dogs left, Teri looked up the number of the electrician and called him on her cell. She didn't trust Jack to have the correct amount of nastiness in his voice. He wasn't there. She left a curt message.

She closed up her cell phone and drove home. The setting sun blinded her vision, its shafts on the road like lines of blood, and she thought about the case again and felt a vague disquiet that she couldn't quite pin down.

3

The first thing Glynis did when she got home was what she did first thing when she got home every day, and that was to turn on the computer and hit the TV remote. While both screens brightened she plugged in the tea kettle. The evening news soon filled the silence. She walked through the dining room and into the little sitting room parlor that was her bedroom. She changed out of her work clothes and put on a pair of flannel valentine pajamas she had bought on-line.

As she was folding and smoothing her work sweater, she examined a spot on the front. She flaked at it with her fingernail, but it looked like it was embedded in the fabric, probably from lunch. That table of little kids must have been throwing food. *All those kids...* Stop it, she said, closing her eyes. You're becoming like your aunt. She folded the sweater carefully and slid it into a clean plastic bag. She'd drop it off at the dry cleaners during lunch tomorrow. Her one treat to herself was fine clothes. She was very tall and buying clothes off the rack was often difficult. She usually had her clothes made or bought them on-line at places that featured tall sizes.

There was a time when she made all her own clothes. It was her mother who had taught her. On good days, her mother would patiently show her how to cut fabric, line up the seams, and how to fit things properly on her tall and slender frame.

She sat down on the edge of her bed. She was tired. She had talked so much today, had said more words to a single person today than she often said in a week—her whole history with Kim, everything about Gil. Things about her aunt. She was so exhausted she felt she could lie back down on her bed and just sleep, but she had at least four hours of e-mail to attend to before that.

The kettle was whistling, and on her way to the kitchen she opened her e-mail program. While she scalded out her teapot with hot water, spooned in loose Earl Grey, and filled it with more hot water, her e-mails messages flowed onto the screen one by one.

The tea steeping on the dining table behind her, she sat down at her computer. She had seventy-eight new messages. There was nothing from Kim, but she noted with delight that there were four from Chasco, three personal ones plus a group one. She also had e-mails from KarenP, Brainbrian, Sewinglady, Lark7, and a few other Internet friends. And of course there were her listservs. She belonged to a lot of listservs: listservs for Christian women, listservs for single Christian women, book discussion groups, on-line Bible studies. Her favorite on-line Bible study was tonight at nine.

She set her computer alarm to alert her at 8:55. Living so far east, most of the chat rooms began quite late. For her health, she tried to be in bed by ten, and usually set her computer alarm to remind her when it was time to go to bed. If she didn't get her sleep, she paid for it the next day.

Her tea satisfactorily steeped, she poured some into a china cup and placed it beside her on the coaster advertising a local computer store. While the evening news showed pictures of an earthquake on the other side of the globe, she organized her messages. She had a system. Before she allowed herself to read even one message, she put them all in order. First she read through and deleted the spam. She always read all of her spam. She was proud of the fact that she had gotten herself quite a few free things: cell phones, CDs, and DVDs. It was a small price to pay for an overloaded In box.

Not that she especially needed free things since she was her parent's sole heir. Her father had been a banker and shrewd with his money— a lot like Glynis, her mother used to tell her. Glynis was three when he died. The only memory she had was of big hands holding hers.

Her spam read through and gotten rid of, she went through her listservs: read each message, responded where appropriate, and then organized them into her mailboxes. Someone on her Christian women's group wanted to know something about on-line Bible studies and what did people think of them, and Glynis was able to respond that she found them quite helpful. On another listserv someone asked prayer for a mother who was dying of cancer; again Glynis was able to respond from personal experience. Someone wanted to know the reference of a specific verse, so Glynis clicked into her on-line Bible concordance and was able to find it for him.

Partway through her single Christian women listserv, and an ancient rerun of *Friends,* Glynis heated herself a frozen chicken cacciatore dinner in the microwave. While that cooked, she toasted a slice of wheat bread and topped it with Cheez Whiz and peanut butter. Supper. She ate while she worked through the messages. *Friends* was over and *Entertainment Tonight* was on. While she watched, she wrote what she hoped was a thoughtful response to a question about what churches can do to better minister to singles.

By quarter after eight she got to her personal e-mails. With enthusiasm she opened the first one from Chasco.

> Dear Gwyneth88,
>
> I'm writing this in the a.m. I know you're at work and you won't get it until you're home, but I'm writing anyway and as I write this, it's with a kind of strange trepidation because I don't know how you'll take it, but I'm realizing that I miss you. And it's at this moment that I find I need someone to pray for me. Someone like you. I know you're such a prayer warrior. I'll write later. I need to spend some time with God.
>
> Love,
> Chasco

She read it twice, her heart racing. He missed her. He *missed* her. They had been friends for maybe six months. Good friends. But was he hinting at more?

In his second e-mail he was back to his cheery, friendly self, asking her what she thought of the latest *Lord of the Rings* movie. She was Gwyneth88 in all her e-mails. Gwyneth was the name of a female heroine in a novel she and Kim had devoured when they were teenagers. Gwyneth was beautiful and wild and romantic with flowing yellow hair. Straight hair. Not like hers. Glynis always wanted to be Gwyneth. It was a much prettier name than the prissy sounding Glynis, like people had a whistle between their teeth when they said it, like the hiss of a snake. And it was such an *old lady* name. Her middle name was no better. Maylene. And let's not even talk about her last name. She and Kim graduated from high school in 1988, hence on-line she was Gwyneth88.

Just before nine, her computer alarm sounded. She drank the last of her tea, cold by now, got out her Bible and clicked her way into the chat room while on the screen beside her an episode of *CSI: Miami* began.

Gwyneth88: Just signing on. Anybody here yet?

Glynis knew that Chasco's real name was Charles Coburn and that he was a youth pastor in Minneapolis. This on-line Bible study was the culmination of a dream for him, he told them, which was to develop a truly on-line church, Chascoministries.com. Beside this Bible study, he had three others. Glynis went to them all, even though one was devoted to teenagers. But Chasco appreciated her joining in. He told her he counted on his older participants to give "wise counsel" to the teens.

Chasco also moderated four listservs. Glynis was a member of three of them. She didn't qualify for the Christian Single Men one or she would have joined that one as well. Because of the time difference she even attended the on-line Sunday morning church. She found that if she slipped out of real church during the singing of the last hymn, she avoided the press of people, which she didn't like anyway, and was home in plenty of time.

By 9:05, everyone was assembled: Sewinglady, MissWinters, Lark7, Phillo, Bub, KarenP, PainterQ, Brainbrian, Crossofheaven, Cassie, Toad30, No666, Evangelistjoe, bloodofthelamb, and of course Chasco. Those were the regulars, and there were always those who joined on occasion. She recognized those names, too; Christianrider, Lightwatch, Marieann204, and Mexicanbob. Glynis opened her Bible to Hebrews 9, tonight's passage.

Crossofheaven: Hey, Gwyneth88, any news on your missing friend?

Gwyneth88: No. Nothing. I've hired a private detective.

Crossofheaven: Hey, way to go!!

Gwyneth88: I hope I did the right thing. It *feels* like the right thing. But I've never hired a detective before. She's a Christian detective and goes to my church.

Glynis could type very fast. Plus she had devised a lot of shortcut keys that she had learned from watching the court reporters.

Brainbrian: We'll keep Kim on the prayer line, then.

Gwyneth88: Thanks.

Chasco: Hey gang let's get to prayer requests after the Bible study. We have a lot to cover tonight.

Christianrider: The leader speaketh.

Following a format Chasco had established, they commented on his study of Hebrews that they were to have downloaded from his website and studied prior to 9:00 P.M. Glynis hadn't really had a chance to look at it. She had downloaded it before work, but during her lunch hour when she would have normally studied it while eating a sandwich at her desk, she was meeting with the detective. While the others commented, she quickly scanned her printout and her Bible. She hated to be so unprepared. She would have to post soon. Chasco had a pretty strict format to the discussions. He had to, he said. On-line chat could get totally out of hand if strict rules weren't followed. You could post, but you couldn't post again until everyone had had a chance to make a comment. In that way, he ensured there would be no lurkers. Lurkers were not welcome in Chasco's Bible studies. That was written right on his website.

She posted, and her comments were received well and she was encouraged. Chasco made everyone feel as if their comments and ideas were special and important. That wasn't the case in a lot of chat rooms, where people regularly flamed each other. She'd been on some of those. But no more. She'd had enough of that!

An hour and a half later, too soon as far as Glynis was concerned, the Bible study was over and it was time for prayer requests. Glynis mentioned her missing friend. Christianrider was still looking for work, and Sewinglady was making quilts with Bible verses on them. She had set up a new website and wanted people to check it out and see if it was a good witness. Crossofheaven was still on probation, but Jesus had so taken over his life and he was praising God all day. He had been in jail for arson, but now, he wrote, the only fires he was going to set were in the hearts of men! Amen, everyone wrote.

Then they prayed on-line. Another one of Chasco's ideas. They went around, just like you did in a group, but in this group they went in alphabetical order. When it came to her turn, it didn't take Glynis long to write a couple of sentences. She specifically asked that Sewinglady's quilt ministry would reach lots of people and that God would give Chasco strength to carry on with all of the ministries and things he was involved in.

It wasn't always this easy for Glynis to pray in a group. She was never one of those people who prayed out loud. In their home Bible study, Kim and the others seemed to have no trouble, but when it came around to Glynis's turn, her hands would shake and her voice refused to formulate coherent words. But with Chasco's patient encouragement, Glynis had been gradually able to pray on-line.

Not two minutes after the Bible study ended, her e-mail icon flashed. Chasco!

Hey Gwyneth88,

I just wanted to reiterate what I know I have said many times before—I really appreciated your helping out. You strike me as such a woman of God. Thanks for your input tonight.

Love,
Chasco

Woman of God! She wrote back immediately.

Dear Chasco,

I think the Bible study went well tonight. I think you are
doing a great job. I really admire your willingness to take on all
these people. They really look up to you. I'm glad that you
are my friend.

Love,
Gwyneth88

They conversed back and forth for a while until Glynis glanced at
her computer clock and realized how late it was. When she signed off,
she realized she hadn't gotten together all of the e-mails the detective
wanted!

With the late night news on the television, she went through her
archived messages and forwarded them to Teri.

Then she turned off her computer and washed up her few dishes,
brushed her teeth, washed her face, and went to bed in the little room
off the dining room. Glynis did not sleep upstairs in the room her
mother had slept in. Nor did she use the room she had occupied as a
child. Instead, she had moved her things into what her aunt called the
parlor. She read a novel from the library for a few minutes until she
drifted off to sleep.

4

Teri was laughing. "Here's a guy wants to live in a tree house on the beach."

"What?" Jack looked up from the plate he was wrapping in newspaper.

"This on-line dating service...they have to write down in their profile a place they'd like to live and here's a guy who says he wants to live in a tree house on the beach. Do they even *have* tree houses on beaches?"

It was Saturday and she was sitting at the kitchen table at her computer while Jack packed. Earlier, Glynis had dropped by Teri's door with a manila envelope.

"You didn't have to come all this way," Teri said.

"I wanted to speed up the process," Glynis said. "Get you going on it quicker. I'm quite worried about Kim. Did you get all the e-mails I forwarded?"

Teri said yes, she had.

Inside the manila envelope were some color pictures of Kim, an envelope with flowers on one corner, and her check. It was one of those art checks, the kind that cost more, totally embossed with flowers, birdbaths and butterflies, and ladies with long dresses and parasols sitting in gardens. At a time when most people were using debit cards and ATMs, Teri found this quite charming. They looked like the kind of checks they would have used in Victorian England.

She had her tape flags and colored pens out and had organized her files and set up her computer database. She had a color-coded system. Notes highlighted or tape-flagged in pink were possible points of interest, blue was for people, and yellow meant vitally important. Something yellow highlighted along with a yellow tape flag meant drop everything else and get to this pronto.

Later, Teri would print out all of Glynis's e-mails and make two photocopies of each. The originals she would lock in her safe. She would keep one copy as a spare, and one would become her working copy. She would head out to Staples later and get that done. But for now she was searching through dating websites for Gil Williamson. Or men that looked like Gil Williamson. It was like looking for a needle in a haystack.

"Didn't Glynis tell you what website he was on?" Jack asked.

"She did. I checked. Gil Williamson is gone."

"Stands to reason if he's found his true love he would take his picture off."

At the other end of the table, Jack was packing boxes and taping them with a tape gun, while on public radio there was a documentary called "The Bard in Time of War." Teri knew this only because she'd asked him earlier what in the world he was subjecting her to and what was wrong with the light rock station she'd had on earlier?

"But this is good. This is important. This is fascinating stuff," he said, squawking the tape gun across a packed box.

"And so, what's a bard?"

"A poet. Of epic proportions," Jack said.

"Oh, you mean like a fat poet?"

He chuckled. "No, not like me, no." Then he'd gone back to packing, but every once in a while his packing was interrupted by Teri's exclamations.

"I should think that would be quite romantic, a tree house." He held up an empty mason jar. "Do we need this?"

She pointed with her pencil to the porch. He took the jar outside, along with an armload of Tupperware lids twisted into gargoyles by the microwave.

They had a small screened-in porch off of the kitchen that had become the repository for garage sale fare and garbage bags. He threw the works into the garage sale boxes.

"No one's going to want those old things," Teri said.

When Jack came back inside he asked, "So, have you found him, or anyone who looks like him?"

She shook her head. "I can tell you one thing, this guy does not live in El Paso. I have called every engineering firm in the entire city. No Gil Williamson. No one knows him, or has ever heard of him."

"He might be on his own, work out of his house or something." Jack was packing cutlery now and it clinked.

"I would think that engineers were like teachers or lawyers. Like there would be some sort of brotherhood or something. Like they would know each other, at least."

"Maybe he's not in El Paso but some town close by." He picked up a slightly discolored glass serving dish with a chip, studied it, and frowned, while on the radio someone was reading poetry in a monotone. "Don't think we need this, do you?"

"Actually, I've never seen that thing in my life."

He took it to the porch.

While Jack unearthed things from backs of cupboards, Teri looked at pictures of Kim. Here was Kim in a cap and gown and standing next to a red flowering plant. Here was another picture of her next to a house. There were group pictures, and Teri recognized some of the people in the church. There were none of Gil. Teri shuffled through them like a deck of cards. Kim was pretty, sweet-looking with short, cheek-length, glossy brown hair. Her chin was small and pointed, her face heart-shaped, her eyes full of energy. In some of her photos she was wearing narrow wireless frames. In others she was without glasses.

"How about some lunch?" Jack asked her.

Teri looked up. "I don't know. Yeah. Lunch would be nice. You cooking in this mess?"

"I was thinking of going to the Market to see what I could scrounge and bring back. I could bring some sandwiches. What would you like?"

"Oh," she leaned back, stretched. "Maybe that ham and cheese one with the sprouts on the dark rye bread." She leaned forward. "I've got a better idea," she said, closing the top of her computer. "Why don't we have lunch there? I was thinking of taking all this work down there anyway, grabbing a coffee and working for a while. I want to read through this stack again. See if I missed something. Do you ever remember meeting this guy when he came to church?"

Jack shook his head. "I think it was before our time."

She put her computer into her leather satchel and slung it over her shoulder, and they ended up walking the half mile up the road to the coffee café known to locals as the Market. Its name, however, had never made any sense to Teri, since all you could buy there was coffee, teas, pastries, and sandwiches between eleven and three.

It was late summer, and already a few tops of trees along the road were turning red, looking as if they had been turned upside down and dipped in red paint. And even though it was only August, you could already feel a tinge of coming winter on the edges of the breeze. She and Jack were both in shorts, but halfway there, she realized she could have happily worn jeans.

The Market was a busy place this morning, as it always was on a Saturday. Almost every one of the little circular tables was filled with Saturday kibitzers. Sections of the *Bangor Daily News* were on tables, folded to various sections. Teri liked the coffee here. The Market featured Green Mountain Coffee, which was, in Teri's estimation, the best coffee in the world, plus a variety of sinful desserts, and of course, lots of healthy things like brown bread sandwiches with sprouts and odd-colored pieces of lettuce. No matter the time of day, one could always find a university student or two, sitting at a table, deep into study. While her own office was a mass of boards and unfinished walls, a little table in the corner by the window had become her temporary office. Teri would miss this place when they moved.

A colleague of Jack's, Harvey Bestletter, smiled heartily and motioned for them to come join them. Teri pulled up a chair while Jack waited in line for sandwiches. Next to Harvey was his wife, the clog-wearing Lydia, and next to Lydia was a young woman who looked to be about Teri's age. Lydia introduced her as Shauna Cole from Vancouver, British Columbia, who was beginning a doctoral degree in Fine Arts. She would be working as a TA in the department. Nice to meet you, Teri said. Nice to meet you, too.

Shauna was draped in some sort of chunky wrap that looked as if it had been made on a loom by a very inexpert weaver. Loose bits of brown yarn poked through oddly in places. Her brown hair was long and tied back, and tiny, narrow dark-framed glasses gave her a studious look. She told Teri that she'd arrived yesterday after a grueling cross-country drive, and wasn't it serendipitous that she came down here and just happened to bump into Harvey and Lydia here at the Market. And now James Addison.

"Are you James Addison's partner?"

"Wife," Teri corrected. "And no one calls him James expect tele-marketers."

"And what do you do at the university?"

"Me? I'm not with the university. I have my own business."

"Business. Ah. A business person."

Teri glanced at her husband, who was counting out change at the counter. "We have a mixed marriage. He's an academic; I'm not."

This little bit of humor elicited a half smile from Shauna. It was obvious Teri was being sized up. New, young wife of Dr. James Addison, senior English professor. The English professor poet wid-ower who had written a whole book of poetry for his first wife after her death, a book that was well-known, not only in literary circles but in grief counseling circles. And he picked *her?* Teri knew exactly what Shauna was thinking. She would have been thinking the same thing had she been in Shauna's shoes.

"So, what do you think of our little town?" Teri asked.

"It's nice." Shauna wrapped her shawl around her. "Small, but nice. I'm used to the city. This will be quite a change. But I love the quaintness of it. The simpleness. Everything in one place."

"Hmm," Teri said.

Jack was back with the sandwiches. Hers was ham and cheese and sprouts on rye. His looked like tuna on whole wheat. The five of them chatted about the university, the city, the fading summer, and fall plans for the English department. Harvey and Lydia wanted to know how the house was coming along, and Teri and Jack groaned in unison.

Half an hour later everyone left, including Jack, who kissed her briefly and said he'd head over to the university with the Bestletters and Shauna. Teri watched the four of them leave, watched Shauna, the way she looked up at Jack.

When they left, she got herself another large Mexican coffee and took it back to her favorite table beside the window, which had been recently vacated by a boy with a Green Day T-shirt and a girl with a headful of yellow beaded braids. She organized the e-mails by date, and then began a thorough reading, one by one, the earliest ones first.

Glynis's e-mails were long, meandering things that printed off to several pages. Typically, Kim's were short, and actually got shorter as her disappearance neared. Kim never wrote more than one e-mail a day while Glynis wrote two, three, sometimes five per day on the weekends. As well, Teri noted, there were very few e-mails that gave any indication at all of where Kim actually lived. Teri read this one dated May 31 and sent at 3:21 A.M. and tape-flagged it in yellow.

> Hello! We went across the river into Juárez, Mexico yesterday. Gil is such a ham, trying to speak Spanish when he hasn't got a clue. LOL. Had a great time. I'll write more about the trip later. Love, Kim

But she hadn't written more later. Not that day, anyway. Even with her limited geography, Teri knew that Juárez was across the Rio Grande from El Paso. So, they *were* in El Paso. Or at least according to the e-mail they were in El Paso. Kim was using a Hotmail e-mail account, so no help there. Maybe she had disappeared, or maybe it was merely a case of trying to get away from Glynis, who wrote e-mails like,

> Where ARE you, Kim??? I'm beginning to worry. Church is just not the same without you. I also haven't been back to the Bible study. Where ARE you?? Just answer me so I know everything's okay.

Sometimes Teri wondered why she was in this business when half the people she found really didn't want to be found in the first place. On more than one occasion, she had received sarcastic letters from the found people saying thanks a lot. Thanks a WHOLE lot. But it was the other kind, the birth parents, birth children, long lost lovers, the ones that were truly happy at finding who they were looking for that made it all worthwhile.

Kim's early e-mails were short ones, describing her plane ride, describing the scenery.

> I'm writing this from Gil's computer, and I don't have much time. We're going to dinner tonight and to the movies. Tomorrow's the job interview. Pray for me!

And then:

> Had the interview today. It went well! I'll tell you all about everything when I see you next. There's a lot to tell, and since I'm dependent on Gil's computer time, I don't want to wear out my welcome.

And then just a few more, giving flight numbers and times and thanking Glynis for offering to pick her up. And then, the day before she was to fly home:

> Hi Glynis,
>
> Well, you'll never guess what! My plans have changed. I've decided to stay after all!! Gil and I had a long talk and we're even talking about getting married!! I'm so excited. So, don't come to the airport! I won't be there! I've decided to take the job after all. I'll write more later.

Here was a woman who loved her exclamation points, thought Teri, leafing through the rest of them. From here on in, they were filled with wedding plans and asking Glynis's advice and help. Glynis's return e-mails included links to wedding planner websites and pictures of dresses. Two young women planning an upcoming wedding. Nothing so out of the ordinary there. And then abruptly Kim had stopped writing.

An hour and a half later Teri was satisfied with her work so far. Later, when she got home, she could get on the Internet and begin what she called her Extreme Search, where she found everything about

Kim and Gil that could be found from all sources. Teri knew how to get into these data banks on the web. She belonged to a number of PI sites where you could pay for this information—she, in fact, used to work for such a company—but she always tried the free ones first.

She got out her cell phone and called Ken, the pastor of the church she and Jack were now attending and where Kim and Glynis attended. His wife told her that he was out mowing the lawn.

"Maybe you can help me, then. I'm trying to locate Kim Shock."

"Kim? She's moved to Texas. I received an e-mail some time ago that she'd decided to stay."

"Would you happen to have that e-mail?"

"I might. Why?"

"I've been hired to look into her disappearance."

There was silence. "She disappeared?"

"Yes."

"And you're looking for her?"

"I'm a private investigator. I was hired to try to locate her."

"You're a private investigator?"

"Yes. Could I come and talk to you and your husband about Kim and Gil?"

"Certainly. Come now. This is awful. I never realized."

5

Ken and Cheryl lived in a white bungalow, the front lawn newly mown and smelling green. Ken, in faded chinos with grass-stained knees, was wiping his forehead with an American flag bandanna. Cheryl wore green gardening clogs, and there were dirt smudges on one cheek. She handed Teri a couple printouts of e-mails and invited her around to the back where they could sit and talk. On a back deck, they sat in shiny red slatted wooden chairs.

Teri glanced down at Kim's last e-mail to them, which was exactly two lines long.

> Hi Ken and Cheryl,
>
> I've decided to stay here in El Paso. I've got a great job. Gil and I are getting married. We'll let you know times and places. I'll write more later.
>
> Love, Kim

Teri looked up. "This is it?"

"That is it, yes," Ken said.

"Were you surprised by this?"

"Very much so," Cheryl said. "I didn't think she'd jump into anything so quickly. Kim was always impulsive, but also levelheaded."

"Do you have any kind of a phone number or address for her there?" Teri asked.

Cheryl shook her head, and Ken put his hands on his dirty knees and leaned forward. "Are the police involved?"

"Not yet."

He frowned and thin lines appeared on his forehead.

Teri asked, "What kind of a person was Gil?"

Ken pressed the points of his fingers together. There were

smudges of grass on his thumbs. "I actually had a good talk with him. He was an engineer and a minister."

"Nothing concerned you?" Teri asked. "No red flags?"

"No."

"I disagree." Cheryl sat up suddenly, her palms on her knees. "There was something about him, I don't know. Just something that, ah, rubbed me the wrong way. He had one of these, I don't know, these overpowering personalities. Mr. Personality."

Ken looked up. "You never said anything at the time, Cheryl. I didn't know you felt like that."

She combed her fingers through her short hair. "I don't like to make a habit of going around talking about people, Ken. I didn't think it was my place to be criticizing him, especially when Kim seemed so set on him. If I had any idea that this would've happened, I would've said something at the time. When she sent that e-mail, I e-mailed right back asking if she was sure she wanted to stay, and would she come home to Maine just to give it some thought. She never answered me back. Has not answered me to this day. I figured I stepped on some toes. I decided to let it rest."

Teri asked, "Did you know Kim's first fiancé, Martin Monday?"

"Fairly well," Cheryl said. "He was a great fellow. I had none of the reservations about him that I had about Gil. The last I heard, he was working in Bar Harbor. Construction work."

"Do you have an address for him?"

"Sorry, no."

"How about pictures of Kim or Gil?"

Cheryl shook her head. "That was another thing. He hated getting his picture taken. He told us all he wasn't very photogenic, when in actual fact he was a very good-looking man." She hugged her arms around her as a sudden cool breeze wafted through the backyard. "What could've happened to her? Do you have any ideas?" Her eyes looked fearful.

"That's what I'm going to try to find out," Teri said.

"We had lunch, the two of us, before she left." Cheryl sighed. "I advised her to give it some thought, and she said she knew what she was doing, and basically to mind my own business."

"She said that?" Ken asked.

"Not in so many words, but I did get that impression. I apologized to her before she left, and we had a good hug and a cry. Her last words to me were, 'Don't worry about me. I'm doing the right thing. You'll see I'm doing the right thing.' And then that e-mail. That's why I've kept this to myself."

Teri wrote down the names and phone numbers of Kim's friends from a dog-eared church directory, the kind with pictures. "Can I borrow this?" she asked.

"You don't have one?"

"My husband and I haven't been coming long."

"I know. And we've been meaning to have you two in for a meal."

"We'd like that."

"How about Sunday dinner, say, a week from tomorrow?" Cheryl said.

"Well, okay, sure, fine," Teri said while Ken went inside. He presented her with a brand-new uncreased directory. "We had these done a while ago. Some of the pictures might be out of date, but you're welcome to it."

"Thank you." She flipped through it, and with the help of Cheryl placed an asterisk beside Kim's friends: Mike, Ashley, Marcie, Glynis, Marguerite, Michelle, Sandy, who was a guy, and others. Teri recognized the portrait of Kim, the one Glynis had of her, the pixielike smile, the narrow nose. Cute. That's how you'd describe Kim, cute. She turned to the *P*s and looked down into the face of Glynis. It was obvious that she had tried to smooth down her hair for the picture, but one side was springing up oddly. She would be very pretty were it not for her hair, Teri thought.

"I haven't seen her in a while," Cheryl said, seeing Teri's glance. "And she's hard to miss. She's over six feet tall. Have you seen Glynis lately, Ken?"

"She sits in the back and leaves during the last hymn. By the time I've made it to the back, she's out the door."

"I didn't know that, Ken. You should've told me. I thought maybe she was going to a different church now. With Kim gone and her aunt gone. And I didn't want to interfere if she'd made a decision to go elsewhere. There are so many times that I feel like I'm interfering that sometimes I just try not to."

"No, she's still here as far as I know."

"We should have her over for a meal, too," Cheryl mused, "find out if anything's wrong."

Teri said, "Did you know Kim's parents..." Teri consulted her notes. "Glen and Susan Shock?"

"They never came to church. Well, Christmas and Easter maybe, but that's all. We weren't here then, but I think Kim started coming to church with the Pigotts."

"This church was almost entirely built on Pigott money," Ken said. "That's what we were told."

"Pigott money?"

"Glynis's grandfather had money. He was in the railroad business. His son was Glynis's father. He died when Glynis was quite young."

Teri shifted in her chair. "Do you remember the King James Murders?"

Ken nodded. "Kim's brother. It happened a number of years ago, before we came. But we certainly heard about it."

Cheryl said, "The people here were still reeling from it when we arrived. Kim's father died shortly after their son died. It's so sad, which is why I try very hard not to step on Kim's toes. She's been through a lot, that girl."

Teri also asked if they knew the name of Gil's engineering firm in Texas, Kim's law firm, Kim's mother's address or phone, an El Paso street address, or the name of the church where they were attending in Texas. They came up empty on all accounts. She left her card with Ken and Cheryl, asking them to call her if they thought of anything else.

At home Teri changed into her sweats and running shoes and took Kelly for a long run down by the river. Later she called Kim's friends. All said they missed her. All said they still attended the Bible study that had meant so much to Kim. All said they were surprised, but not really, by Kim's decision to stay. Poor girl's been through so much, they said. If she's found true love, well, good for her. No one had a Texas phone number for either her or Gil, and no one knew the name of the company she worked for.

They all knew Glynis, too, but no one had seen her recently. Most assumed she was now worshiping elsewhere. People do that, you know, they told her, switch churches at the drop of a hat. It can get hard to keep track.

Mike Wordman added that it was difficult befriending some people because they demand so much.

"Glynis demands so much?" Teri asked.

"Glynis is, sort of, I don't know, maybe I shouldn't say this, but she's sort of the clingy type."

Ashley called Glynis needy and high maintenance. Michelle said that she had cut ties with Glynis, because she was working on some self-discovery issues and was cleansing herself of toxic relationships.

After Teri got off the phone, she sat on the couch and stroked Tiger's ears until Jack got home. Of Kim's friends, no one particularly thought it strange that she had decided to stay. And no one seemed particularly worried.

No one except Glynis.

6

It was cool in the backyard where Teri sat at the picnic table. She had come outside and set her files on the table, looking through the e-mails Cheryl had given her. It was early evening, warm and still light. Besides, it was too depressing inside with all the boxes and assorted clutter.

Jack was at the university leading a special poetry session for his grad students. During the year this group met monthly in their living room, but during this time of upheaval and lack of furniture, he reserved the student lounge at the university. Probably, even now, Peter would be bonging on his congas, which he took with him everywhere, and Stephan would be setting out copies of his chapbook *submerged,* poetry he'd written while scuba diving.

No doubt Shauna would be there with her skinny, dark-rimmed glasses down on the end of her nose, wrapped in her nubby shawl and commenting on the utter *smallness* of the place. Altogether about a dozen showed up for the monthly poetry sessions. Teri didn't usually attend, but joined them afterwards for refreshments, which ranged from drippy, high cholesterol cake to skinny slices of organically grown fruits. The students took turns with the food. She'd miss them this evening.

Another group she was missing this evening was their weekly Bible study group, which normally met on this night, but had been canceled for the summer. If it started up at all again in the fall, it wouldn't be until late September, early October. People were so busy this year. Witt, another of Jack's colleagues who came with his wife, Mavis, would be teaching a course in Victorian literature that evening, plus Mavis was taking a postgraduate night course. They both feared too many nights out. Andrea and Ben Silver's daughter was in ballet and it was several nights a week. It was getting more and more difficult to find a night suitable for all. Because the Bible study incorporated members from several churches, it had been a place Teri felt safe, not like in Jack's old church where everyone still missed Jenny and Teri was nothing more than "Jack's second wife."

Teri would also miss Andrea, who was becoming a good friend. The two of them met several times a month for coffee and to talk. "Even if Ben and I have to bow out of the study for a while, that's no reason that you and I shouldn't get together," Andrea had said. But she knew it wouldn't be the same.

Andrea was a seamstress who designed and made clothes. "If I had tons of money," Teri told Jack once, "I'd get Andrea to make all my clothes."

This having a close female friend was new to Teri. When her mother died, Teri began shutting herself away from people, until years later it had become a habit. Her cop friends were just that: cop friends, drinking buddies, and party pals. Jack was the first true friend since her mother died, and Andrea was fast becoming her second.

She wondered about Kim's so-called friends. Teri hadn't seen Glynis in church yesterday. The sanctuary had been filled with smiling people, and many that Cheryl had pointed out as Kim's friends were there, including Marcie and her husband and daughter. But toxic, needy Glynis wasn't there. There were people in Teri's old life who would have described her as toxic. She was sure of that.

She turned to the e-mails Cheryl had given her. It looked like she had received only one before the e-mail indicating that she was staying.

Dear Ken and Cheryl,

Just to let you know I arrived safely. The job interview is day after tomorrow. I'm staying in a lovely old hotel, and Gil and I are having a great time! I'll let you know what happens.

Kim

The next e-mail, the one Teri had read earlier, came ten days later:

Hi Ken and Cheryl,

I've decided to stay here in El Paso. I've got a great job. Gil
and I are getting married. We'll let you know times and
places. I'll write more later.

Love, Kim

It was the lack of specifics that Teri noticed in all of the e-mails
Kim had sent to everyone. No mention of exactly where it was that
she was working. No mention of the name of the church. Wouldn't it
be normal, especially when writing to your pastor, to at least mention
the name of the church you're attending? And what was with all the
exclamation points?

7

Teri was meeting with Marcie this morning. While she waited for her to arrive, she sat in a corner in Wellingtons with a large mug of coffee. She and Jack had discovered this place a few months previous after a morning spent arguing over house plans. Teri wanted the fireplace against the back, and Jack was settled on the east wall. The casual atmosphere of Wellingtons allowed them two hours of uninterrupted time when Jack could draw his house diagrams on backs of napkins, presenting her with arguments based on the location of windows and where the cats would eventually take up residence. Teri presented an equally strong case for the fireplace on the north wall, based on the placement of her houseplants and the available light. Though both of them had made a resolution to cut back, between the two of them they consumed two blueberry muffins, a couple of plate-sized blueberry cookies, and a blueberry fritter that Jack cut in half and Teri argued that he got the bigger section. It was blueberry season in Maine when they'd discovered this place.

The food at Wellingtons was mostly of the cholesterol-laden type: oozing cheese Danishes, blueberry fritters that were more blueberry than fritter, and all manner of oversized cookies with humongous chocolate chips and immense nuts. The coffee was the good Green Mountain variety, which was served along with a variety of teas and a refrigerator full of cold drinks.

Wellingtons seemed to be the watering hole for all of Coffins Reach. It reminded her of the Market, but while the Market catered to a very upscale university clientele, Wellingtons was for the locals: fishermen, lobstermen. At any given time of day, you could find two or three people sitting around opinionating about the state of the country, the state of fishing, the state of lobstering, the state of their neighbor and their neighbor's wife. And whereas in the Market you could buy healthy sandwiches with whole grain breads stuffed with organic sprouts, in Wellingtons, the three basic food groups were sugar, fat, and caffeine.

At the table next to her, three men were talking about some poor fellow who'd broken his arm at sea and how they made a splint for him out of an old broom handle and duct tape and how he stayed out for another three weeks tuna fishing. The consummate eavesdropper, Teri sipped her coffee and listened.

In a little while a big woman in a loose gray T-shirt came in carrying a little plate with an oatcake and a white mug with a tea bag string hanging over the edge. Teri's grandmother would have described Marcie as a "big, handsome girl." She sat down across the table with an exaggerated sigh.

"I checked my e-mail before I came over here," Marcie said, leaning her forearm on the table and dunking her bag up and down in her mug. "I hadn't realized it had been so long since Kim left."

"Did it concern you at all when Kim decided to stay?"

Marcie shrugged. "Kim knows what she wants and has never been afraid to go for it."

"And what she wanted was to stay with Gil?"

"I assume so. I guess she loved him."

"You guess?"

Marcie shrugged.

"When's the last time you heard from her?" Teri asked.

"I got that e-mail that she was staying, when, maybe two months ago now? That was the last time I heard from her. You have to understand Kim. It wasn't unusual for her to go that length of time without communicating with anybody."

"Really? Not even her closest friends?"

Marcie shrugged, her heavy shoulders rising and falling, the exaggerated sigh.

"What about Gil? What was your opinion of Gil?"

"You mean, was Gil the kind of person Kim would run off to Texas with? In a word, yes. Here's what I think," and Marcie leaned forward and spoke more softly, more conspiratorially. "Running off with a guy, well, it's just not something a nice Christian girl does. But when I heard she'd decided to stay, I didn't say it out loud, of course, but a part of me said, 'You go, girl! Good for you!'"

"Why would you feel like that?"

"You see, a lot of so-called Christians wouldn't approve of, you know, running off with a guy like that. That's why she's kept it so hush-hush. I'm willing to bet that Kim and Gil will come back here, married and all respectable."

She was engaged before, Marcie told her between gulps of tea and pieces of oatcake. It didn't work. It was a disaster. Marcie wasn't the least surprised that Kim would want to "try on" marriage before the real thing again, and that sort of thing didn't bother Marcie in the least. Kim was a big girl. Kim could make her own decisions.

"So, basically, you weren't worried about her?"

"Not at all. When Kim wants to reconnect, we're all here. Kim seems strong, but she's had a sad life. I brought some pictures." Marcie handed a few snapshots to Teri and then bit into her oatcake, sending a shower of crumbles down the front of her T-shirt. She flicked away the crumbs and said, "I have more if you need them."

Teri flipped through them. Here were Kim and Marcie in a Mexican restaurant, sombreros together, huge smiles. Here was one of Kim with a beach towel wrapped around her, one hand on her hat to keep it from blowing away. There was another of Kim standing alone in front of the church, another of Kim at a barbecue with a group of women. What with Glynis's pictures, she was getting quite a collection of photos.

"None of Gil?"

Marcie was the only person Teri had ever met who ate while she talked. She literally chewed and formed words in her mouth at the same time. "Gil? He hated getting his picture taken. It was a thing with him. I mean the guy's a total hunk and he doesn't want to get his picture taken? Give me a break. Guy like that should be all over the camera."

Teri raised her eyebrows. "So, I take it your opinion of Gil was not all that great."

"Mike Wordman tried to take his picture. Gil took his camera, threw it on the ground, and stomped on it. I kid you not. I mean, when it happened, we're all like, huh? What's going on? And then he's apologizing and apologizing. He replaced the camera, of course. I think he even got Mike a way better one in the end. I mean here's this guy who brings flowers to Bible study, and he's smashing a camera on the ground!"

"Flowers to Bible study?"

"Yeah, he brought flowers to Bible study. Gave them to the hostess of the night, I think Marguerite."

Teri wrote that down.

"He was very charming," Marcie said. "Or he could be when he wasn't smashing cameras."

"How was he charming?"

"He was like this total charming person. Like holding the door for her charming. Like flowers charming."

"Did you know Martin Monday?" Teri asked.

"That was the biggest mistake of Kim's life."

"So, in your opinion, he was another loser?"

"No. Not at all. That's not what I meant! Her biggest mistake was in letting him go! It was Matt and me who introduced them. Matt, that's my husband, worked with Marty. Hey," she said suddenly, "you know, I just might have a picture of Gil after all."

"Really?"

"We were at this last party before Gil left, and Matt was videotaping everybody? I think he might've gotten a few of Gil unawares. I was like, 'Matt, give me that camera! You want Gil to smash it?' and then Matt says to me, 'That's what I'm hoping for. I got my eye on a brand-new digital movie camera.' I could check for you."

"Thanks."

Marcie also promised to give Teri Marty's number and address. She was sure she had this at home. She'd just have to check.

8

G lynis mailed the envelope on her way back to work after lunch. Normally she ate lunch at her desk and prepared for whatever Bible study she would be a part of that evening, but today she had an important letter to mail. She didn't want to merely drop it in the box next to the office, but wanted to drive to the main post office in Bangor and send it Express Mail. It needed to get there. Chasco's ministry depended on it. He counted on people like her, people who could afford to help out with the good work he did with the youth. It didn't bother her in the least that he didn't have charitable donation status. That was something he was working on. He had told her in a private e-mail, though, that it was the fault of the liberal bureaucrats who didn't see the good work he was doing as important enough. He was getting fed up. By return e-mail she told him not to worry, she would still send money to his on-line church. She considered it her tithe now, and that it was a *true* gift, she wrote to him, because she didn't expect anything in return, not even a tax receipt.

She was giving half to her real church and half to Chasco's church. But lately she'd been toying with the idea of sending it all to Chasco's church. KarenP and Sewinglady thought it was a good idea, especially if she wasn't altogether happy in her regular church. Which she wasn't. Lark7 was a little more cautious and told her that she needed to examine a full financial statement of the organization. She asked Chasco for one and he sent her one. She got the names and e-mails of a few of the board members, and when she queried them, she got immediate replies. One even hinted that they were looking for board members on the east coast, particularly New England, and would she consider it at some later date? She wrote that she didn't feel qualified for that. When she was told that Chasco had the utmost respect for her, she replied, "maybe."

Gradually, by degrees, she was leaving her real church. The funny thing was, no one had called her to say they missed her. Not Marcie, not Michelle, not even Mike Wordman, who was always friendly to everyone. The pastor's wife, Cheryl, hadn't even called.

They hadn't called her, and yet her on-line friends couldn't get enough of her. If she missed a day with KarenP or Sewinglady, she heard about it. Where are you, Gwyneth88? I miss our talks. I rely on you. And Chasco never failed to tell her how much he appreciated her.

In line at the post office, she shifted from foot to foot. If she didn't hurry, she wouldn't make it back to work on time. She waited and waited while the man in front of her asked about commemorative stamps. The postal clerk was nodding, while more and more people lined up.

Maybe Chasco was right. Maybe she needed to find an easier way to send him money. Lately Chasco had been haranguing against the post office. One night God woke him with a vision of Satan himself sitting atop the post office, and now he didn't trust the mails. He had suggested in his last e-mail that in order to save time and avoid a "wasteful government devil-run post office" that she give him her bank account number, and he could just take the money out as per her instructions. But Glynis was reluctant to do that. You never know who's hacking in on e-mails, she wrote to him. You really don't know how safe they are. What if I gave you my account number and some-one read it and it ended up in the wrong hands?

Smart girl, he wrote. I never would have thought of that. But then I've always been too trusting. That's why I've been taken advantage of so many times (which is why I need someone with your kind of practical business sense on the board.) Okay, a check is fine. God bless!

Every week or so, Glynis sent a personal check. On the way back to her car, she breathed a prayer that the money would get there quickly and that Chasco would use it for the furtherance of God's kingdom.

There was a strict rule at her work: no personal e-mails. Ever. It was a rule Glynis mostly abided by, but this afternoon no one was back from lunch yet, so she logged on to her Yahoo! account and sent

Chasco a quick e-mail that she'd just sent him a check for $700 by Express Mail. Then she went into the lunchroom and got a pot of coffee going. It was still expected that Glynis make the coffee. Kim used to rail at that when she was here.

"Glynis, you shouldn't have to make coffee. You shouldn't let John Egan push you around like that."

"It's okay. I don't mind."

And Kim would give her that raised eyebrows look, the look she'd given her ever since they were girls.

Glynis worked for a group of four lawyers. John Egan and Barton Smith were the senior partners. She was always a little afraid of those two crusty old men who demanded so much of her, yet never seemed really to see her. She once told her on-line friend KarenP that she could work all day naked and she doubted those two would even raise their eyes. They would just come over to her desk with letters to type.

Tom Rose had been hired along with Kim, and he was okay, if a bit loudmouthed, plus his womanizing ways were well-known. Glynis kept her distance, even though he had never come on to her at all and was nothing but a gentleman around her. Most men were put off by her height.

Clara Winkel, Kim's replacement, wanted to know Glynis's qualifications and seemed surprised that Glynis wasn't a certified paralegal. Whenever she could, she would urge Glynis to take further training, leaving pamphlets on her desk, talking to her, urging her to attend this conference or that. But when it came right down to the crunch, John Egan never came up with the money for her to go to any professional development conferences. If Glynis wanted to pay for it herself, well, that was another thing entirely. They'd give her the time off, no problem. Clara, like Kim before her, just shook her head and said that wasn't the way you did things.

John Egan returned from lunch, nodded curtly to her, went into the lunchroom and poured himself a coffee, came out, told her it was too weak as usual, and then went into his office and closed the door. Even after all these years she didn't know how to make coffee. John Egan and Barton were the only two who drank lunchroom coffee anyway. Tom and Clara brought in their own designer coffees in paper cups with brown sleeves.

With John Egan safely in his office, Glynis logged back on to her e-mail.

There was a new one from Chasco with the subject line: URGENT PRAYER REQUEST. She looked over her shoulder and around her. John Egan was still on the phone behind the heavy closed door. Tom and Barton were in court, and Clara was at lunch with a client. She clicked on it and opened it.

> I have a real emergency here and I hope you're able to get this at work. First of all, thanks for letting me know about the check. That will benefit the ministry in ways you can only imagine. I thank God for you, Gwyneth88. But now I have a rather urgent matter of prayer. It concerns Melissa, a young teenager, a member of my youth group. Maybe you've heard me mention her.
>
> She was acting onstage last evening in a play that our ministry team was putting on in churches, when suddenly she collapsed. We called 911, and when the ambulance came she was rushed to the hospital where it was diagnosed that she had suffered from an aneurysm. An aneurysm, and she's only fifteen! She has a long road ahead of her, and we almost lost her. There's the problem too, that she is one of the street kids that I brought to the Lord and she was a wonderful witness, but she basically has no family, and these medical bills are going to be exorbitant! So, what I'm asking for is prayer. No, not money! DON'T think this is a plea for money, Gwyneth88, it's NOT! You're too generous as it is! We know God will supply that. That's nothing for God! But pray for Melissa that she will be restored to full health and that God will be glorified through all of this. This is really affecting the other kids.

Glynis hit reply and then wrote: "I'm so sorry to hear about Melissa. I will pray for her. Can I send her a card?"

He must have been on-line because he wrote back immediately:

"Do you want to go to chat?"

She answered: "I can't, Chasco. I'm at work right now and shouldn't be checking personal e-mail anyway. Love, Gwyneth88"

He got right back to her with Melissa's e-mail saying that maybe an e-card would be nice. He ended by writing: "When you think of it can you pray? We'll e-mail more tonight. All my love, Chasco"

All my love. *All my love!* Had he ever written that in an e-mail to her before? John Egan's door opened, and quickly she trashed both messages and their replies and then emptied the trash, her fingers trembling. What was wrong with her accessing Yahoo! at work? The Internet was connected all the time anyway; it's not like they were paying per call. If Chasco were counting on her for prayer, she should be there. And it wasn't like she was hurting anyone. It was still her lunch hour and her time, after all.

Clara walked in then, breezy in a floral skirt and scuffed brown sandals. Clara always looked unmade; blouses untucking from skirts halfway through the morning, hems catching on things and ripping out, buttons loosening and falling off. She was forever asking Glynis for a needle and thread or nail polish to stem a run in her panty hose. She certainly didn't fit the stereotype of a ladder-climbing female attorney. Kim always wore suits, her hair perfectly combed. Clara's no-color hair wisped out in all directions in no particular style.

"I've organized the new client files for you," Glynis told her. "I found the similarities you were looking for, all males aged twenty to thirty who'd gotten off on that same charge. I put them on your desk. Plus, there's fresh coffee."

"Glynis, you are a godsend. I wasn't able to get any on my way in. Too rushed. Is John Egan in?"

Glynis pointed.

Clara walked into her office and sat down behind her desk to check all her personal e-mails, of that Glynis was sure. Partway through the afternoon, with the lawyers safely in their offices and with nothing else to do for them, Glynis checked her e-mail. There was a new one from Chasco.

Dear Gwyneth88,

I'm sitting here, my face bowed low before God because I
don't know how we're going to pay for any of this. A nurse
came over with forms for me to sign. She asked me if I was
the next of kin. I said no, that I was merely the minister. She
asked me if Melissa had insurance. So, I'm asking for prayer,
Gwyneth88, that God will supply money from heaven. He
owns the cattle on a thousand hills. Nothing is too hard for
our God! Pray with me. I'm sure by the time I e-mail you
tonight the money to pay for her entire surgery and then
some will be supplied. Our God is an awesome God!

All my love,
Chasco

There it was again. All my love. Glynis e-mailed him immediately:
"I've been praying whenever I think of it. Is there anything else I
can do?"

He wrote: "Things are still pretty much touch and go. What I
would really like for Melissa is a strong female influence in her life,
someone to look up to and provide spiritual guidance the way I, as a
man, cannot. Would you consent to be that for her?"

"Me?"

"Yes, you."

"I don't know. I've never been that to anyone before."

"Well, Gwyneth88, it's time you started. I consider you a real
woman of God."

No one had ever called her a real woman of God before.

9

Sitting at her computer at the kitchen table, Teri learned that Kim had worked at Smith and Egan until June when she moved to Texas. There were no infractions on her driver's license, her credit history was good, and she didn't even have any overdue library books. Her last known address was her apartment in Bangor, an address that Teri already had.

Teri flagged one item: Kim Shock had taught a course at the university on small business law. It looked like she taught the course only once, a year ago.

Her search on Glen and Susan Shock yielded nothing that she didn't already know. Glen Shock had died of an apparent heart attack shortly after their son Barry died. The address given on the Internet for Susan Shock was the one behind Glynis's house. An old one. She'd have to do a bit more digging.

She decided to work her way through the e-mails she had earlier flagged. One that particularly caught her attention was written two days after Kim left for Texas.

> Hi Glynis,
>
> I made the right decision in coming here. Someday we'll sit down and I'll tell you all about it. There's so much to tell.
>
> Kim

But it looks like she never got to tell Glynis much of anything. There were just a few more e-mails after that. But Glynis kept writing. Long e-mails like,

Hi Kim,

Did you go to the website I mentioned in my last e-mail?
You should, because there are lots of good ideas on it. I was
sort of thinking that the peach looked nice with that shade
of green. Plus a hint of apple blossoms in the bouquet. Isn't
that unique? What do you think? Follow the *wedding colors*
link for *peachy green* on the website and you'll see what I
mean. If I had the time I would love to sew these gowns. But
I'm so busy these days.

Love,
Glynis

And then the next one, two days later:

Glynis,

I don't have much time to write this, so if I'm cut short, I'll
try to get on again. I just want you to be careful Glynis, and
guard my stuff well.

Love, Kim

Guard my stuff? Another flag. She phoned and left a message on
Glynis's answering machine. She also thought it might be important
to know the specific cases Kim was working on before she left, so she
asked that as well.

The e-mails quit then, but a week later they started up, and they
were decidedly more upbeat. These were the ones filled with exclamation points. Kim was so happy!! She'd made the right decision!! And
couldn't wait to get married!!

Teri flagged one:

There was a flash flood here! I'm not kidding! A car was
washed right off the road. I've never seen anything like it!!
I thought we got storms in Maine, but this was nothing like
that! What an experience!! I haven't been to the wedding

website yet, but I'm sure anything you pick out will be fine.
I have so much faith in you.

Your best friend,
Kim

Teri logged on to the Texas meteorological website and discovered
that on that date in Texas there were no flash floods. None. The entire
southwest was reporting drought conditions for that entire month.
Somehow that didn't surprise her, and she didn't know why.

And then another:

Hey Glynis,

How're things at church? We've been going to a nice big
church here! We've been enjoying it!

Kim

Again, no church name, no denomination. But at least the hint
that it was big. While Teri was poring through the El Paso business
directory for big churches, Stephan walked in and saluted from the
door. She waved and turned back to her computer while he poured
himself a cup of coffee from the pot and put it in the microwave.

"You're not going to want to drink that, Stephan. It's like nine
hours old."

"Well-aged then," he said. In the microwave the coffee came to a
roaring boil, frothed up over the rim of the cup, and spilled onto the
microwave tray. She stared at him when he took it out, cleaned the
microwave with a paper towel, and added four heaping spoonfuls of
sugar. "Just how I like it," he said.

"Remind me never to take you to Starbucks."

"Jack around?"

She looked at Jack's dishes, washed from breakfast and neatly
stacked in the drying board by the sink. Jack never used the dishwasher.
She, on the other hand, always did. "Actually, Stephan, if he ever

deigned to take his cell phone with him, I might know where he is. But, as you know, he is a total Luddite. In actual fact, I suspect he's out at the house arguing, or at least I hope he's arguing, with the electrician."

"What's the matter with the electrician?"

"What's not the matter with him? He was supposed to be finished more than a month ago."

"My dad's an electrician."

"Your dad? Really?"

He was rooting around in the bread box, an old wooden painted thing, whose grooves were grimed with years of toast and other food. This was one item that would definitely *not* make it to their new place. "In Augusta. But you could call him. All right if I make myself some toast?"

"Go ahead. There might be a few pieces in there that aren't moldy."

After he pressed the down button on the toaster, he found a pen near the telephone and wrote down the name and number on a cereal box flap. "Tell Jack to call him."

Then he made his way past packed and taped boxes, half-packed boxes, and other debris into the living room and sat down on the couch to watch television.

"Cable's unhooked," Teri said. "Sorry."

Stephan clicked off the remote. This is what Jack's students were like. They just made themselves at home. She didn't mind it here at this house that she considered Jack's anyway. She wondered how she would feel in their new place.

10

There were several phone messages for Glynis that evening. She'd get to them after her e-mails. She would go against her established routine and read Chasco's first. No one had ever called her a *woman of God* before. No one. Her aunt had called her lazy, and her mother was usually too sick to call her much of anything.

She dropped her mail on the dining room table. She'd get to that later, too. Mostly bills anyway. There was the latest copy of *Vogue Patterns* magazine. She still got the magazine, even though it had been a while since she had ordered any of the patterns and sewn anything from it. Still, as she laid it down there was a momentary flicker of longing. She used to like the feel of fine fabric between her fingers, the anticipation of laying out the pattern pieces on top of it, the creative wonder of the finished product.

She put the magazine down and turned on her computer. A cup of tea in hand, she read. It was a long one from Chasco, all about his youth group, all about his day, all about the series of Bible studies he was planning. He ended with:

> I'm so glad you're willing to help Melissa. I knew you'd come through. You always do, Gwyneth88, and that's why I respect you so much, why I hold you in such a high place in my heart. You asked earlier about a woman from my church helping her, well, I'm afraid that Melissa is one of those kids that the mainstream church has failed. I'm finding more and more people disillusioned by the church, Gwyneth88, which is why I feel led by God to establish this on-line ministry.

A high place in his heart? Her fingers flew over the keyboard as she answered. I'll try to help. I'll do my best.

Then she told him about her day and that she was feeling good that she was doing something tangible to help find her friend. She told him about her bosses, about the fact that she could never make the coffee to their satisfaction. She wrote about how good it was to be finally home, that it was still early and she had a whole evening ahead of her to get caught up on her e-mail. She hit Send and then went into the kitchen and put in a microwave chicken dinner. By the time she was back, there was an answer from him.

Hey, you're there. You want to go to chat?

She clicked her way into the program. She couldn't stop the fluttering in her stomach. For the next hour they chatted. He told her about Melissa, and she commiserated over the trouble he was having with her hospital bills. Was there anything she could do? You've done so much already, Gwyneth88, he told her. Just being her mentor is enough. No, no, that's not enough. I have money, she wrote to him. My parents are both gone, and my father, even though I don't remember him, was a good investor, my grandfather, too. My mother never had to work in all her years. What is all this money good for but to help others? No, Chasco, I'm going to send you a check. Wouldn't it be easier, he wrote, if you just gave me your bank account number? No, Chasco, I don't trust the e-mail that much to tell you that information on-line. No, checks are safer. I'd rather use checks and cash.

Well, Gwyneth88, you obviously know what you're talking about. I'm such a numskull with money anyway. It just doesn't mean that much to me, I guess.

After she reluctantly signed off from Chasco, she wrote to Melissa.

Dear Melissa,

Chasco suggested that I write to you. I understand you've had quite an ordeal lately. I just wanted you to know that I'm a friend of Chasco's and both of us are praying for you. You can e-mail me anytime you want, and I'll try to answer

as quickly as possible. I may not have gone through something as horrible as what you went through, but I really had
to trust God when my mother died. I know how hard life
can be sometimes.

Love,
Gwyneth88

Dear Gwyneth88,

Chasco said you were nice, and now I believe him. If this e-
mail seems weird it's because I'm on all this medication...

The e-mail went on to describe in detail her ordeal, how she was
on stage one minute singing praise choruses and the next she was in
an ambulance and being rushed to a hospital with the worst headache
she could ever imagine.

They went to the chat program and chatted for twenty minutes.
In the corner, the television was on, a rerun of *Home Improvement*.
Glynis muted the volume and clicked into her on-line Bible, and tried
to find the verse that talked about all things working together for
good. It was times like this that she wished Kim were here. Kim
would know what to say. Kim always knew the right thing to say.

> *Melissa:* Sometimes I get so scared! Like is God really there
> at all? Why did he let this happen?
>
> *Gwyneth88:* It's for a reason. Everything's for a reason. God
> has a plan for everything.

And then she found it, Romans 8:28. She copied it and pasted it
into her note to Melissa. She was pleased with herself. This was
exactly the sort of thing that a godly woman would do.

> *Melissa:* Thanks. Maybe this IS for a reason. Maybe I just don't
> know that reason yet.

Gwyneth88: I'm sure that's it. We just have to keep praying.

Melissa: I'm not supposed to know, but I know Chasco is worried about my hospital bills. Maybe you can calm him down, tell him everything's going to be okay.

Gwyneth88: He shouldn't worry. God will supply. You'll see.

Melissa: I hope so. I really hope so.

After she said good-bye to Melissa, she told KarenP that Chasco was answering his e-mail now with *all my love* and did she think that *meant* anything?

Dear Gwyneth88,

Oh, I'm sure it does mean something! Well, if you have snagged Chasco, everyone on the singles Bible study is going to be jealous!

She wrote to Lark7 and Sewinglady; they all said the same thing to her. Chasco was a catch. And yes, *all my love* definitely means all my love. Chasco was too smart to put that in and have it not mean anything.

Her ten o'clock computer alarm sounded, and before she signed off she checked her voice mail and sent a couple of e-mails to Teri answering her questions.

In her bed that night she thought about Chasco. She hoped he was tall. She prayed he was tall. Wouldn't it be nice if he was tall? Really, really tall?

11

S nare crunched his empty beer can and flung it at the garbage can. It missed and hit the wall. The loud clang made his head hurt. He cursed and pressed his palms into his temples for a second. Control. Control. Be calm, he told himself. But it was getting harder. He would be like his father. And lose all control one day and...

"Forget about the money." He could hear Beamish tell him in that phony accent of his. "You know the trouble with you? You don't know when to cut your losses and run."

But it wasn't about the money anymore. It was about revenge. It was about betrayal. A few things Beamish, in his fancy cars and fancy houses and all his money, knew nothing about. Snare's teeth hurt and he massaged his jaws, opened his mouth, yawned, willing the pain to leave. There were random points of pain all over his body: his teeth, the back of his head, the ends of his fingers, the side of his stomach, a spot above his eyebrows. Every day a new place.

He had only seen Beamish a few times since the horrible thing happened, and both those times, Beamish swore he didn't have the money. At first Snare believed him. But now he was having doubts. For all he knew, Beamish could be teamed up with the girl! He tossed that idea around in his head for a few minutes. Well, of course. She was pretty, a lawyer even, and Beamish...well, Beamish was Beamish, superrich, mysterious. Well, Snare held the cards now. The girl was his now. Safely locked in that basement and far away from him. And if Beamish had the money, he'd get it. He'd find it. He'd tear Beamish's huge house from top to bottom. He'd find it.

It was Beamish's fault that the money was missing in the first place. It was Beamish's fault that he'd rotted in jail for two years. And if there was one thing he had learned from his father, it was that if people did you wrong, you made them pay.

His e-mail icon flashed. Good. This was something he was good at. This is where he even had it all over Beamish. This is where he shone. He cracked his knuckles, leaned forward, and began.

12

Glynis e-mailed Teri that yes, Kim had left a box of her stuff in Glynis's attic for "safekeeping." She'd brought it over the day before she left for Texas. Glynis added that she was going to check on Kim's old cases at work, and she'd let Teri know.

Teri shot back a quick thank you. Next, she wandered around the FBI Most Wanted website for a while, frustrated at the slowness of her connection and longing for the day when she would be in her brand-new office with high speed Internet. While she waited for the faces to download a line at a time on the monitor, she thought about Kim. About Gil. About Gil and Kim. It didn't take a rocket scientist to conclude that something wasn't right in paradise.

She looked at the faces on her screen, this representation of the worst in society. If the sheep and goats would be separated by God at the end, these people wouldn't even make it into the goats category. Criminal homicide. Rape and aggravated assault. Terrorism. Armed and extremely dangerous. Do not approach. *Made in the image of God.*

The same feeling crept over her that always crept over her whenever she looked at faces like these. How did they get like this? What twisted set of circumstances played out in their lives to turn them into people who killed, kidnapped, burned buildings, and built bombs? People who would just as soon kill themselves as anyone else.

She followed the links to what she really wanted, which were the con artists, particularly those con artists who lured victims on dating websites. Particularly, rich young career women. Young pretty female lawyers in particular.

She read about a husband and wife team wanted for a string of burglaries at all-inclusive beach resorts. Clad in appropriate beach-wear, they would wander onto the resort, conveniently forgetting their IDs in their room, get chummy with the guests, and eventually gain access to rooms where they stole jewelry and money. She read about Internet scammers who were accessing people's credit cards on-line. And then there was that famous Nigerian money scam, and people still falling for it. And phone scams promising special medical cards good for prescriptions, which were virtually worthless. There were others. And there were more warnings and places to report if you'd been scammed.

She didn't know what she was looking for as she worked through the pictures and sites, clicking from one to another. Finally, she logged off and went back to her phone calls. She had widened her territory to a hundred miles around El Paso, looking for engineering firms or law offices. And that included Mexico. She used to be a fairly good speaker of Spanish. Trouble was, she didn't get a lot of practice in Maine. So she muddled through several calls to Mexico, and then decided that Gil was probably in the U.S.

Near evening, she made a hit. She called a small firm—Davis Electronics in Las Cruces, New Mexico—and was greeted with, "Oh yes. Gilbert Williamson. He worked for us."

"Really? He did?" Teri was immediately on alert, pencil poised.

"Yes."

"As an engineer?"

"Yes, an engineer. Is he okay? Did you find him?"

The pencil lead on Teri's mechanical pencil ran out, and she was rapidly trying to insert a new one while she asked, "When did he work for you?"

"Let me see. It would be more than a year ago. From January until about August."

"So, he wasn't there very long."

"Not really, I guess. Who is this?"

"My name's Teri Blake-Addison. I'm an investigator looking into, ah, into his disappearance. Do you by any chance have an address for him? Or a forwarding address?"

There was a pause. "So, it's official then."

"Official?"

"He's officially missing. It's really true. Are you the police?"

"I'm a private investigator."

"Did June hire you?"

"June?"

"His fiancée. June Redfeather."

Teri scratched her head.

"She said she was going to hire a detective. I'm glad she finally did."

Teri said, "Tell me how and when he disappeared."

"He went to California on an art buying trip, and he never returned."

"An *art* buying trip?"

"Oh, he was quite a collector. He bought and sold art. I think that's why he got on so famously with June. She owns a gallery right next door to us here. He left for California about a year ago and never returned."

"The Gil Williamson I'm looking for is tall, midthirties, fair hair, and an engineer."

"Sounds like our Gil Williamson."

"And he collected art?"

"Oh yes. It's why he and June hit it off."

"Did you call the police?"

"Yes, but nothing ever came of it. I think they thought he just ran away. But Gil wouldn't do that. He and June were so *devoted* to each other."

"You wouldn't happen to have the name of the art gallery he was going to in California?"

"No, but June might."

"Did Gil ever mention anybody by the name of Kim Shock? Is that name at all familiar to you?"

"Kim? Not that I can recall."

"Can I ask you something else—was he, ah, a good engineer?"

"Everyone around here liked him, if that's what you mean."

"What I mean is, did he do any actual engineering, building bridges, the sort of things engineers do?"

"We're not that kind of firm. We mostly do small things. Not bridges."

"Would you say that Gil was good at what he did?"

"Yes. Of course. I've said that before. What's this about?"

"How about his résumé? Do you have one on file for him?"

"Yes, we do. We always keep those things."

"Can you fax it to me?"

"If that can help find him, of course I will."

"I also want June's address and phone number. Plus, I'd like to speak to one of the engineers who worked closely with Gil, if that's possible."

"Hold on a minute. I think Mark Byers is in. I'll transfer you."

She drew stick men on the top of her paper while she waited. If Gil was the con artist she was beginning to suspect him of being, why would he take his second fiancée to precisely the same place he left his first fiancée?

"Mark Byers here."

"I assume you were filled in on why I'm calling?"

"Yes. How can I help?"

"I'd like to know the sort of work that Gil did with your firm."

"We worked together on several large projects. He was easy to get along with and had lots of good ideas."

"What about his actual engineering skills, would you say he was competent? Did he ever go to Barbados, say, and build bridges?"

There was a laugh. "Where did you get *that* from?"

"What do you mean?"

"I mean those precise words."

"I don't understand."

"That was a joke with Gil. He'd often say, 'Send me to Barbados to build bridges.' It was a joke. His way of saying, 'Get me out of here,' or 'Thank goodness it's Friday,' something like that. What's this about?"

"So he was good at what he did and worked out well for you?"

"He was very good at what he did. His skills on the CAD were very solid."

"Were there any red flags? No problems?"

"None."

"Is the name Kim Shock familiar to you?"

"No. Should it be?"

"It's the name of the person he was last seen with."

"Well, sorry, can't help you."

After she hung up she heard the whir of the fax machine, and in the living room the fax spewed out a page from its perch on the top of a half-packed cardboard box. She noted with disappointment that there was only one sheet, with a scrawled note.

His résumé appears to be missing, along with his previous employment record, but I do have this list of character references for him. Hope this helps. I'll see if I can find his résumé proper for you.

His résumé appears to be missing. Why am I not surprised?

It contained three character references with addresses and phone numbers, plus the name of Southwest Arts, June's gallery. She called, but June was out. The girl who answered had been there less than a year and had never heard of Gil Williamson. June was away on a buying trip and wouldn't be back until the end of next week. Then she tried the other references. The first was for Rev. Henry Snare, minister at First Baptist Church on Front Street, Austin, Texas. She was informed that the number was not in service. A quick Internet check revealed that there was no First Baptist Church on Front Street in Austin.

Then she tried another name on the character reference list, a Frank Dooley in Arizona, and lo and behold someone actually answered the phone.

"Yeel-lo."

"Mr. Dooley?" Teri began.

"Yep?"

"I'm calling in reference to Mr. Gil Williamson. You're listed as one of his character references."

"Who?"

"Gil Williamson."

"I don't know anybody named Bill Whoziewhatsits."

"Gil Williamson."

"Never heard of him."

"You're name and number are on his list of references."

"I don't care what your so-called reference says, I never heard of him."

"Do you perhaps have a relative by that name who might know Mr. Williamson?"

"Nope. Nobody but me named Frank Dooley in this family."

"Are you sure?"

"Of course I'm sure."

"Sorry for your time."

She hung up the phone and tried the final reference, someone named Andrew McRae, and was informed that Andy had died six years ago at the ripe old age of ninety-seven after suffering with dementia for many years. His daughter couldn't be sure, but she was fairly certain her father had never known anyone by the name of Gill Williamson, but if Teri liked, she could look through her father's papers.

"I don't think that will be necessary," Teri said.

She hung up and looked down at the one grainy photo she had of Gil and Kim.

"Who are you?" she said out loud to him. "Who are you?"

The doorbell rang. It was the Millers, the couple who had bought their house, and could they come in and measure for carpets and drapes?

"Now?"

"There are some things we need to check out," said the woman with a flounce of glossy auburn hair.

"We'll be out of here in two weeks. The place comes with the drapes and carpets. The living room drapes are brand-new," Teri said.

"The place is going to need completely new window treatments," the woman said, walking past her. "And we want to do all new carpets throughout. We have a completely different color scheme in mind."

Before Teri had a chance to protest, the woman was kneeling in the front hall measuring the entryway, motioning for her husband to write down some numbers in his handheld organizer.

"We'll be here a few minutes," she said to Teri. "You can go about your business. Don't let us disturb you."

"Okay then. I'll be in the kitchen." Teri pointed. "Working."

"That's fine. We won't be needing to work in the kitchen today."

While they measured and talked, Teri called Marcie and asked whether her husband had found that video of Gil and Kim yet.

"Oh, forgot. Totally. I'll make sure I talk to him when he gets home tonight. I'll see if we have it. We may have even recorded over it. I can't rule out that happening. I'll have to check. Any news on Kim?"

"No."

Teri wandered outside and yelled at Kelly to quit digging holes in the yard and arrived back in time to hear the woman say, "We really have to get rid of that mantel. The room is so old-fashioned, but I love the high ceilings. We can easily turn this place into nouveau old."

Kelly bounced toward them, sniffing. The woman jumped away, raised her arms, bracelets tinkling. "Dogs," she said.

"Kelly! Down!" Teri said.

Kelly tromped off to the kitchen, and the woman sighed and lowered her hands. Then, "This place is going to be more work than we initially thought. We're going to need to get started on things before we move in."

"Get started on things?"

"The fireplace is going to go." She put a hand on her hip and frowned.

"We'll be out in two weeks," Teri said.

"No." She shook her head. "That's not acceptable. We will be *living* here in two weeks."

Teri looked around her. If they wanted to work in the living room, she supposed all of their boxes *could* be moved into the kitchen. And the couch, well, it could be covered, she supposed. What was she thinking? This was *their* house for two more weeks. "No," she said. "I'm afraid that's impossible."

Barbie Doll Hair pouted and looked at her husband. Really, she pouted. Her lower lip came out just like a child's, and Teri tried not to roll her eyes.

Mr. Dutiful Husband shrugged inside his designer suit and said, "We promise not to be too much of an inconvenience. We'll tell our contractor to keep the mess to a minimum."

"We can't," Teri said. "Both my husband and I are working. I've just taken on a project that's demanding my time. We don't need the added pressure of— I'm sorry. Two weeks. We'll be out of here in two weeks."

The two of them marched grumpily out the door and down the walk. Before they got into the car, they stood for several minutes talking with animated hand gestures. When they left, the car tires spouted up gravel behind them.

13

Glynis arrived at work three-quarters of an hour early. The detective wanted to know what cases Kim had been working on. She also wanted to know what was in the box Kim left with her and seemed genuinely surprised when Glynis said she didn't know.

"It's just a few things that I don't want to leave in my apartment," Kim had told her. "Can I leave them with you?"

And Glynis had said fine, no problem. It never occurred to Glynis to look through Kim's papers. She just wasn't the sort of person who'd do that. Which is why she found it so strange to be snooping through Clara Winkel's things.

It was quiet in the office. No one was there. Clara wouldn't be in until afternoon. John Egan would be in later, but he'd sit in his office all day with the door closed. Tom Rose and Barton Smith would be in court all day.

She had always liked this office, Kim's office, and according to Glynis, the best office in the place. Theirs was an old, downtown building with high ceilings and ornate moldings and big windows that actually opened, unlike the kind of office that Sewinglady told her she worked in, with no opening windows and bone-chilling air-conditioning in the summer and too much blowing heat in the winter. As Glynis walked around the room, she was already thinking of how she would describe this to Sewinglady in the evening.

> There I was! In the office! I'd broken into my friend's former office, feeling like some sort of detective! It was a scary feeling. I don't know how people could do this for a living! I was actually sick to my stomach.

Clara had moved Kim's desk against the wall. Kim used to have her desk right beside the window, which Glynis thought was nicer because you got to look outside. On her desk were pictures of her family. Glynis never thought of Clara as having a family, yet there she was in a photo sitting next to a big, chunky, light-haired man and two chubby, towheaded boys.

The metal file cabinet in the closet was the one that Kim kept her files in. It was unlocked, thankfully, and Glynis easily opened it. The files were organized with the most recent cases near the front. Those would be the ones Clara was working on. In the back, she saw Kim's name on a few of the papers. She found a couple of files, but was this the sort of thing the detective wanted? She looked through a few of them. One file was especially thick and bore Kim's name on every page. She pulled it out and put it in her bag. She was closing the cabinet door when she looked up and there was Clara standing in the doorway, staring at her.

"Oh," Glynis said.

Clara continued to look at her.

"I'm sorry. I was just...I was looking for those cases you wanted me to organize...I thought I could get a head start. No one was here. I'm sorry. I was just—"

"You were getting files?"

"Yes. Those files...those things you wanted...You weren't in and—"

"Those files in the closet? Those are mostly old cases. You should have been looking through this file for the recent ones. I'd like to talk to you, Glynis."

"Sorry. I'm so sorry."

"Are you okay?"

"I was just..."

"You look so pale. Can I get you something? A glass of water?"

"No." She swallowed several times.

"When you're able, I need to talk to you about something, Glynis. Sit down."

Glynis sat. "I'm sorry about the...about this..."

"It's not about this. It's about your use of the office computer for personal e-mail."

Glynis looked up at her. "I only use it during coffee break and lunch."

"I know. And it's a stupid rule. But a rule nonetheless. That rule was made plain to me by John Egan. I balked at first too, Glynis. I tried to tell him how little sense it made, but you know John Egan. Set in his ways. So, I must abide by the rule if I want to work here. And so must you."

"But..."

"I know, and I totally agree, but John Egan thinks that personal e-mail will distract us from our work here. That's his reasoning."

Glynis gripped her hands tightly in her lap to keep them from trembling.

14

"This is a person who never uses her telephone," Teri muttered. It was through e-mail that Glynis had contacted Teri in the first place. It was through e-mail that Glynis and Teri set up their first meeting. And it was through e-mail, now, that Glynis and Teri were corresponding about the case.

> Teri,
>
> I have a file of Kim's that I brought home from work. I think it's all her old cases. What I do know is that Kim did a lot of pro bono work. She was really good with people. She was always very concerned about fighting for the rights of the disadvantaged. If you would like to come over tonight, I'll give you this file. You could look at Kim's box at the same time. I get home around five-thirty. I'll be busy with my Bible study later on, so I won't be able to go through it with you, but you're welcome to look through it yourself.
>
> Glynis

That was fine with Teri. She'd rather look through the box by herself anyway.

Jack was at the university this morning getting things ready for the start of a new semester, while Teri sat at the kitchen window thinking about Kim and looking out at Kelly digging in the yard. What would make a smart young lawyer give everything up to run off with a guy she met on the Internet? She had put Gil's name into a few of her PI databases, but so far Gil Williamson didn't exist prior to Davis Electronics.

The sun was out this morning, the day golden. Maine may get cold and rainy springs and cold and rainy summers, but autumns were beautiful and went on and on and on. She had spent the morning working on the mystery of Kim and now decided she needed a break. She whistled for Kelly and the two of them climbed into her Honda, Kelly in the passenger seat, head up, nose working, alert for any adventure. When she got to their log house, lo and behold an electrician and a plumber were both working happily away.

"Hi there," Teri said.

"Hey," they said back to her.

"You must be Stephan's father," she said to the one working on wires in the soon-to-be downstairs bathroom.

"I am. And you're Teri?"

"Thanks for coming on such short notice. We can't tell you how much we appreciate this. We're supposed to be in here in two weeks, and you can see how far it is from being habitable."

"Oh, we'll have this ready. Don't you worry about a thing."

This rough-edged, gimme-a-chain-saw type of guy did not look like he could have fathered the serious, sad-eyed scuba diving poet who was working on a master's in Fine Arts.

"Stephan tells me you're some kind of Sherlock Holmes."

Teri laughed. "Not exactly."

Upstairs she greeted the plumber, who was lying on his back under the sink. "Hey!" she said. "This is really coming along."

He scooted out. "Downstairs is done. This will be soon, too. Not much left."

"Great."

Before she drove home, she took Kelly for a walk around the edge of their property. Elizabeth, kneeling in her garden, looked up and waved, and Kelly gamboled over to where William and Harry sat serenely on the grass beside their mistress.

Later, at supper, Jack told her how much of an asset Shauna was going to be in the department. Not only was she eager to please, but she really knew her stuff and was going to work out fine as a TA.

"How serendipitous," Teri said.

@ • @ • @

Glynis's house was in an old section of Bangor near the I-95 on-ramp. It was a neighborhood on the verge. Well-groomed homes with freshly mown lawns and well-tended flower boxes sat next to houses with broken-down cement porch steps and lawns overgrown with dandelions.

Glynis's house had elements of both. The lawn was mowed, but there were no flowers, and blue paint was flaking here and there. The grates on the basement windows looked new.

Glynis met her wearing very wide cotton pants pulled in at the waist with a drawstring and a loose fitting white cotton shirt. The bulkiness of her clothing accentuated her thinness and the wild mass that was her hair. Tall as she was, she could be willowy if she wouldn't slouch, thought Teri. Her narrow feet were bare and looked too small, somehow, for her long body, as if there weren't enough infrastructure to support her and she would topple over.

She led Teri inside, rearming a security system behind them. Glynis's kitchen was very tidy, but the dining room, although clean, looked lived-in. Papers, several fashion magazines, a popular study Bible, and assorted letters and bills were in organized stacks on the maple dining room table, which, devoid of a cloth, revealed several water stains from cups. Against the far wall was a computer on a small table, and next to it a television. The television was on, muted and tuned to an old rerun of *Seinfeld*.

Glynis told Teri that Kim's box was upstairs in the closet in the last room on the left. She was welcome to go on up there. Her Bible study was scheduled to begin shortly, so she wouldn't be able to accompany her upstairs.

The box was where Glynis said it would be, sealed with clear tape and in the bottom and back of the closet with "Kim Shock" in black felt-tip marker on the top. But Teri, being Teri and a PI after all, decided to do a little exploring before she had a look at its contents. A good PI looked at everything. Clues sometimes came from the most surprising places.

The upstairs consisted of four large rooms and a bathroom. Three of the rooms had beds, dressers, and closets complete with clothes. The first bedroom contained a double bed covered with a dusty chenille spread. The clothes in the closet were for a woman like Glynis, very tall and thin. But these old-fashioned flowery dresses would not be what Glynis would wear. The smell of some kind of cinnamony perfume clung to them as she moved her hand through the closet. They were all good quality. Nothing from Wal-Mart in this closet. The second bedroom contained a bed and a dresser, but no clothes. In the third bedroom was a single bed with a pink spread. A dresser with three drawers was empty. Likewise there were no clothes in the closet. Glynis's girlhood room?

The bathroom obviously hadn't been used in years. A gray lump of soap clung to the top of the vanity, and an orange bottle of shampoo leaned against the back. Teri picked it up. Gee, Your Hair Smells Terrific. There were a few odds and ends in the medicine cabinet. A square tin of aspirin, some Band-Aid bandages in a metal flip-top container, a can of White Rain hair spray, and a paper container of hair nets.

The room that held Kim's box was the emptiest. The only furniture it in were a chair and a child's desk. A mirror hung crookedly on the wall. Most of the silver had worn off so that reflections were scratched and out of focus.

She pulled out her Swiss Army Knife and opened the box. There were several jewelry boxes filled with various kinds of costume jewelry, an expired L.L.Bean credit card, a couple pairs of sunglasses. Mostly junk. She rummaged through crummy jewelry, wooden bracelets, clunky bracelets, a few rings. Why would Kim want Glynis to take care of this? At the very bottom was a dusty green backpack, the kind favored by the military, with its many flaps and loops and places to hook on canteens and tents and extra jackets and guns. She pulled it out and untied the top and looked inside.

It was filled with money. Lots and lots of money. Fifty dollar bills all rubber-banded together in bunches. She kept picking up bundles of fifties and staring at them. She did a quick calculation and guessed there was at least fifty thousand dollars here. Maybe more. She felt around at the bottom of the pack. It was all money. Nothing but money.

Back downstairs, no one had yet arrived for Glynis's Bible study. Teri said, "Glynis?"

Without looking up Glynis said, "I just have to finish this one thing."

"I'll wait." Teri sat down at the table. Although she tried to read the computer screen, she couldn't see what Glynis was focused on.

A few minutes later, Glynis looked up. "Did you find anything that might help?"

Teri hesitated, then said, "Are you aware that Kim left a sizable amount of money?"

"Money?" She put her hand to her neck.

"Yes. Money and lots of it. Perhaps you'll want to take it to a bank. I don't think you should leave this amount of money in your house."

"I didn't know that."

"I think you should put it in the bank for her."

"No," she said. "No. That was Kim's. If she wanted me to put it in a bank, she would have told me to do that. She told me to take care of it. There must be a reason why she gave me that box rather than put it in a bank herself. I should respect that."

"When exactly did she give you that box?"

"Just before she went to Texas. She said she didn't want to leave it at her apartment. She told me it was important papers."

"Important papers, hmm," Teri said. "How did she seem when she gave you this box?"

"Nervous, excited. Let me think. I thought she was excited because she was flying out to see Gil again. She said she'd be back soon and could I take care of this for her."

"I can't impress on you enough that you really shouldn't leave that in your house." Especially in this neighborhood, Teri thought but didn't say. "If she's missing, maybe we should figure out where this money came from. Do you have any of her bank books or records?"

Kim had an account at the bank near the law office, Glynis told her, plus the one near the hospital.

"So, as far as you know, Kim banked at just two banks?"

"Yes, I'm pretty sure."

"Do you think it was money she withdrew from her accounts at those banks?"

Glynis thought. "Maybe. Kim didn't say."

"What about personal papers, letters?" Teri asked. "Do you have any other papers of Kim's?"

"When Kim left she asked me to pick up her mail for her. So I did that. Until they packed up her apartment. I should have thought of these sooner, but I think her mail was mostly flyers, that sort of thing. If it was bills, I paid them for her." She got up. "Let me go get the letters that I do have."

While she was gone Teri glanced at the computer. It appeared that she was in a chat group, and unless Teri moved closer she wouldn't be able to read the messages. She was about to get up when Glynis came back with a few unopened envelopes and handed them to Teri. There was a preferred customer notice for a ladies' dress shop, several L.L.Bean catalogs, a twenty-dollar rebate check for a cell phone she purchased, a handful of identical postcards with the message on the front, "I'm praying for you." On the back were various messages: "You were such an encouragement to me when I decided to go for it and try for that job, thank you!" and others thanking Kim for things she had done in the church, signed by various people. Teri recognized a few of the names: Michelle Tandy, Mike Wordman, and two others. Teri looked questioningly at Glynis.

She shrugged. "We had this encouragement thing going in our Bible study. We were supposed to pick one person and write an encouraging note to them."

"Oh." She returned the cards to the stack.

There were also four personal letters, all in the same handwriting with no return address.

"Do you know who these are from?" Teri said turning them over.

Glynis shook her head. "I don't open Kim's letters."

"Since she's missing, maybe we should," said Teri, slitting open the first with her miniature Swiss Army Knife.

The first one was dated two months previous and from someone who signed her name "L."

Dear Kim,

You say I'm in danger, or that I could be in danger. But at this point I feel safer here than anywhere else. Even with you, although it's nice of you to offer. On the streets I know the best places to hide. I know the honest people. I really appreciate all you're doing for me. My only goal is to be safe and away from him.

Love,
L

Dear Kim,

I know that you think what I did was stupid and I admit it was, but I wanted to prove my point. I'm safe, though. I'm in a safe place. I'm not ready to tell anyone. Thank you for thinking of me.

Love,
L

"Any idea who this 'L' is?"

Glynis shrugged. "I don't know."

The other two were essentially the same, all from L, all saying that she wasn't ready to leave the streets, but if she did she'd let Kim know. One contained the line, *Don't worry, he's not going to find me.*

"You have no idea what this is all about?"

"Kim helped street kids. She was their advocate. She got to know a lot of them through her parents. They were foster parents. Maybe it's one of those kids."

Teri reinserted the letters into their proper envelopes and put them in her satchel.

"You're going to take them?"

"Yes," Teri answered. "I'll make photocopies and make sure you get the originals. You want me to find Kim, right?" Then she said, "How about those cases Kim was working on before she left? You said you had information on them?"

Glynis handed her a manila envelope marked with her name. "I took these from the office this morning. Plus, I found Susan Shock's address. It's in there."

Teri skimmed the file, which appeared to be letters and e-mails to Kim, all from victims of cons or scams. Included in the file was a letter from a woman who had lost three thousand dollars when she paid to get vinyl siding put on her house. Another complained that money he and his wife had forked out for their dream cruise had vanished, and the cruise company was no more. Still others complained about phone scams, and luxury vacations they had supposedly won that never materialized.

"So Kim was working on behalf of people who'd been scammed in one way or the other?"

"Yes. She had me do bits of research on the subject, too."

"What did you do?"

"Phoned people. Followed up. Here's the ad she used." Glynis held it out for her. It was business card size and read: *Have you been scammed? Are you the victim of a con? Call me, write me, e-mail me. Reasonable rates. Special consideration.*

Teri put the letters back the file, thanked Glynis, and left.

15

Since it was still fairly early, Teri decided to do a little neighborhood door-to-door. At the house next door to Glynis's, a woman who said she was good friends with Susan Shock told Teri it was the murders that tore that family apart. "Susan and I go way back. We've been friends a long time. You heard about the tragedy, did you?" She shook her head and made tsk-tsk sounds. "It was the loss of that boy of theirs, the way he got into that religious group and did what he did. You never know, do you? You just never know."

Teri agreed. You just never know.

"Before her boy died? Well, a more gracious and wonderful person you would not find. I mean she would get out there with all those kids and play with them like she was one of them. Quite a character, she was. And the way she dressed. All that color and scarves."

The woman, however, had no idea where Kim might go and had not met Gil.

She next went to the house beside the Shocks, where a man with an oily face and a pencil behind his ear said he'd lived there for ten years. "Everyone knew Susan. Or knew of her. Her reputation was legendary." He described her as loud and flashy, with dozens of kids running through the yard all the time.

"You know how in every neighborhood there's one house that all the kids flock to? Well, Shocks' was that place."

"Did you know Kim?"

"A lot like her mother, that one. The two of them a pair. Last I heard she was engaged to some fellow over Mount Desert Island way. You might check over there."

At the house on the other side of the Shocks, a woman remembered Barry. "My kids were that age. He was a nice kid. Quiet, serious. Very intelligent. What a loss. They say something in him just snapped. Happens with these adopted kids sometimes. I saw a show about it once. I remember he used to get all the kids together for plays. Glen even built a sort of stage where Barry and the others could act out their Romeo and Juliet."

"How about Kim Shock? You wouldn't have any idea of where she might go if threatened or in danger?"

"She was independent, that one. But I wouldn't know. You say she's missing?"

"She appears to be."

"She'll be found. She's too smart. Too smart for her own good most of the time, that one. That's what we all used to say about her. Sad how it ended. This neighborhood has a lot of sad stories, it does. Then there's that poor Maylene Pigott. If she'd've lived, there would be things they could do for her now instead of the terrible way she died. All alone like that. Killed herself, she did." She clucked her tongue and moved her head from side to side. "And the poor daughter. Living all by herself the way she does. Now, there's a sad case if there ever was one."

The house the Shocks had lived in was occupied by a young couple with a baby and a puffball of a dog underfoot who yapped the whole time Teri stood at the door. They had never met the Shocks. The house sale was completed through a broker, and they never met the original owners. She'd heard about the tragedy, of course, but that had nothing to do with the house. A house was just a house. They didn't believe in ghosts.

At each place she left her business card and instructed them to call her if they remembered anything.

16

While the detective had been thumping her way around upstairs, Glynis had been trying to figure out where Chasco was. The Bible study for teens was supposed to have begun ten minutes ago. She was already in the chat room and had been for twenty minutes. Three of the teenagers—Velour, Jazz, and Chemize404—had joined the chat room.

> *Velour:* Do you know where Chasco is? Do you know what we're supposed to be studying?

> *Jazz:* What should we do, Gwyneth88? If Chasco doesn't show up, will you be leading it?

> *Gwyneth88:* I don't know. Usually Chasco handles it. I haven't heard from him.

> *Chemize404:* The Bible study wasn't on his website today. I kept checking. He always has it up two days before the study.

Three more had joined the chat room, and still no Chasco. A young man with the username Freefire said that he had a friend who wanted to join the Bible study and could Gwyneth88 approve him?

> *Gwyneth88:* Usually Chasco approves new members, I'm not sure. We should wait for him.

> *Freefire:* He really wants to learn about the Bible. I've told him all about you and Chasco.

> *Gwyneth88:* Okay then. Have him join just for tonight, and then I'll submit his name to Chasco.

And so now there were seven on-line. Gwyneth88, Velour, Chemize404, Jazz, Freefire, his friend Work4God, and another young man with the username of Philemon5.

Soon there would be upwards of a dozen young people and no leader! Even though Glynis didn't know what to do, even though her hands shook as she typed, even though a thin line of sweat was forming on her upper lip, she felt, for the first time in a long time, energized. That these young people would be looking up to her (to her!) for advice and strength made her feel something she had never felt anywhere else.

Glynis made a decision then. She knew Chasco wouldn't abandon these kids. He loved these kids. It had to be some sort of an emergency. She keyed in: "Chasco's had an emergency." She paused in her writing. "We need to pray for him." She paused again. "How about if we pray right here, like we normally do."

And they prayed around alphabetically. They actually prayed. She did it. She had called them all to prayer. It was a wondrous feeling! When prayer was ended, she asked them what they wanted to do. There were even more teenagers on-line now.

> *Jazz:* Why can't you do the Bible study, Gwyneth88? You should do a Bible study on your own, anyway.

> *Velour:* I agree. Have you ever thought of that? Of leading your own on-line Bible study? I think you're good enough. Everyone thinks so.

> *Gwyneth88:* Oh, not me. I just like to help Chasco.

> *Journey2:* Everyone is amazed at how smart you are. You should have your own web page and Bible study. Call it Gwyneth88.com. I know lots of people who'd help you set it up.

Others agreed, and Glynis leaned back and wondered casually what the people in the church would think if they knew she had actually been asked to lead a Bible study! She had ever lived her life only in her best friend's shadow. She felt what it was like to kiss a boy after Kim described it in great detail when she stayed overnight. She felt what it was like to be in love when Kim told her about it.

Even the vacations Kim took—downhill skiing at Marmot Basin in western Canada, snorkeling in the Caribbean, hiking up Mount Katahdin, sunbathing on the beaches of the Bahamas—Glynis lived it all via Kim's descriptions.

But now she was being asked to do something on her own, and she wondered what the people at work would say if they knew. What would John Egan say if he saw her? Or Tom Rose? Or Marcie or Mike Wordman from church? All those people that barely saw her. All those people in church who hadn't written her a single encouragement card.

And here she was, on-line, leading a group of teens through a study guide on dating! She had purchased a study guide, along with a pile of others, when the local Christian bookstore had a warehouse sale. She was writing to the kids about dates she had had, experiences she had had with boys, about mistakes she had made, about how she always put God first in all her relationships, and how He had blessed her because of it.

None of this had technically happened to her, of course, but Kim had shared so much with her and in such detail that Glynis felt as if she herself had lived it.

Glynis had been on very few dates in her life, probably because the pool of eligible boys in youth group was vastly diminished by her height.

Her first date had been a disaster. It was a double date set up by Kim with two boys she'd met at summer camp. They were both sixteen and it was summer. Her acne-faced date was more interested in animated Kim than quiet Glynis. And it was plain that he was sulking that he had gotten Glynis in this double-date lottery.

They'd gone to see *Back to the Future*. Glynis was painfully aware that two seats over, Kim and her boyfriend for the night were holding hands, whispering, and giggling, while Glynis sat with her hands in her lap, pretending to be engrossed in the film, while the boy next to her ate the bucket of popcorn without offering her any. Afterward in the car, Kim talked and flirted and laughed, and Glynis wondered how her best friend could be so at ease with boys. Was it something you learned? Something you practiced? Glynis was so nervous that her mouth was dry and she kept swallowing. At least her date was the same height as she was. At least she didn't tower over him like she did everyone else in the world.

Later, while the four of them were sitting in a noisy Denny's drinking Coke, Glynis said she enjoyed the movie.

"Hey, it talks!" her date squealed. "The Jolly Green Amazon actually talks!"

"He's a jerk, Glynis," Kim told her later. "A class-A jerk."

But the name stuck.

If he could see her now, that pimply-faced kid who started that nickname, he might not be so quick to call her that. There were people here who actually respected her, people who waited to hear what she had to say. Yes, she missed Kim, but she had so many on-line friends now: KarenP, Sewinglady, Lark7, Chasco. Especially Chasco. Those days of being Glynis the Jolly Green Amazon were over. On-line she could be Gwyneth88, the romantic heroine with the long blond hair. She could be herself, or a better version of herself.

The Bible study was over, and she was going through and deleting spam and cleaning up her mailboxes when her mail icon flashed. She noted with delight that it was from Chasco.

Dear Gwyneth88,

I'm so sorry that I missed the Bible study. Velour just e-mailed me saying that you did a tremendous job. What a wonder you are! I've been up to my ears in hospital stuff with Melissa. What a mess! No money and huge bills! And enough red tape to circle the globe. But, I've no doubt that God will provide. Please, if you are e-mailing Melissa, don't tell her any of this. I want her to think God has *already provided* for her needs. Thank you for the money you sent. God will reward you for this.

All my love,
Chasco

She read it over several times. All my love! She e-mailed him right away, told him all about the Bible study and how much she enjoyed it. He didn't answer right away so she wrote an e-mail to Melissa. When Melissa answered right back, Glynis suggested they go to chat.

> *Gwyneth88:* How are you feeling?

> *Melissa:* Better. I'm out of the hospital now and staying with a nice Christian family. Their names are Maurice and Corinne Binder and they have two adorable poodles. I'm lucky to be here. My own mother didn't want me.

> *Gwyneth88:* I know what it's like to have problems with your mother.

> *Melissa:* She was a drug addict. I don't even know where she is. If it wasn't for Chasco, I don't know where I'd be.

> *Gwyneth88:* Chasco's a great person.

> *Melissa:* He says you are, too. He says you're one of the nicest women he knows. He talks about you all the time.

> *Gwyneth88:* LOL! We've never even met!

But before she turned off her computer, she realized that she had forgotten to tell Chasco about the new Bible study member, Work4God. So she e-mailed him again, turned off her computer, and went to bed.

17

I'm hoping you can help me," Teri said to the bank teller on the phone in the morning. "I did this really stupid thing. I'm supposed to deposit this money into my cousin's account? For this couch I bought from her? But I'm like, *duh*, so stupid. I wrote down her number? But I lost it. In the move and all? So, I'm wondering if I send you the check, can you put it into her account for me? I can't send it to Kim 'cause she's like, out of the country by now."

"That should be no problem. What is your cousin's name?"

"Kim Shock."

There was the click of a keyboard. More clicking. Then, "How do you spell Shock?"

"S-h-o-c-k. Like what happens when you stick your finger in a light socket? Or when you scooch across the carpet and then touch somebody?"

"Are you sure she banked with us? I can't seem to find any information on her."

"Yeah. I'm pretty positive. We were driving by the bank one day? And she told me that was where she had her account. Oh man, I'm thinking about something else. Did she like close her account there already or something?"

"It looks that way."

"So, she like had an account there but doesn't anymore? Like I'm too late?"

"Yes. Kim Shock closed all her accounts two months ago. We received an e-mail authorizing us to do so."

Thank you very much, bank teller lady.

Teri did the same song and dance at Kim's other bank. So Kim Shock had closed all her accounts prior to leaving. Had all that money Teri found in the green backpack come from Kim's closed accounts? Had she managed to save that much? Was the law profession truly that lucrative? If not, where'd that money come from?

Next she called the university's Cooperative Extension program to find out about the class Kim had taught once on small business law. Teri asked to see the class list, but was told by a chatty person that they normally didn't give out that sort of information. But when Teri told her she was a detective looking into the disappearance of the instructor, well, that was a different matter entirely, and she should have said that right at the beginning. She faxed the list to Teri at once. It was always amazing to Teri how easily she got information. Honest people don't even question. Only criminals demand warrants.

She leaned on boxes in the living room and scanned the list of students in Kim's class. One name stood out. Lou Cohen from the bagel shop Teri used to live above.

For six years prior to her marriage to Jack, she lived in a small but comfortable apartment above a kosher bagel shop in downtown Bangor that Lou ran. Her apartment window looked right down on the Kenduskeag Stream. She could lean her head out the window and look down on the annual canoe race that went right past her building.

Lou was surprised but delighted to see her. He came out from behind the counter, wiping his hands on his white apron.

"So you decided to leave that university professor of yours and come and marry me?"

She laughed. "You're so sweet, Lou. I *do* miss your coffee and those wonderful blueberry bagels, but I'm here on business, detecting business. I have a question for you."

"Quest away."

"I'd like to talk to you about an instructor that you took a course from a year ago. Kim Shock. Do you remember her?"

He frowned in concentration. "Oh that, yeah. The university was offering courses to the downtown merchants. It was on some sort of grant or pilot project. It was almost free, so I went. So someone's finally caught up with her, have they?"

"Caught up with her?"

"Yeah, caught up with her. For plagiarizing."

Plagiarizing? Teri whipped out her notebook. "Do you have a

minute, Lou? Can we talk?"

He pointed to a table in the corner by the kitchen. "Sit. I'll get you a coffee."

She swung her satchel over the back of the chair, took out her notebook, and sat. The place hadn't changed much. Still the same rectangular wooden tables with picnic benches, which made the place look like a dormitory. Still the sought-after round tables and cozy chairs in the raised section by the windows. Still the same posters on the walls. Still the same music on the loudspeaker, an odd eclectic mix of eastern sounds and polkas. Teri always figured it was somehow Jewish.

He came back with a coffee the way she liked it with lots of cream, a warm blueberry bagel, and a mountain of cream cheese.

"Tell me about this plagiarism," Teri asked between bites.

"Her course. The one-day, waste-of-my-precious-time course on business law." He leaned forward, his forearms on the table. "I have this book on small business practices, and basically that book was her course. She taught it as if it were her own material. I don't know how many people picked up on that, because of course no one would say anything, her being so cute and all."

"She was cute?"

"Does the name Ally McBeal ring a bell? She had the short skirts, the hair, this cute little smile. You should talk to Iris Pepper about it. She was fit to be tied. She was going to complain to the university. I don't know if she did or not." He shrugged. "I was talking to Roy Peterboom from Book Nest. He took the course a year earlier and thought it was great. Someone else had taught it then. Maybe she was just having an off day." He shook his head and frowned. "So you back working for the university now? They hired you to look into this?"

"No. Kim Shock is missing."

"Oh hey, that's not good. Scratch all the bad things I said about her."

They talked more about her course. Kim had secured some sort of grant and the only cost was five bucks for the handouts. From his office Lou produced the book Kim had plagiarized. Teri borrowed it. They ended up chatting. She told him all about their new log house on the Penobscot and how he should come out and visit when they got moved in, and he told her about the rowdy new tenant now living in Teri's apartment who threw his empty beer bottles out the window into the river.

After she gave Lou a good-bye hug, she walked across the street to Pepper's Clothes, but was told that Iris was on vacation in New Hampshire and would be home at the end of the week, but could the assistant manager help her? Was the assistant manager acquainted with Kim Shock? When the assistant manager shook her head, Teri said she'd call when Iris got back.

There was a message on the machine for her when she got home. It was from Shauna, of all people.

"Hi Teri, I just thought that if you're not too busy, maybe we could get together sometime."

Shauna wants to get together with me? Teri raised her eyebrows.

18

Glynis was very cold during lunch. Almost shivering. She wished people would keep their houses warmer, but no one ever did. It was raining, and for about the fifth time that afternoon, Glynis wondered why she had ever consented to come to the minister and his wife's place for lunch. She was missing Chasco's on-line Sunday morning service, and that made her nervous. When she had said yes, she'd like to come to lunch on the weekend, she had thought Ken and Cheryl meant Saturday. By the time she realized they meant Sunday, it was impolite to back out. Yesterday she had e-mailed Chasco that she wouldn't be there and explained why. He understood, or at least said he did.

Chasco: Promise me, that you'll e-mail me the MINUTE you walk in your door. I want to hear all about your lunch.

Gwyneth88: I will.

Chasco: You've never told me about your minister. What kind of a person is he?

Gwyneth88: Fine. Nice. I've never been one of those people who are super involved in church. For a long time it was because my mother was so sick. And then when she died and my aunt moved back to Boston and I was on my own, well, it just seemed like I wasn't getting all that much out of it.

Chasco: I know what you mean. There's so much wrong with our present-day system of "doing" church. So many are disillusioned. That's why I'm so actively involved in on-line ministry. I'm surprised you're sticking with your church at all.

> *Gwyneth88:* I don't know how much longer I'll be able to
> stick with it. Nobody's very friendly there.
>
> *Chasco:* That's the beauty of an on-line church. People are
> much friendlier, because most of us know what it's like to be
> shunned by the church.

Last night Chasco had sent her a picture of himself. She was surprised to see that he had red hair and freckles. There was a picture of
Chasco on his website, standing behind a podium at the front of a
long auditorium of young people. It was a long shot and difficult to
tell the color of his hair. She never knew he had such red hair. And
freckles! How endearing. How boyish. She looked at it again and
again. She had printed his picture and tacked it on her bulletin board
beside her computer. She studied his picture as they wrote notes to
each other far into the night.

> *Gwyneth88:* Thank you for your picture. I hope you don't
> mind, but I printed it off.
>
> *Chasco:* I'm flattered that you printed it! ☺ It's your turn,
> now. Do you realize that I've never seen a picture of you? I'm
> almost beginning to wonder if you are who you say you are.
> Ha-ha. People can be who they want to be on the Internet.
> I'm opening my soul to you (I've a good feeling about you.
> I've been praying long and hard about us), but it's time for
> you to let me into your life a bit. How about a picture?

When they signed off she felt vaguely disquieted because of
course she was deceiving him. She was not Gwyneth88, the romantic
heroine with the long blond hair; she was Glynis, the Jolly Green
Amazon.

She had stayed up far too late last night chatting with Chasco and
was paying for it now. She stifled several yawns as she looked around
her and tried to enter into the conversation. She wished she were anywhere but sitting in Ken and Cheryl's living room.

She was also distressed when she realized that this wasn't just a little lunch but a regular party. Her detective, Teri, was there along with her husband, a balding, semipaunchy sort of fellow with a beard who smiled a lot. And then there were the minister's three children, two girls and a boy.

They were in the living room, and Teri's husband was talking to the youngest, a serious looking boy with glasses. The other two were teenage girls who sat in the living room with them and chatted with the adults as if they were comfortable doing so. When Glynis was that age she was nervous around adults.

It was sort of funny when she thought about it. She always said to herself that she didn't relate to young people, yet she was relating to the young people in Chasco's Bible study just fine.

"And so how do you like working in a law office?" It took Glynis several seconds to realize that the eldest of the minister's children was addressing her.

She looked over and blinked. "It's fine."

"Rachel here is thinking about becoming a paralegal," Ken said.

"Oh, nice."

"Do you work with criminals who come in and all?" asked the younger of the daughters.

Glynis smoothed her skirt. "Not very often. It's not that kind of law practice."

At lunch they sat at a large dining room table and talked, all of them at the same time. Glynis wasn't used to this, being an only child. Her mother's sister monitored every morsel of food Glynis put in her mouth, and every word out of turn elicited a strong admonition.

Glynis found her thoughts moving around in odd patterns— drifting off the curtains, reflecting on the professor's glasses. She was watching them talk, watching their lips move, the daughters laughing, the young son cracking jokes, the mother smiling, Jack and Teri chatting happily and filling their plates. She watched them and thought about Chasco. She was thinking about his picture, his smile, his impossibly red hair. She found herself wishing he were sitting here beside her, being a part of this group, and she a part of a couple.

"Are you cold, Glynis?" Cheryl's hand was on her shoulder.

"You're shivering. I'm going to close that window. You're getting a draft right on your back."

"I'm okay," Glynis said.

"I hear you're a tea drinker. I have Earl Grey. I hear that's your favorite. Can I fix you a cup? I'm also making coffee for the coffee drinkers in the group."

Glynis pulled her sweater around her shoulders. It was summer still, yet she could not stop the shivering. "Yes. Tea would be nice."

Later, when tea and coffee and dessert were served, Cheryl asked Teri if she had any new leads on Kim. Teri said no, but that she was working on it. It was obvious that Teri hadn't told them that Glynis was the one who had hired her. She was at least glad of that. She wouldn't have to answer any uncomfortable questions.

"That is such a mystery," Cheryl said frowning. "This has us so baffled." Then she turned to Glynis. "Did you know that Kim is missing?"

Glynis nodded.

"She's such a nice young woman," the minister's wife was saying. "You knew her fairly well, didn't you?"

Glynis nodded again. The minutes dragged. She wanted to be home. When the dessert dishes were finally cleared, Glynis felt fingers in her hair. She jerked forward.

"Oh, I'm sorry." Rachel, the minister's oldest daughter, was behind her. "You probably didn't know I was here. I *love* your hair. It is *so* cool. I wish I could get mine to do that. Is it permed or something?" The girl was continuing to smooth her hair. "Every time I see you in church I think you have such cool hair."

19

In the morning Teri woke to the sounds of hammering, thudding, crunching, things falling and breaking. She got up out of bed, pulled her robe on, and looked out the window. Jack's car was gone, and in its place sat a white truck with the words *Renali Brothers* along the side. She quickly pulled on sweatpants and one of Jack's T-shirts and ventured downstairs. In the living room two men in white overalls were banging at the fireplace with sledgehammers.

"Hey," she called.

They didn't hear her.

Louder. "Hey!"

They stopped, looked at each other. Schwarzenegger look-alikes with sledgehammers.

"What are you doing?" she demanded.

"You're home," said the one on the right.

"We thought you were out."

"I was sleeping."

"If we'da known you were sleeping..."

"What are you doing?"

"Our orders were to demolish this fireplace," said the one on the right.

"And to redo the molding. For the window treatments," said the other.

"I told the new owners that we would be out in two weeks. It's not two weeks yet. Who told you you could do this?"

"Your husband let us in," said the one on the left.

"The Millers, they asked your husband and he said no problem, just go ahead," said the other one.

Teri stomped upstairs and shut herself in her bedroom. "Jack, you *totally* exasperate me sometimes!" she muttered to herself. "And since when are they called window treatments? What happened to the perfectly good word *curtains?*"

There was a note on the dresser she hadn't seen before:

Teri—Sorry I missed you. Harvey and I are showing Shauna the ropes today. We're planning to go out for dinner tonight. I'm hoping you can make it. Call me. By the way, the Millers called and asked if they could start renovating the fireplace. I said sure, no problem. Love you, J.

Teri threw on some clothes, grabbed her computer and her satchel, and hopped into her car. At the Market she found herself a table in the corner.

The place wasn't crowded on a Monday morning, and she had plenty of time to enter relevant data and conversations into her database. Internet surfing would have to wait until she was home, but she figured she had enough to keep her busy. As she made notes, a picture was emerging of Kim. She had helped street kids, as evidenced by these letters from "L." She had a special interest in people who'd been scammed, as evidenced by her ad and the e-mails and letters she'd received. Yet she had plagiarized a course that she taught. Why?

She flipped through the letters again: women who'd been cheated out of their life savings and begging Kim to take their case; men who'd been lured by the promise of property and lottery winnings in foreign countries; individuals lured to on-line gambling, which had destroyed their lives; parents whose children had been kidnapped or lured by strangers on the Internet. She picked up a copy of Kim's ad. Then turned it over. There was a piece of paper, another ad she hadn't seen before:

Have you or a loved one been the victim of an Internet predator? Call me.

Was this the sort of thing lawyers did? Was she trying to drum up business? Is this how she afforded her expensive clothes and a huge savings account?

When she was a cop, Teri worked with all kinds of lawyers: prosecutors, public defenders, high-priced criminal defense lawyers, and lots of shysters. But looking into the sort of thing Kim was probing was usually the fare of police investigators, not lawyers. She puzzled over that while she drank her coffee and watched the couple next to her, their heads almost touching while they looked at pictures in a magazine.

She called Marcie on her cell. No, she hadn't had time yet to look through their pile of videos for the one of the party. They had so many videos, it would be a chore to go through them. She'd have to plug each one into the VCR and see. That would take forever and she'd been so busy, you know, with work and Madison's school. They were having problems with one of Madison's teachers. That was their priority now.

"This is pretty important," Teri said. "Kim's missing, you know."

"I know. I know. I'll get on it tonight. Come and pick it up tomorrow. I'm writing it down on my bulletin board right now, as we speak. There, it's done. Okay. I'll get to it tonight."

"Another thing, Marcie, were you able to find Martin Monday's address and phone?"

"Now, that I did get. I had my address book in my purse the whole time."

Teri wrote his phone number and address in her notebook. She ended by saying, "I'll be over first thing tomorrow morning for that video."

"That's if I can find it."

Teri called Martin Monday next, and he expressed dismay that Kim was missing but agreed to meet with Teri tomorrow. If she wanted she could drop by his work site. He wanted to help all he could, he said.

20

Dinner with the Bestletters and Shauna wasn't as bad as Teri expected. She was still fuming at Jack for allowing their fireplace to be dismantled, but Jack, the old softy, tried to placate her by saying that the place was a wreck anyway. Starting tomorrow he was going to begin driving loads of boxes over to the new house. Harvey's son had a truck he could lend them, plus people from church had offered to help. Some things are just not worth worrying about, Teri, he told her.

They were seated at a table in the rear of the noisy restaurant, Jack and Teri on one side, Shauna and Lydia on the other, and Harvey at the end with a chair pulled over from an adjoining table. A table full of rowdies in the center were raising mugs of beer in various toasts. Their waitress told them it was a birthday party. In the corner a young woman was sitting on a stool and playing a guitar and singing something that sounded like blues, but even with her microphone she could barely be heard over the din.

Dinner conversation revolved around the university, the town, the people, the literary scene. Shauna was full of questions, mostly directed at Jack. She flicked her dark hair as she talked about poets she knew and her latest project, a prose poem about the life of Lizzie Borden.

"I hope an improvement on the original?" Jack asked.

"Oh indeed," she said, stretching out *indeed* to three syllables and looking at Teri. Teri still hadn't gotten back to her about lunch and the "something" she wanted to talk about.

"What fun!" said Lydia, clapping her hands.

Then the four of them, Harvey, Lydia, Shauna, and Jack, talked about some new course that was going to be offered in the English department.

"Oh, but we're leaving Teri out of the conversation," Shauna protested.

"Oh, don't mind me," Teri said, picking up a French fry and

dipping it in ketchup. "I like listening."

Teri was often uncomfortable in social situations. She knew how to work a room when she was on a case, but when she wasn't on the job, she was often quiet, bordering on shy.

"What will I say to those people?" she had asked Jack a couple of years ago. They were engaged at this point, and she was accompanying him to the annual university Christmas dinner.

"Just be yourself," he told her.

"Myself is an introvert. Myself is a loner. Myself doesn't talk to strangers."

"Yourself is a person who can go up to complete strangers and extract needed information. Yourself is a consummate actor when trying to get the information you need."

"That's different," she said. "That's for the job. When it's just me, it's different."

"So, Teri," Shauna was asking her now. "Are you on the trail of some elusive ne'er-do-well?"

"Always," she said.

"I'd love to hear about it," Shauna said. "This Hercule Poirot pursuit of justice."

Lydia turned to Shauna. "Teri's an amazing researcher. We were sorry to lose her at the university."

Shauna looked at her. "Seriously? You worked at the university? I thought you said you didn't."

Teri nodded. "Strange as it may seem, I did. For a time."

"What did you do?"

"Looked up things. A lot like I do every day."

"Well, isn't that something."

When they were getting ready for bed that evening, Teri told her husband, "She doesn't like me."

He laughed. "Of course she does. She's just a little eccentric."

"But she likes you."

"Oh. Well. That's not true."

"No, Jack, seriously. I see the way she looks at you."

But he laughed and told her that was ridiculous.

21

Teri wondered if she'd made a mistake in coming here. To get to where Martin Monday was working, she had to press a call button at an iron gate at the end of a long driveway. She waited primly in her car. No answer. She pressed it again. Still no one there to let her in. She got out of her car and walked toward the gate. It was a black iron gate attached firmly on either side to a ten-foot fence, the bottom six feet cement and the top a kind of wrought iron pattern with black, ominous-looking spikes. The whole thing was ornate and meant to look decorative, but its function was to keep people out. It could well have been topped with prison wire for the message it sent.

She'd called Martin Monday's office and was told by a chirpy secretary with a California accent that Martin was on Mount Desert Island, past Northwest Harbor.

"He told me I could come see him on the job site."

"He'd love to see you. He's just out working on a house."

A house. Whatever was beyond that fortification was certainly not any house in Teri's living memory. Old-timers were fond of saying that they knew Mount Desert Island when it was merely a lovely place for locals. Only locals knew about its unspoiled reaches of forest, its soaring cliffs, its majestic vistas. Now Mount Desert had become a rich kids' spot, a place where Hollywood types increasingly built huge summer homes behind high walls and gates with buzzers. Gates like this one.

Just for fun she pushed on the gate. It wasn't locked. She looked at it in surprise. She could leave her car here, hike up, talk to Martin, and hike back down again. No, she'd open the gate all the way and drive up. Her first rule of being a good PI: Pretend like you own the place—followed quickly by the second rule: It's easier to get forgiveness than to ask permission.

She opened the gate wide, drove through, and got out and closed the gate behind her, smiling and waving happily at a slowing motorist.

The long winding driveway was paved and clean and lined on either side with pine trees in regimented rows. A few minutes later the forest opened to reveal a hotel-sized mansion. Carefully maintained gardens surrounded it, and in each window was a flower box. Not a weed, not a blade of grass out of place.

So this is how the rich live.

Off to the side was a white gazebo. Again, more flowers. She was obviously in the wrong place since this building most definitely was not under construction. And she wondered vaguely what story she would concoct when the rabid groundskeeper threatened her with a shotgun. She was also aware that she was in grubby jeans and that her Honda Civic desperately needed a bath. At the edge of the circular drive she saw the ocean. This house was right smack on a cliff, and ahead of her the Atlantic gleamed and shone and sparkled and danced. "Man!" she said aloud. "Wow!"

She got out of her car, not bothering to lock it. She walked around the front of the house, the side that faced the water. There were decks at every window with more flowers, more swings, more little garden patches out on the grass with white wrought iron tables and chairs. In a far garden she saw someone bent over and made her way toward him.

"I'm looking for Martin Monday," she said to the fellow, who stood up when she approached.

"Oh. Over there." He pointed toward the framework for a small building at the far edge of the property.

"Thanks!"

She waved and smiled and trudged off toward the construction as if she owned the place.

A whole crew was there, and she asked the first person she saw to direct her to Martin Monday.

"Hey! Marty! Someone here wants to see you."

Teri waited. The man walking toward her in the sunlight, a tool belt slung low around his waist, his shirt partially opened, dark, curly hair falling carelessly on his forehead, looked as if he were walking off the cover of a romance novel. He held out his hand for her to shake, and she looked into his eyes, which were a piercing blue. "You had no trouble getting through the gate?"

"None. It was open."

"That's good. I was afraid someone might've locked it. We're in and out with supplies these days and the family's away, so we're leaving it unlocked."

"This place is amazing. What are you building? A stable for the horses?"

He laughed. His laugh was low and deep and cheerful. *Kim, you have no brain in your head to let this guy go.* "Not really. What we have here is a guest house."

"That's a *guest* house? What's wrong with a guest room? What, does that family have twenty-five kids? No room for guests in that place?"

"Amazing, isn't it? This guest house is miles bigger than my regular house. And I've got a really nice regular house. I built it myself."

She shaded her eyes with her hand. "So who lives here anyway?"

"Some rich guy named Max Beamish. And you want to know the really sad part? He comes to this place one week in the summer. That's it. One week." They were walking around to the front of the structure he was building. She could see it was going to be a miniature of the big house. "You want a soda or something?"

"Okay, yeah. That would be nice."

There was a cooler near a pile of boards. He grabbed two cans, and she followed him to the gazebo.

"We might as well sit in there. You say Kim's missing? That's what you're here about?"

"It appears that way," Teri said, sitting across from him and flipping to a clean page in her notebook.

"I'd like to help all I can, I really would. I just don't know what I can add. She and I have been out of touch for quite a while."

"I understand that," Teri said. "What I'm looking for is anything about Kim—her habits, what she was like, where she might go if frightened or in trouble. I'm developing a bit of a picture of her, but it's a confusing one."

He smiled, sighed. "She's a confusing one. She was always on some sort of crusade."

"What do you mean 'crusade'?"

"She did a lot of free work for people. Pro bono work."

"Before she left she was interested in helping people who'd been conned out of their money. Do you know anything about that?"

He leaned back, folding strong forearms on his chest. "When I knew her she had one goal and one goal only, and that was to clear her brother's name. Of course, I knew her right after it happened, right after he died. It was uppermost in her mind then."

"Now it appears she's interested in finding people who've been scammed."

He was thoughtful for a while, his hands on his knees. "I'm surprised Kim would stay in Texas like that. It seems so unlike her, but I would be willing to bet it has something to do with Barry."

"Really? You think so?"

"I think so."

He leaned back, took a long drink of his Coke. "I often wonder if Kim and I would've made it if we'd met at a different time and under different circumstances. She was so angry that her brother could've gotten himself in a religious cult like that. She was determined to find out why and how."

"Was he religious?"

Martin shrugged. The sun made crisscross patterns on his face through the gazebo's latticework. "She was convinced that someone hypnotized him, or brainwashed him, that he wouldn't knowingly do what he did. Both she and her mother didn't believe the police reports that he had that adoption syndrome the media made such a big deal over. I think from the beginning our relationship was doomed. She clung to me after a particularly bad time, and for me, it was nice to be leaned on, nice to be needed. I'm not sure now that I was ever in love with her. Or she with me."

"Do you have any idea where she might go if she was in trouble?"

"I don't know. Maybe her mother's? They were close."

"I have her address. I'll check that out."

When he found out that Teri went to the same church that Kim went to, he asked, "How is Glynis?"

"Glynis?"

"Do you know her at all?"

"I do, actually. She's worried about Kim. Why do you ask?"

"No reason. Just curious. I could never figure out those two, the friendship they had. Glynis has so much to offer in her own right. She's very talented and extremely creative, yet hangs on Kim almost for dear life. I think she looked to Kim as someone with a normal childhood when hers was so tainted with tragedy. Her mother committed suicide. Did you know that?"

Teri looked at him.

"Her mother was quite sick, dying in fact. I can't remember what she had, but it was one of those debilitating things. She took her own life before the pain could get too bad. There was a kind of strange ostracism that Glynis felt then from the church and other Christians. I think instead of people reaching out and embracing her, she and her aunt were shunned in a way. The only one who really was there for her was Kim. And then her aunt moved back to Boston and ended up blaming Glynis for driving her mother to suicide."

"Glynis told you all this?"

He nodded. "We were good friends. Both of us were trying to help Kim through that dark time in her life. Tell her I said hello when you see her, will you?"

"I will."

She made two stops on her way home: Marcie's for the video, and the apartment where Kim had lived. Marcie wasn't home, but Matt, a big guy in a sweatshirt with cutoff sleeves, gave her the video after rooting around in a plastic laundry basket full of loose videos.

"I'm pretty sure this is the one." He eyed it. "Yeah, I think so."

"Can you check it first?" Teri asked. She didn't want to get all the way home and find out it was their kid's piano recital or figure skating show or Sunday school program.

He plugged it into the VCR, watched one minute, and told her yes, it was.

"Thanks. I'll make a copy and get it back to you."

22

Kim had lived in a town house apartment near the law offices of Smith and Egan. The sign advertised the place as Luxury Town Houses, but after witnessing the once-a-week summer home of one of America's richest entrepreneurs, Teri thought these apartments looked sad and run-down and hopelessly small. She pulled in, parked in a spot with VISITORS painted in yellow in capital letters on the pavement. She walked through a door marked "Office," which opened up to a kitchen complete with appliances and decorated nicely with a maple table and hutch. Some sort of a showroom, she surmised.

"Hello!" she called. She heard scuffling from the back.

"We're full up," said a man emerging from a doorway. He wore faded chinos and an undershirt. "Even got too many on the waiting list."

"I'm not here about an apartment. I want to ask you some questions about a former resident."

"You got a warrant?"

"No. I'm a private investigator. A young woman lived here a while ago, and she's now missing."

"Kim Shock."

"You remember her."

"Of course I remember her. Nice person. Always paid the rent on time. She goes away, and all of a sudden I don't know where she is and the rent's due. And then I get a letter with a check asking me to pack up her things and send them on, so I did."

"That's it?"

"That's it. She left nothing. It's all gone."

"Nothing else in storage?"

"Nope."

"Furniture?"

"Sold. Like she asked."

"And you did all this?"

"She paid me."

I bet she paid you well. "Do you by any chance still have the letter she sent?"

"Nope."

Teri sighed. "Where did you send these things?"

"Someplace in Texas. El Paso."

"You don't have that address anywhere, either?"

"Nope."

"And you don't remember it?"

The phone rang at that instant and he answered it. Teri left and headed home.

Before she could watch the video, she had to locate the VCR. She eventually found it two boxes deep in the downstairs bathroom, then went in search of the television. The bodybuilders were still at it, dismantling the mantel as she waded through the debris in the living room.

"Hi," she said.

They waved in unison and said hi in stereo. But the television wasn't in the living room. Nor was it in the dining room. She finally found it in the room she had started in, the kitchen, behind a stack of chairs and covered with a raggy quilt she'd never seen before.

The previous evening, Teri and Jack, with the help of Stephan and Harvey's son, had moved most of the stuff from the living room into the kitchen to give the house wreckers a place to wreck from. With their living room gone, it meant no more television or stereo until they got to their new place. Lately, they were taking nightly trips out to the new house with boxes of stuff. Teri was immensely pleased that the television and VCR hadn't been among them. She pulled the VCR out of its box and plugged it into the back of the television. Next she had to find an extension cord long enough to plug the works into an outlet above the counter. She remembered seeing one at the top of the stairs earlier. All of this took a most frustrating half hour to accomplish, and when she finally made a place for herself on the dirty kitchen floor to watch the video, she was coated in dust and sweat. The day was warmer than it had been for many weeks. Murphy's law: When you move it's either the coldest day of the year, the hottest, or the wettest. It looked like this was settling in to be the hottest.

She sat cross-legged on the floor, wiped her damp forehead with the bottom of her T-shirt, and leaned her back against a box to watch. On the screen was a group of people in a backyard with several of them standing in front of two barbecues. The video was complete with running commentary, which came, Teri guessed, from Marcie's husband, Matt.

Teri recognized Marcie, heard her large laugh, her voice ordering people to go this place and that for their burgers, and where the lemonade for the kids was. And then the camera moved closer and closer and finally Marcie's hand went up to the lens. "Don't take it now," she was saying. "Don't take one of me. Get a few of the kids. Or of Madison."

There were children there, lots of them, little kids running around at knee level with hot dog buns in their hands, and dogs their own size chasing after them, hoping for a few leavings. There looked to be around twenty there, many of whom Teri recognized. When they noticed Matt, they either put up their hands and moved away or hammed it up. Glynis didn't seem to be there.

And then the camera moved to a side porch where a couple sat on the top step. Matt whispered, "And over there, completely unaware of the hidden camera, are the two lovebirds, who are the reason for this party in the first place. But you'd never know it by the fact of their marked absence from the mainstream of the party, but we'll forgive them that. They are obviously in love, folks, obviously in love. But we'll forgive them that, too. They'll get over it. Ha-ha. On the left you have Gil Williamson, engineer extraordinaire, and on his right our lovely lawyer Kim Shock. And I have to be quiet. I don't want the man of the hour destroying *this* camera, even if he *can* afford to buy me a new and better one. On second thought, maybe I should get him to break this one."

The camera moved closer and closer. Kim was one of those tall, long-legged beauties. And Gil, in a white golf shirt and jeans, looked pleasant enough. Certainly not as handsome as Martin Monday, but pleasant enough.

They were sitting next to each other, and Kim had one knee up, her bare foot on the edge of the step. She was looking at him, away from the camera, and they were talking intently.

Then Gil leaned back, his hands on the porch behind him, and laughed. Teri watched his face, the way his mouth was when he laughed. He reached over and touched Kim's hand.

"And what is our magical couple talking about with eyes only for each other?" Matt was saying quietly.

Kim pulled her hand away. She wasn't smiling.

"Okay, lovebirds, time for me to get back to the party."

And then Matt imperceptibly backed away, and was again panning the party, making comments. There were no more pictures of Gil and Kim.

Teri ran the video back, looking at the one clear shot of Gil's face. She kept looking into the face. Tomorrow she would take this video to a computer guy she knew and ask him to make some stills of Gil.

She rewound the video again, this time concentrating on Kim. At the way she sat there, hugging one knee, the manicured, painted toenails. There was something odd about the way she looked at Gil. Not like someone in love, but what? Amusement? And pulling her hand away from his like that, what was *that* all about?

Teri replayed the video several more times, memorizing the way Gil's eyebrow shot up; the frown lines on the left side of his mouth; the curve of his lips; the small mole or discoloration underneath his right eye; his hair, thick and fair.

She was running the video back and forth, slow-forwarding it again and again. She heard a sound from somewhere behind her.

She turned. Shauna was there, her long legs in wide khaki pants.

"This is a wonderful old house," she said when Teri looked up. "Jack was telling me about this place."

Jack? When did the two of them become so chummy?

"Jack's not here," Teri said rising.

"I'm not looking for Jack. If I were looking for Jack, I'd go to the university."

"Right."

"I came because I wanted to talk to you."

"Okay. Yeah. Sorry I didn't get back to you," Teri said, wiping the kitchen dust off the back of her pants. She felt grubby and hot. And there was Shauna looking so cool, so clean. She ran a hand through her hair, sure to bring up pieces of dust or chunks of plaster from above the living room fireplace.

"I came because I want to talk to you about crime. You are the expert in crime, or so Jack tells me."

"You want to talk to me about crime?"

"I mentioned that story I want to write about Lizzie Borden. Well, there are other crimes I want to write about."

Teri turned off the television and rewound the video.

"You were watching a video in here?"

"Yeah. Got bored packing. Decided I needed a break."

Shauna cocked her head.

"Just kidding," Teri said. "It's for my work."

"Is it a case?"

"Well, yeah. A case."

"It must be quite mesmeric being a private detective."

Teri nodded seriously. "Mesmeric. That's exactly how I would describe it."

Shauna raked her hands through her long hair. Teri noticed that she wore a different earring in each ear. "I should think it would be quite fascinating. The allure of it. The danger. Do you enjoy reading detective stories? I bet Jack does. Since he married someone like you."

Teri suppressed a grin. "Jack hates mysteries. He prefers literary stories all about people and angst."

Shauna was on the stool, leafing through a copy of Stephan's chapbook of poetry that had been on the top of a stack of papers.

"You've seen Stephan's book?" Teri asked.

"Oh yes. I've read through most of his stuff. He's quite gifted, wouldn't you say?"

"He's a nice kid, too. It helps to be gifted *and* nice."

"You see that little computer there?" Shauna pointed at Teri's iBook, which was on the counter. "That's you and me in about a billion years."

"Say what?"

"That's the next step of human evolution. We came from apes, then Lucy, and soon, the next step, the next logical step is computers."

"Lucy who?"

"Lucy, the prehistoric woman who lived three million years ago."

Teri blinked. Then lifted up her iBook. "And so now you think we're all evolving into computers? With the amount of time mine spends crashing, I'd say that was a step backwards."

"It's something I believe." Shauna was serious, and Teri forced herself not to roll her eyes.

"I'm a transhumanist," she added.

Teri blinked. "Okay." *There are actually people who believe this?* "So, you don't believe in God, then?"

Shauna spread her arms wide. "Depends on your definition of God. God is a concept. God is a place. God is the ability to create technology that will wipe out human suffering. God is the ability to alter DNA for the benefit of all people." She sat back down.

"And we're all going to turn into computers?"

"Laugh if you want. I mean we've come this far, what's the next logical step. They're already implanting DNA into microchips. It's there, the technology is there. Clones. I see it making us better than we are."

"You don't believe there's anything beyond this earth then? No eternity. No God out there. Nothing but us and our DNA and our ability to create computers?"

"I know you're a Christian. Jack and I have talked about this, and I'll tell you what I told him. I tried Christianity once. It didn't stick. I think I'm too much of a free thinker for organized religion. I like exploring ideas. I mean the God of Sunday school is so pathetic."

Teri said, "Probably you're right, if the Sunday school God is some namby-pamby Santa Claus in the sky—you better watch out, you better not cry—then, yeah, I think that's pathetic, too. But what about a God of awe and mystery, a God that you can't define and write theories about."

"But science and a belief in God are at odds with each other. I've chosen science."

Teri laughed. "First of all, I don't think science and God are at odds with each other, and second, I think God is beyond science."

Shauna cocked her head and looked at her. "I'm jealous of you, Teri. I'm jealous of you. You have it all together—a new house, a husband, and a religious system you actually believe in."

"That's not so hard, Shauna."

But Shauna was backing out the door. "I've got to go."

It wasn't until after she left that Teri wondered why she had come.

23

When I woke up at Georgina's that first morning, I thought of all the things I could buy with the money. I could get a car, some new clothes, maybe even find an apartment of my own. Something nice. I could open a savings account. I'd never had a savings account. I lay on my back, the backpack under my head, and looked at the ceiling and dreamed and dreamed about all the things I could do with the money.

It was quiet. I liked that. My two roommates, Estelle and Fiona, were gone already. Georgina was an exotic dancer who ran a kind of rooming house as a tenant landlady. You paid minimal rent, often had to share a room, and her rules were strict: no visitors in the rooms at night; you had to be in by eleven (unless you'd made prior arrangements with Georgina); no cooking in the rooms, not even a kettle; and absolutely no alcohol or tobacco. If people didn't like those rules she would say fine, leave. Lots did. And if you were caught breaking any of the rules, one of her bouncer boyfriends wasn't opposed to dragging you out of bed in the middle of the night and throwing you out into the street.

But I liked it there. I felt safe there. And I mostly kept out of everybody's way, same as I did out at the farm, making my meals at times when no one else would be in the kitchen, and taking my showers when I knew no one else would be wanting the bathroom.

When I was sure that I was alone in the house, I carried the backpack into the bathroom and locked the door. Then I dumped the money on the floor. I had never seen so much! I threw it up in the air like they do on those lottery commercials. Whee! I said out loud. And I threw it up and let it rain down on me. I must have done this for ten minutes saying Whee! Whee! the whole time.

"What's going on in there?" Georgina was banging on the door. "There better not be any hanky-panky."

I stopped dead still and a shower of bills settled on the floor. "Sorry," I called through the door. "I'll be out in about five minutes."

"It better be sooner than that. I got an appointment."

So I stuffed the money as fast as I could back into the backpack. Georgina scowled at me when I skittered past. When she left, I took the money back into the bathroom and set about to properly rebundle it. It was all in fifties. I actually lost count after about sixty thousand dollars. Can you imagine having so much money that you actually lose count?

Then I put it back in the pack and took the pack downstairs to a place in the basement that I knew about. I'd been down there hiding once when one of Georgina's bouncers was going to throw me out for making tea. I knew about a hole in the floor behind the furnace and under some metal shelves. I pulled up the piece of loose cement, dug in the dirt a bit, and buried the backpack. Then I put the cement back on top.

I never spent a penny of it. You would've thought that I would at least have taken maybe a couple hundred out for myself, but I never did. It's hard to explain, but I never felt right about it. I kept thinking of Coach and the girls and how the money was all a part of their death. I couldn't spend it.

Thinking about it, the most fun I ever had with that money was the day I stood in the bathroom and for ten minutes threw it up and let it shower all over me.

24

Glynis wasn't pretty. No matter how much she looked at herself this way and that in the dressing room mirror at Pepper's Clothes, no one would ever mistake her for being pretty. She could be well-dressed. She could be smart-looking, handsome, but pretty? She was far too tall. Her hair was too unmanageable, her eyes too deep set and dark, her face too intense, her shoulders too narrow, her arms too skinny, her fingers too long, her knees too bony. There were a million reasons why she wasn't pretty. She would buy cashmere sweaters and shirts, the best wool suits and fine leather shoes, but underneath it all she was still Glynis. And Glynis was the Jolly Green Amazon. Even her aunt called her that.

Don't call her that, her mother would say to her. Don't call my daughter that. Why not? It's true, isn't it? No man's going to want a woman all skin and bones like that and taller than he is. What kind of kids would they have? Amazons. Maybe it was something you ate during your pregnancy, Maylene. Did you ever think of that? And then she would laugh.

When she was a little girl, she prayed every night that when she woke up she would be shorter. She wanted to be five foot seven. The perfect height, according to her aunt. All clothes look good on you when you're five foot seven, her aunt would say. You can wear anything when you're five foot seven. Kim was five foot seven.

But it never happened.

"How does that fit, Glynis? Can I bring you some more of those skirts?" Outside of Glynis's dressing room, Iris Pepper had a handful of skirts.

"I'll probably buy the one I have in here," Glynis said. "And maybe one of those sweaters. Thank you," she said, opening the door. "Those skirts are nice. I'm so glad you have fashions for taller women."

Iris stood back to look at Glynis. "That looks wonderful on you, dear. Do you know how many women would give anything to be as thin and tall and as stately looking as you are?"

Glynis didn't say anything.

"How is your aunt doing these days?" Iris asked. "Ever hear from her?"

"Not very often. No."

"You tell her hello for me next time you see her."

Glynis smoothed the skirt. When Iris closed the door, Glynis pulled the sweater over her head, sending her hair into winging spirals. Stately? Her reflection mocked Iris Pepper's lie: her skin all pasty, her wrists knobby at the ends of the sleeves. With her left hand she held her hair back severely off her head. And now Chasco wanted a picture of her. She hated getting her picture taken. She avoided it whenever possible.

No, she was not photogenic.

More than twenty years ago, she and Kim had been at the Sunday school picnic. Their church always went to a lake in June, with water too cold for swimming, but all of the kids swam anyway, while the moms sat on lawn chairs under umbrellas on the grassy beach and the dads got the barbecues going. Her aunt and her mother were both there, her mother silent and unmoving in her wheelchair.

Somewhere Glynis probably still had the picture of the two of them, she and Kim standing in water up to their ankles. Later she would look at that picture and wonder what mistaken bit of information, what circuit had shorted in her brain to make her think she looked good in that bathing suit. It was a new one, something her aunt had brought home for her from an exclusive women's store. It came with a matching cover-up, which Glynis wore proudly.

Next to her, Kim was in a faded pink hand-me-down bathing suit that drooped on her. It also had a finger hole along the side seam, but Kim didn't seem the least embarrassed by it; in fact she seemed to constantly draw attention to it, poking her finger in the hole and laughing as they stood there, the water over their ankles.

Kim stood, one hand on her left hip, the toe of her right foot pointing forward. Glynis tried to copy that pose. While it looked natural on Kim, later looking at the picture Glynis realized how affected the pose looked on her, and how foolish the cover-up looked with her big fluffy hair and her chicken neck and her height miles taller than Kim.

And when the Sunday school boys came over, it was to Kim they went, to Kim they talked. Kim with her droopy bathing suit was the one they splashed water on. Not Glynis with her new suit and matching cover-up. Kim, earthy and sexy, even at thirteen.

"Just hand me out those things and I'll ring them up for you," Iris said.

At the counter Glynis handed Iris her Visa. Yes, it was a warm day. And yes, it would be nice if the nice weather held. No, she wasn't looking forward to winter either, but at least she had this nice sweater. And yes, she would be back; she loved the fact that Iris could get clothes in extra tall.

"I used to tell your mother that you should be a supermodel," said Iris, folding the sweater. "You know, there are lots of tall women. Sigourney Weaver, now she's your height, I think, or close to it. And Geena Davis, she's at least your height. There are lots of famous beautiful women who are tall. Someone was just asking me the other day, who is that tall, beautiful girl who comes in here sometimes? And I had to say, oh you must mean Glynis Pigott."

It was kind of Iris to say these things even if they weren't true.

"I'm looking for a photographer," Glynis said. "One of those places that makes you up to look better than you are. I need to get a picture taken."

"You need a picture?"

"Yes."

"Let me see..." Iris flipped through some business cards and handed one to Glynis. "Call this number. He sometimes does our fashion shows. He's wonderful. He'll take one look at you and flip."

"I'm sure he will."

When Glynis got home her answering machine was flashing, but her e-mail messages came first. She made herself a pot of Earl Grey and sipped while she savored the two long e-mail messages from Chasco. The hospital was still after him for money. The bill was huge. Brain specialists are some of the highest paid specialists. Did she know that? But that wasn't why he had e-mailed.

> Whenever I see that there's an e-mail from Gwyneth88 in my box, I have to say that I find my heart doing all sorts of strange things. Do you mind my saying this? I feel we have a connection that I can't deny any longer. It's funny that I should feel this way and I've never even seen a picture of you! You asked me how tall I am. I'm 6'3".

She wrote back to him. She told him it was a beautiful day, and then she wrote a long note about her mother. She was beginning to tell him the things of her heart, things she had told few people, how it was when she found her mother and how she always felt less than adequate. He wrote back:

> I missed you yesterday. Whenever I e-mail you and you don't answer right away I find myself missing you. Everyone is still e-mailing me about the great job you did with the Bible study. Just one thing, however, and it's an arguably small thing, and I almost hate to mention it, but all members of the Bible study have to be approved by me. ☺
>
> Chasco

She wrote back and apologized. After she clicked Send, she wrote to KarenP and Lark7 and told them all about the new clothes she bought and how she was beginning to feel things for Chasco that confused her.

After she logged off, she listened to the phone message. It was from Martin Monday, of all people.

"Hi Glynis, this is Martin Monday. I hope you remember me. I heard that Kim was missing. And it got me to thinking, and I was just, ah, thinking about you. And just wondering how you're doing.

Give me a call sometime, or maybe I'll try calling back. Bye."

She raised her eyebrows and erased it.

Before she went to bed she buttoned her new pink sweater to her neck and stood in front of the mirror. She pushed her hair off her face and stared at herself. Maybe there was a photographer somewhere who could make sense of her wild hair and dark eyes.

25

Pepper's Clothes featured handmade and designer clothes for real women. Tall women, big women, short women, women who wanted something different than mall clothes. Teri had been in Pepper's Clothes only as a casual observer. Usually the prices made her want to flee, her hands in her hair. A 70 percent off sale might bring Pepper's Clothes down to where they fit her budget.

Today, however, she brushed past racks of overpriced cashmere suits and hand embroidered blouses to where Iris Pepper stood behind the counter writing in a notebook.

"Iris Pepper?"

She looked up. She was midseventies but with that vibrant health and energy women that age have if they've been fortunate enough to escape major illnesses. Teri's friend Andrea Silver, who sold the clothes she made here, described Iris as a "bundle of energy." She was a small woman with iron gray hair nicely styled and small silver hoop earrings. If there was one word that came to Teri's mind to describe her, that word was *classy.*

"Yes?" she said.

Teri extended her hand. "I'm Teri Blake-Addison. I'm a private investigator looking into the disappearance of Kim Shock. I understand you took a one-day course she offered to local businesspeople."

She snorted. "Biggest waste of my valuable time."

"Why's that?"

With jabs of her pen on the paper, Iris basically told the same story that Lou Cohen had. She ended by saying that there was something "odd" about the whole day.

"What do you mean by 'odd'?"

"She was a very lovely young woman. And the entire time she was talking I had this feeling she was smarter than she let on. It was as if this were some big joke with her."

"Really."

"It was like she was having us all on."

Having us all on. Teri puzzled at this on the drive home. In her kitchen, she cleared a space at the table, shoving aside a stack of casserole dishes that needed wrapping and packing or putting in the garage sale box. *Garage sale box,* she decided, carrying them outside. After all, how many casseroles can one make at one time?

The Renali brothers were working quietly today, their radio tuned to a country music station. At the table she took out copies of the letters "L" wrote to Kim, the plagiarizer. They were all postmarked Bangor. Teri called a social worker she knew from the inner city and asked her if she knew a street kid who had the first initial L. "I'm assuming it's female, but I can't be positive," Teri added.

"You're joking, right? You don't have an age, you don't even have a gender, no name, just an initial? It'd be like finding a needle in a haystack."

"I guess when you put it like that..."

"I can do a lot, Teri. I can work a lot of miracles, but I need a bit more than a first initial."

"It was a long shot. I admit it. But if you twig something would you give me a call? It's important."

"Sure."

Jack walked in then with a bunch of empty boxes, and after she hung up he asked her how it was going.

"I'm looking for a needle in a haystack. I see you got more boxes."

"I've got a bunch of students coming over later to help pack."

"Speaking of students, do you know that Shauna thinks we're all going to turn into computers?"

"I know. She really believes that. We've talked about it."

"Do you guys talk a lot, Jack?"

"We work together, Teri."

"Don't you think she's a little strange?"

"Not strange, just lonely, just looking for validation. Like we all are. She's way out here, far from home for the first time, and feeling like a fish out of water." He piled the boxes on the porch. "These probably won't even be enough. We've got the whole basement yet. I'll go get more."

After Jack left, Teri went back to her computer. She'd put "L" aside for the time being.

The money. Follow the money. If Teri's years on the police force had taught her anything, it was to follow the money. Find out who controls the money and you'll often find not only motive but suspect.

The money in Glynis's possession was a worry. On a clean sheet of paper she ran through various scenarios:

1. Gil was a scammer and the money was his and gotten through various scams. Kim was obsessed with bringing scammers to justice. So she stole the money from Gil.
2. Maybe this was money she managed to get from the con men she'd investigated at some point, and she was planning to give it back.
3. Maybe she was a con artist herself. Maybe that explained that plagiarized course she taught.
4. Maybe the money was rightfully hers. She'd earned it and for some reason (?) wanted to leave it with Glynis.

It was only morning and already she felt tired. She ran a hand over her face, wondering why her eyes wouldn't focus. Teri had gotten her computer friend to make copies of the picture of Gil and had sent it out on a few of her private PI listservs. It was grainy, but a bit better than the indistinct one Glynis had given her. She dialed up her modem and idly searched through some of her data banks for something, anything about Gil.

An on-line PI friend from Toronto thought Gil looked like a deadbeat dad she was currently trying to track down. Another one from the West Coast said his face looked an awful lot like Troy Duncan, a man he'd investigated in connection with two sisters who'd been bilked out of close to a quarter of a million dollars. The two lived in Arizona. Anything remotely near Texas put it in the running. Teri shot him an e-mail. Another PI working in Florida said the case reminded him of a con man by the name of Julius Dumain, who was posing as a faith healer and offering healing and positive energy (whatever that was) for a price. His location was El Paso. She made a note of that. Another said the picture looked a little like a man who passed himself off as a medical doctor, but took people's money and did phony medical procedures. Those that sent pictures, she downloaded. She compared stories. She made notes. She printed off the pictures. All of it quite interesting. None of it leading her any closer to Kim.

Partway through the morning she did something uncharacteristic for her. She called Andrea.

"Hey," she said. "I'm up for a coffee break; are you?"

"Sure. When and where?"

Fifteen minutes later they were sitting at an outside table at the Market and talking about Teri's coming move. Teri was tired and stressed. Andrea was tired and stressed. Teri had a case she couldn't solve. Andrea had a big wedding on the weekend and one of the bridesmaids had gained a bit of weight since her last fitting and there just wasn't room to let out the seams. And of course everyone was blaming the seamstress. She might be faced with cutting out an entire new bodice.

Forty-five minutes later they parted promising to "do this more often."

On her way home, Teri thought how lucky she was that in the space of two years, not only had she found a husband, but now a woman friend.

26

The day was beautiful, and Glynis was on her way to get her picture taken. What would it be like to be a minister's wife, she wondered as she drove down unfamiliar streets to the address on the business card. Maybe she could talk to Cheryl about it. *Stop it. You're getting way ahead of yourself! All he does is sign his e-mails with* love *a few times and you're head over heels!* But no, it was more than that. Wasn't it more than that? They were exchanging pictures. They were e-mailing two and three times a day. She was telling him things she told few people, and he was sharing equally with her. It was only a matter of time...

"You positively sparkle!" said the man who would be her photographer. He was short, much shorter than Glynis, but he looked up at her and said, "It will be a joy photographing you. Pure joy. You are very photogenic. But I don't need to tell you that. You already know that, I'm sure."

Glynis thought of the picture of her in the awful bathing suit. "I just need a small picture," she said. "It's to go on-line."

"A website! And you're a model! We can do a whole workup, a whole portfolio. Did you bring clothes?"

"Just what I'm wearing. This sweater." She touched the neck of her new cashmere from Pepper's.

He hustled her through the reception area and down a narrow hallway whose walls were decorated with framed photographs and posters. A quick glance and you could tell that this was no ordinary photographer. No smiling family groupings, no grad pictures. These were art shots: models draped in wisps of black and posing dramatically, several nudes, strange still lifes. One particularly caught her eye, a La-Z-Boy recliner, old, patched, and cracked and sitting in a hay field, a few green sprouts growing out of its crevices. Glynis wondered if she was in the right place. All she wanted was a simple head-and-shoulders.

On either side of the hall, doors opened into studio rooms with props piled up or laid out artistically. In one of them, someone was using a garden sprayer to spray what looked like a hamburger on a plate while someone else photographed it.

"Chloe!" called the little man, strutting in front of her. "We need some makeup. And hair. Now." And he clapped his hands twice.

"Come, come," said Chloe, taking her arm. Chloe was a husky woman with dangling silver earrings who smelled of some undefined perfume, or maybe it was hair gel. The makeup room looked like an ordinary hair salon, only smaller and cluttered with racks and racks of clothing, crammed together and sticking out at odd angles. On the floor were parasols, shoes, and a box of what looked like feather boas. The room gave off a slightly used-clothing smell. Glynis sat in the chair.

"Oh what hair, what hair," Chloe said, working her fingers through. "So much curl."

"Frizz, more like," Glynis answered.

"You may want to try some straighteners. I could suggest a few. I could give you some names of people who do wonders with your kind of hair."

"I usually let it do whatever it wants to do," Glynis said.

"I have another idea for today. It will really bring out your cheekbones and your eyes. Those eyes." Chloe slicked Glynis's hair back with gel and tied it in a knot at the nape of her neck. "Not many women can do this," Chloe said, "but you can. Your face is smooth, your skin is good, your head shape classic. Good bones. You could shave your head and still look beautiful."

Glynis laughed. "I don't think I would go that far."

"You have classic facial bones. You could pull it off. Not many could."

Glynis moved her head from side to side. "It seems a little severe. What about a few little tendrils at the side. Just something."

"You don't like it so severe? Okay, we can do tendrils." She combed out a few wispy curls around her face. "We don't want too much. You'll end up looking like a Victorian heroine. We don't want that. We can't have that. Plus, when you do this it has to look messy, not contrived. Mess, mess, that's what we want here," Chloe said, scrunching up a few stray strands until they did, indeed, look messy.

"It's going to be the same for your makeup. Smudgy and messy is the look we want. You have such dreamy eyes. Has anyone ever told you that?"

Glynis laughed. "Dreamy? No. Never."

"Dreamy. Drowsy, and I think that's the look we'll go for. Make it look like you just got out of bed."

"I look *terrible* when I just get out of bed."

"It's a look. It's a look. Let me tell you something," Chloe said, arranging various pots of color on the tray in front of her. "I was a makeup artist for movies for a number of years. And you know the look when the movie stars are just getting up in the morning? Well, that look takes a lot of doing. My biggest challenge was a few years ago, the heroine was supposed to look like she had a cold. She had to look sick, beautiful, cute, and vulnerable all at once. *That* was a challenge. Now if that movie star really *was* sick, she would probably look as dreadful as you and I when we're sick, but for the movies it has to be different."

She talked nonstop while she used the tips of her fingers to apply colors to Glynis's face. When Chloe was finished, Glynis looked at herself in the mirror. The effect was quite startling. She looked brooding and dark, your typical unsmiling runway model. With no hair. But in an odd way, she did look beautiful.

Then it was into various clothes, drapes across the shoulders, blouses, and Glynis almost believed it when the photographer kept moving her this way and that, going on and on about how photogenic and classic she looked. She ended up ordering the whole photo package, although for what purpose she had no idea. The prints would be ready in about a week, but she was free to take the disk now, they told her.

"This will get you the job," the photographer said.

"The job?"

"The modeling job. You'll have the best website out there, the best portfolio."

Her exhilaration, the feeling that she was on top of the world, was short-lived. When she tried to dial up her modem later that afternoon, the little hourglass kept filling and refilling. She tried again. She restarted the machine. Nothing. And then she remembered. Her server was down for a bit of "regularly scheduled maintenance in order to serve you better," the e-mail had said. She read a few e-mails that had come before the shutdown, and wrote answers that would be delivered as soon as her server was up and running again. She loaded one of her pictures on the computer and got it ready to send to Chasco.

It was getting darker out. She sat sullenly at her dining room table and aimed the remote at the television. Chasco needed her tonight. He needed her for the Bible study. And she wasn't there. She read and reread his last message to her, sent that morning.

> I look forward to the Bible study tonight. How I rely on
> your expertise.
>
> All my love,
> Chasco

Suddenly, a kind of loneliness clutched at her like an invisible hand around her neck, causing her to actually choke. She turned up the volume of the television, letting the loudness drown out her solitude. Without e-mail she was cut off from her friends, the people she needed, the people who needed her. She watched the news. She got up and wandered around her house. In her bedroom, she changed out of her good clothes, washed all of Chloe's makeup off her face, and got into her valentine pajamas. She grabbed a novel but couldn't concentrate. She kept thinking of Chasco's Bible study and how she wasn't there.

At eight, the time when she would normally be deep in conversation with KarenP or Sewinglady, she sat numbly in her chair while an episode of *Law and Order* played itself out in front of her. She was almost glad when her computer alarm sounded and it was time to go to bed.

27

Hey Gorgeous!

It was in the subject line of her e-mail, the first thing Glynis saw when she logged on to her computer at five in the morning. Her Internet provider had promised that her connection would be restored by the early hours of the next morning, so Glynis had set her alarm for five. And now, at ten minutes after five, she was sipping tea and watching her many messages download one by one onto her screen.

> **Hey beautiful!**
>
> I got your picture. Wow! Thank you for sending it. Boy with those eyes of yours I'm sure you have to fend the guys off. I never realized you were so beautiful, the way you write about yourself as thirty-two and still unmarried. Now, I know why you're still unmarried. You have so many offers you can't make up your mind!
>
> All my love,
> Chasco

Glynis smiled, grinned actually, as she drank her tea. It was happening. It was finally happening for her. "Kim!" she said out loud. "I have a boyfriend, Kim. I wish you were here; I'd tell you all about him. He's handsome, a youth pastor and taller than me, and most of all, he likes me!"

She was reading through Chasco's e-mail now. He was telling her about his youth group, about Melissa who was doing much better, although he was still being hounded by the hospital for money. He also talked about a new project he was starting. He wanted to buy Bibles for all the teenagers in the city.

> I had a dream last night, Gwyneth88. In my dream every teenager in Minneapolis was reading a Bible. I woke out of my sound sleep and it seemed that God was saying to me, This is my dream for you. And I said, *Lord, what do I do about this? I don't have the money to supply Bibles for every single teenager. That's a huge undertaking.* And God told me. *God's people will supply. You just sit back and wait.*
>
> So, Gwyneth88, I'm stepping out in faith. I'm trusting God. He's never let me down. I know he won't now. I'm not telling a lot of people about this dream. I feel the Lord very definitely telling me not to put the plea on my website. Most people tell me I'm off my rocker. That I'm beyond crazy! So, I'm asking you to keep all of this in confidence. Of course you will. Me and my crazy dreams! Next you'll be calling me Joseph!
>
> I know you understand. You're one of the few that do. I feel so free to share my thoughts with you, things I've told no one. I have to tell you that I've been praying about us. About you and me. That God will make His way plain for us. That when we finally meet—and we shall, and it shall be soon— that it will be God's timing and in his plan.
>
> Love,
> Chasco

And the next one that came last night:

> My dear Gwyneth88,
>
> I feel so bereft tonight. Where are you??? I miss, miss, miss you! Can you send me your phone number? Should we talk?
>
> Love,
> Chasco

She wrote a long e-mail to him then, apologizing that her server was down. She described getting her picture taken and said that she was glad he liked it. Normally, she didn't wear her hair like that. She thought it was a bit severe, but the photographer said it showed off her facial bones better, and who was she to argue? She said she had to go to work today, much as she hated to. Also, she wasn't sure about sending her phone number. Was that taking the next step for them? Should they wait? Was it too soon? She reminded him they had only been corresponding seriously like this for less than a year. But today she was going to send him seven hundred dollars for his Bible project. She admired his high ideals.

Next she answered one from Melissa, apologizing for not being there for her last night, but that her server was down and there was nothing she could do about it.

She wrote to KarenP telling her all about Chasco and her picture, and asking for advice. Was it too soon to meet? Was it all happening too fast? Did she think Chasco was too good to be true?

She poured herself the last cup of tea from the pot and then went through her listservs, message by message, and then suddenly it was seven-thirty and time to leave for work.

Just as she was about to shut down her computer, a new e-mail popped onto her screen. It was from Mick Kosh. Glynis gasped, opened her eyes wide, and stared at the screen.

When Glynis and Kim were little they made up a kind of language of their own. They turned words inside out, scrambled the letters, and added more to make the word sound right. They would spend long summer afternoons writing down this language in scribblers. If there were too many letters, they just dropped some until the word sounded right. Glynis Pigott became Nilly Goppit. Kim Shock became Mick Kosh. It had been long years since they even talked about this language. But Glynis remembered. And seeing *Mick Kosh* on the screen sent a shiver through her.

She sat down again at the computer and opened the e-mail.

Nilly,

I'm sorry I haven't e-mailed in so long. Things have gotten sort of complicated, and I guess I didn't realize the complicated situation I was putting myself into when I took off to meet Gil. I don't know how much you have heard about what is going on, but things are not as they seem. That's all I can say.

Don't tell anyone about this e-mail. I wonder if you've heard from L. She's going to contact you, I think. I told her she would be safe with you. Also, Nilly, you remember the box I left with you? I probably shouldn't have, but please take that box to a safe place. I know this e-mail doesn't make any sense, but when we meet again I'll tell you all about what's been happening here. This e-mail is just to let you know that I'm okay. I don't have much time at the machine.

I love you,
Mick

P.S. Trash this e-mail as soon as you get it, and then empty your trash.

Glynis looked at the date. Two weeks ago. She'd sent it two weeks ago and it was only coming through now. She hit Reply and sent a quick message, but it bounced back the moment after she sent it.

28

Jack was going to clean out the basement today. Classes hadn't started yet, and while Teri sat in their bedroom and worked on her searches and made calls, she could hear him rummaging around downstairs. Plus, the Renali brothers were constructing and deconstructing with hammers and nails. The quietest place was their bedroom, where she could close the door. Still in her housecoat, she got out the letters to Kim Shock and read them all again. Maybe it would be worth a call to these people.

The first one was a man named Charlie Grantham, who'd e-mailed Kim. Teri introduced herself as a private investigator looking for the lawyer who had handled his case. She'd gone missing.

"So that's why I haven't heard from her in so long."

"When's the last time you did hear from her?"

"Maybe a year. Little less, maybe. She seemed quite interested in helping me. Took down all kinds of weird information from me, but then I never heard from her again. I got to thinking she was just like the rest of them shysters, except she didn't take any money from me."

"What do you mean by weird information?" Teri asked.

"There was all sorts of things she wanted to know: the guy that came, what did he look like? How tall was he? Did he speak with an accent? What was the color of his hair? How did he make the first contact? What did he say? Did he get access to my bank account?"

"And what did you tell her?"

"What do you mean?"

"How tall *was* he? What *did* he look like?"

"You think that's important? The important thing was I got royally swindled out of my money."

"She's missing, so everything's important."

"Okay, I told her the guy was average height, had black curly hair and a New York accent, and drove a PT Cruiser. Maybe she got too close to one of these guys. Maybe that's what happened to her."

Teri spent the next hour talking to the others on Kim's list and got basically the same stories. Kim asked them the same questions about the scammers. What did they look like? Any distinguishing marks? What were their names? She'd followed up on only a few, just e-mails saying she was still looking into the matter and she'd let them know.

She called Mary Kate Springfield in Florida, who'd been conned into purchasing a useless medical prescription card via telephone. She told Teri that when she told Kim that she had never met her scammer, that it was all by telephone, Kim said she was sorry but she couldn't take the case, that she was only interested in scammers that operated person to person.

Teri called someone named Claudia Braithwattle from Toronto, who'd been conned by a man who said he loved her. He even flew to Toronto to meet her, where he systematically ripped her off, stealing her credit card numbers and wiping out her savings.

"The lawyer was quite interested in my story. She wanted to know everything about this man. But then she said she couldn't take the case because it happened in Canada, even though I live in New York now."

The third person she called was Paula Frize, who'd sent a lot of money to a television faith healer with no results. "It's been a year now, and I've sent her more than five thousand dollars and I'm still not healed. How much more do you think it will take?"

Teri blinked, said she should probably not send any more.

Teri called the rest of Kim's list and got versions of the same story. In every case, Kim wanted to know what these scammers looked like and talked like.

Kim, what were you after? She had her chin in her hands staring at her computer screen when the phone range.

It was her friend Andrea Silver.

"How about a walk? I've got my maid of honor's dress remade and I need a break. I thought maybe you could steal a few minutes away from packing and working and go outside. We're not going to get too many of these days again."

They agreed to meet at the park.

Teri called down the basement stairs to Jack that she was taking Kelly for a walk with Andrea.

"Good, Teri," he said. "I'm glad you're getting together with her; she's nice. She'll be good for you."

She left, mildly perturbed that Jack should be so concerned about her finding friends. It was none of his business.

"I'm a loner," she always told him. "It's my personality."

"That's just an excuse," he said. "No one is a loner by nature. God created us to need people."

"No man is an island," she quoted. "I know. I've heard you say that."

Half an hour later she and Kelly and Andrea were walking through a sunny park, still green for the most part, only the most cold-sensitive flowers showing any signs of browning. Andrea was telling her about a customer who was becoming very demanding and refusing to pay the full amount of the dress Andrea was making.

"I mean, I try to be Christian about it, but should I turn the other cheek and let her get away without paying me? Or should I demand payment? She *says* she's a Christian, and I know the Bible says that Christians shouldn't really go to court against Christians. And that's not what I want to do. I want to avoid that, at all costs. Ben says I should just forget about it, but it galls me."

"It would gall me, too. I say stand up for your rights. But in a nice way."

They laughed. They talked about the Bible study then, and Andrea said she didn't see how it was going to work for them this year. "We've decided to put a hold on it, at least for the time being, until we get Isabel through ballet. There's just one thing after another."

"Tell me about it."

"We're out just about every night of the week as it is. And now Community Education wants me to teach a sewing class."

"Are you going to?"

"I might. I enjoy meeting the people, and the money's not bad."

"I'll miss you in the Bible study," Teri said. "I really will. There are not a lot of people I identify with. You're one of the few there my age. Kind of comes with the territory when you marry an older man, I guess."

They passed a few joggers. It wouldn't be too long before the trails would be too snow-covered to jog.

"I never thought of that. Is that a problem?"

"Not really," Teri answered. "It is kind of an adjustment, though. The couples we socialize with are all older, gray haired, the women sitting around the kitchen talking menopause, and here's me, young enough to have a baby."

Andrea looked at her wide-eyed. "Are you telling me something here?"

"No. No, no. No, I'm not. I'm just saying theoretically. I only brought it up because I'm trying to make the point that Jack's friends are all older. I never thought it would be a problem. And it's not a problem exactly, the problem's probably with me. I'm just saying I'll miss you and Ben in Bible study if you aren't able to make it."

"I'll miss being there."

Andrea asked how the house was coming, and Teri told her about their ongoing battles, and also that a current case was keeping her too busy to even think much.

"How's it going?" Andrea asked.

"Did you know Kim Shock at all?"

Andrea stopped on the trail and looked at her. "Is that the one you're looking for? I don't think you told me that before."

"Yes."

"I know Kim. A little. Actually, I know her friend Glynis better."

"You know Glynis?"

"I've made clothes for her. She finds it hard to get clothes to fit. She's six foot one and so slender. Glynis and her aunt used to shop at Pepper's Clothes all the time. I think Glynis still does. I haven't made anything for her recently, although I suspect she's purchased a few of my things at Pepper's."

"I was in Pepper's Clothes just this morning," Teri said. "Out of my price range. I used to live kitty-corner from that place. In the building with the bagel factory."

"I know that place!" Andrea said. "Funny we've been going to the same Bible study for how many months and never connected on this? Great bagels, by the way."

"They are. And good coffee."

"And how many times must I have been sitting in there treating myself to a bagel and coffee after just having dropped off stuff at Pepper's, and you were right there?"

"Probably having coffee at the next table. I used to work down there. I'd take my little computer and sit in the booth by the window."

"You know, I might've even seen you there! Sometimes I was in there alone, sometimes with my best friend. Small world, huh?"

"Small world." But Teri felt choked and tight, stumbling on the words, *best friend*.

29

Teri had not felt lonely for a long time. It was not a feeling she allowed herself, but on the way home she wondered what it would be like to be Andrea's *best* friend.

There was only one time in her life when she had a best friend. Lisa Fenyo in the fourth grade. She remembered her now, with her wide face and bone-colored hair parted down the middle and falling straight down to her shoulder. Her best friend. But even then, having to make sure. Every day.

"Are you my best friend, Lisa?"

"Yes."

"Are you sure you're my best friend?"

"Yes."

"Are you really sure you like me?"

"Yes, but if you keep asking me, I'm going to say no!"

They were friends until they were both fourteen and Teri's mother died. Lisa got tired of the bad place Teri was in and gradually moved on.

Her mother had died. Her best friend had left her. Nothing in this life was a surety. Even God.

So she retreated into herself and went into law enforcement, where she had lots of buddies.

Jack was really her best friend, her only friend, when you got right down to it. But there were times when she longed for women friends. She'd see women friends in malls, drinking coffee, going to chick flicks together, talking, sharing, the animated hand motions, their purchases laid on the tables beside them. Best friends.

Lisa Fenyo had gone on to be one of the popular girls in high school. And in their senior year, when Teri was expelled for a variety of misdemeanors—smoking, insubordination, skipping classes—Lisa became a member of the National Honor Society, the secretary of the senior class, and president of the Yearbook Society. By the night of their graduation, which Teri made by the skin of her teeth, there were not two more different people in the entire graduating class.

"Will you be my friend? Will you be my friend?"

"If you keep asking, I'll say no."

When Teri pulled into their driveway, her husband was throwing black plastic bags into the back of a pickup truck.

"The basement's cleaned out," he told her.

"Our basement? You mean the room that's underneath the house? The one filled with so much junk it's a fire waiting to happen? You mean *that* basement?"

He took her arm. "Oh, ye of little faith. These," he said pointing, "are the remnants."

Harvey's son's rusted pickup was piled to overflowing with black plastic garbage bags, old boards, table legs, several old chairs, a rusted baby stroller with wheels missing, assorted toys too dilapidated to give away, several deflated basketballs, a few headless, naked dolls, an old stepladder with most of the rungs removed, assorted cardboard, slats from a baby crib, bags full of old clothes.

"Wow!" Teri said, and then she looked at Jack and back at the junk, junk that used to be Jack's life. The baby strollers, the toys, Jenny's clothes, now so much garbage. She put her arm around him and rested her head on his chest. They watched as Harvey's son drove the truck away.

Back in the kitchen, he said, "I didn't throw it all out." He indicated two large boxes, one labeled Cooper and one labeled Lily.

"Some things for the kids their mother would want them to have." In Lily's box was a set of rose-rimmed china, Jenny's recipe books, her journals, some framed photos, a couple of dolls with hand-sewn clothes, a ceramic frog. In Cooper's were Jenny's books of poetry, more of her journals, a few photo albums, a couple of Jenny's coffee mugs with her name on them.

"You don't want her journals anymore?" Teri asked.

"No."

She was still holding on to him, her arm around him. After a few minutes he said, "You haven't seen the basement."

She followed him down the rickety stairs to the lower reaches, where instead of clutter it was now swept clean, the floor mopped.

"I never knew there was so much room," Teri said. "You could play floor hockey down here."

"Cooper and his friends used to do just that."

"I'm happy," Jack said to her when they were upstairs again. "We're going to be so happy in our new place. It will be so good." Then he pulled her into an embrace, kissing her. "I love you," he said. "I just want you to know that." And then, "I have to go out to the house. Stephan's father is meeting me there. You should see it, Teri, it's almost wired. Things are really coming along."

And then he was gone and Teri was alone. The recipe books, the journals, the china teacups only reminded her how little of her own mother she had. When her mother had first disappeared and everyone was sure that with just a little more prayer she would turn up safe and sound, her father would allow no one to touch anything. But when she didn't come, when the police determined that the most likely scenario was that she was lured from the parking lot in full view of the convenience store—six feet from the door as a matter of fact—and murdered, he still wouldn't move anything.

And then, one day he got rid of everything without telling anyone. When Teri was twenty she had asked her father if she could have the Christmas decorations her mother had made.

"No."

"No?"

"I don't have them anymore."

"What happened to them?"

"I got rid of them, Teresa. I got rid of her things. It was too painful to hold on to them."

Cooper and Lily were lucky. They had journals and recipe books and photos and things their mother had made. And most of all, they had a body.

The phone rang.

"I got an e-mail from Kim last night," Glynis said. "I've been thinking about it all night. Kim said not to let anyone know, but I think you should know. I'll forward it to your e-mail. I just wanted you to know."

30

Kim's e-mail further reinforced for Teri that she needed to find out who L was and where she was. She tried e-mailing Kim, but the e-mails to her Hotmail account bounced back, as she knew they would. She went into Hotmail.com to see if there was any way to match a name to a location, but of course, there wasn't. Teri looked at her watch. It was still early. She had time to get where she needed to go and be back before dark. She jotted Jack a quick note, stuck it to the fridge with a magnet, and left.

Teri had a certain type of person in mind when she drove down winding potholed dirt roads toward the trailer that fit Susan Shock's address. Before finding this road, she'd stopped at several places in Vanceboro to ask directions. At the Irving, a teenager in loose trousers said he had never heard of where that was. But an older fellow with a pencil behind his ear said that not only did he know the street, but he also knew Susan Shock.

"Jus' about everyone around here knows Susan Shock," he said.

"How long has she lived here?"

He scratched his head. "Couple three years. Maybe more. She came here after some family trouble." He took his glasses off, wiped the lenses on his shirt. "You interested in her plants?"

"Plants?"

"She raises plants."

The directions he gave her were the kind that locals give locals: turn right where the old Hankins farm used to be, then left where the Congregational Church burned down. She had a hard time making sense of them until he scrawled a map for her.

Still, it took her a little bit of time to find this trailer. It was hidden behind scraggly scrub bushes and an unkempt driveway she would not wish to venture down in the winter snow or the spring thaw. But it was the end of August now, and her car bounced over the hard and crusted ruts. The leaves that brushed the sides of her car were so covered in dust, Teri wondered how photosynthesis could possibly occur. The road was narrow, and she was sure she had taken a wrong turn somewhere. Her mission now became to find a place to turn around and go back.

Then the road widened, and she came upon a cleared piece of land and this surprising trailer, freshly painted gleaming white and surrounded by a patchwork of gardens, a small greenhouse, and several cold frames. She parked and got out. Numerous square garden patches were marked by tiny wooden stakes and tied around with ribbons, each one a different color, and blowing gaily in the breeze like race markers.

On closer examination she could see that these weren't colored ribbons, but little rectangles of cloth. She got to thinking that there was probably some significance to the colors. Green for lettuce, orange for carrots, red for tomatoes and so forth. She walked between the garden patches on strips of freshly mown and soft green lawn. It was like a garden oasis in the middle of the poverty and remoteness that was northern Maine.

Around the side of the trailer a woman was bent over one of the beds, head bobbing, humming, and here and there singing the odd fragment of a tune Teri couldn't identify. She wore plaid shorts and a short-sleeved denim shirt with lots of pockets. A white cotton hat was pulled down over her ears. She was barefoot.

"Hello," Teri called.

No answer. The head bobbing continued.

Teri moved into her line of vision and waved. "Hi."

The woman pulled off her Walkman, stumbled back, and clutched her chest. "Oh! You startled me half out of my wits!"

"I'm sorry. I didn't mean to frighten you."

"Not frightened. No, startled. I get listening to my music and the world around me could fall apart, I wouldn't know it. Plus no one ever comes up here."

"Good music?"

"Eagles. Can I do something for you? Are you here for plants? It's kind of late for that, although I have some nice house plants in the greenhouse."

"Are you Susan Shock?"

"Yep. I'm she." The white bell-shaped cloche she wore on her head gave her an endearing look. She was very pretty.

"I'm Teri Blake-Addison. I'm a private investigator. I'm here about your daughter."

Her eyes widened. "Has something happened? Oh no. I need to sit down. Something awful has happened. I just know it. I haven't heard from her in so long, I keep calling and calling. And now you're here. What happened?"

"Nothing happened. Not that I know of, anyway."

"Then, why are you here?"

"Can we talk? Can you spare a minute?"

"Let's go in."

It was a tiny well-kept trailer, comfortably cool with a breeze through the opened windows. A peach Formica table was covered with gardening magazines and a stack of CDs. Susan seemed to favor the music stylings of the Eagles, Genesis, and Chicago.

"Tell me," she said. "Take a seat. That one. I'll sit here. Now, tell me, why are you here? What made you drive all the way up here? What do you know about Kim?"

"She seems to be missing. I've been hired to try to find her. She sent an e-mail yesterday, though it was dated two weeks ago. I'm trying to track down some leads. Do you know anyone, maybe a street kid who has the initial L?"

"Lanny," Susan said. "Lanny Boucher." She folded her hands and put them on the table. "What has Lanny Boucher got to do with this?"

"Who is Lanny Boucher?"

"A special friend of my son's."

"Barry?"

She sighed and looked down at the table, at her hands folded there. They were chapped and dirt creased. She picked at a nail. "He didn't kill those girls. I don't care what anyone may tell me, or what proof anybody puts in my way, I know in my heart that he didn't kill those girls. He couldn't have."

"Tell me about Lanny and your son."

Susan smiled then, not at Teri but past Teri, perhaps at some distant memory. "They were always around. All the kids at our house. Always at our house...You want a beer? I could do with a beer."

"No thanks, I'm driving. But I'll have anything else that's cold."

Susan reached into a small fridge, pulled out a couple of cans, flipped open the pop-top on a beer and handed Teri a can of iced tea. "I'm not driving," she said. "Of course I'm not driving. I never go anywhere anymore, so I can drink whenever I want. Nothing's stopping me." She grabbed half a bag of Oreo cookies and placed them on the table. "Barry's favorite."

Teri didn't say anything. Susan was going to talk, was even now settling herself in to talk. As a PI, Teri knew better than to interrupt anyone who was getting ready to talk.

"I wanted children," Susan was saying. "I wanted a houseful of children. I had Kim, but something happened during the delivery. I had to have a hysterectomy just after she was born. Of course, that was the end of my childbearing. So Glen and I took foster children. And then eight years later we adopted Barry. He came to us when he was two."

She told Teri that Barry and his friends loved nothing better than to act out *Romeo and Juliet* in the backyard on a little wooden stage that Glen had built. They would even charge twenty-five cents admission. Gentle, sweet Barry was incapable of such horror.

But Teri knew otherwise. She'd heard the testimony by psychologists at the trial, that in a small number of adoptions, the children carry scars from their very early years. They may be model children, but then one day something goes terribly wrong.

"What about Lanny Boucher?" Teri broke in. "How does she fit in to all of this?"

Susan sat back. "If Barry had a girlfriend it was Lanny Boucher. We had her for a few months in foster care. But even after that she was around the house a lot. She was a nice kid, a smart kid. She and

Barry did their plays all the time."

"Lanny wrote letters to Kim. Do you know if they might still be in touch?"

"I didn't know that. I wouldn't know anything about that. I can't remember the last time I laid eyes on Lanny."

"Can you tell me your impressions of Gil Williamson. You met him, didn't you?"

Susan snorted. "Excuse me while I laugh out loud. I don't think Kim loved him. He wasn't her type."

"What do you mean?"

"Kim can't stand pushy, know-it-all men, and Gil is a pushy, know-it-all man."

"Why would she stay in Texas with him then?"

She shook her head. "Maybe she looked at me. I'm fifty-six and I'm turning into an old woman who lives by herself and sings 'Hotel California' to her plants." She took a long look at Teri. Outside a bird was trilling. "Let me ask you something. Have you ever lost a child?"

Teri shook her head.

"It does something to you. It changes you. You're never the same afterward. That's how Glen and I felt about losing Barry. He was Romeo. Lanny was Juliet. And here they are, both gone. And Glen, their stagehand, he's gone, too. And now Kim. When will it end?"

31

Killing Beamish had been surprisingly easy. After five years of listening to his smart-aleck comments, he thought there would be more of a fuss. What he didn't expect was for Beamish to just stand there grinning the way he did with those horse teeth of his, those big ears, looking so stupid. There wasn't anyone stupider looking than Beamish.

But Beamish was also smart, probably the smartest person Snare knew. And even though Snare was ahead in the looks department, Beamish never lacked for the ladies. It was the phony English accent. They all fell for that accent of his. And of course, his money.

Yet, even with the gun pointed at him, there he was grinning, grinning, snorting with the effort of it. At one point Beamish had grabbed the barrel of the gun with his knuckly fingers and pushed it away.

"You're not going to shoot me; let's quit pretending."

"I will kill you. It's your fault I ever went to jail."

"Oh come *off* it, let's be adults about this. Blaming me? Blaming me?"

"And you have my money and I want it."

"You still going on about the money, mate? Is that what you're all got up about?"

Everything was a joke with Beamish. That was the problem. Everything was a joke.

"I'll kill you," Snare said. "I've been looking for it for five years, and it all leads me back to you. Five years. The money's mine."

"You haven't learned anything from me, have you?" He sighed theatrically and walked around the room. "All the lessons, all the mentoring. I expected so much from you. First of all, I don't have your blistering money. Secondly, my friend, never do anything out of revenge. Revenge will destroy you. Learn to cut your losses and move on. You've been holding this in for five years? Man, you are already dead."

But Snare wasn't listening. Snare had listened for too long, and Snare pulled the trigger and shot Beamish in the face, blowing those teeth, that raggy hair all over the far wall.

"I'm not dead," he said as an afterthought. "You are."

Snare was winning. He had the girl now, anyway, and a whole lot more scams lined up, things Beamish didn't know anything about. Wigs and phony passports, all kinds of uniforms.

"The marks of an amateur," Beamish always told him. And he would pick up a wig and twirl it on the end of his finger. "Amateur hour."

He's gone, don't think about him, Snare told himself. Snare's favorite was a police uniform that he'd stolen from a theater group. So what if it wasn't from any particular police detachment. It was surprising how little people noticed. He also had a phony badge. It was even plastic. People never noticed that, either. He had a janitor's uniform and a chef's hat. He could also do accents. He could even copy Beamish's phony British accent to perfection.

Sometimes Snare would pretend he was an international operative, someone like James Bond, rather than a petty con man and computer geek, understudy of the great Max Beamish. When he found himself sitting next to some pretty thing on an airplane and they got to talking, he would say, "I'm a spy. Don't tell anyone. Shhh." And he would wink at her and she would chuckle. "No, really," he would protest. "I'm a spy with about a hundred different passports. But let's be quiet about it, shall we? Don't tell the flight attendant. We don't want to upset her."

She would giggle. "What do you do really? Come on."

"Okay," and he'd put his hands up. "I'm a thief. I climb into people's houses when they're not there and collect their things and take them out in sacks over my shoulder. I have this little mask. You want to see?"

And she would giggle some more.

"Okay, fine. I'm not all those. I'm..." and here he would come up with another fabrication—a CEO, a foreign correspondent with Reuters, a venture capitalist, a neurosurgeon. His personal favorite was the CEO of Blockbuster, and when the woman was dutifully impressed, he would offer her a couple of free video cards. And when she would say oh no, that's not necessary, he would make a great show of feeling his jacket pockets, saying he left his free passes in his checked luggage. But never mind, he would say, pulling out a couple of equally phony business cards, this'll do. Then on the back he would write, *Good for three free DVDs*. He'd put this in her hand and say, "Now, you take this to the manager of your local Blockbuster. You get yourself some DVDs, you hear? If he has any questions, you get him to call me. Number's on the front. I want to know you did this, okay?"

"Okay."

If he determined that she was rich or came from rich family stock (as Beamish called it), they would exchange business cards, and he would have the name and address of yet another potential victim to add to his Rolodex.

Sometimes, after a particularly lucrative scam, he rode first-class and told people he was an actor and had auditioned for the part of Ross in *Friends*. The whole thing went right down to the wire; they had only three to choose from, but they thought he was a bit too good-looking for the part. The part required someone who was a little more slouchy. That's what he told people.

"Luck of the draw," he would say. "I could be rich and famous now."

As Beamish lay dying, Snare searched his house. No money. He didn't find it. But he *would* find it.

32

Chasco wasn't on-line. Usually when she got home from work there were two or three messages from him, and as soon as she answered, he would be right there suggesting they go to chat. She had raced home and...nothing!

While she waited for Chasco, she found herself idly surfing through the on-line phone listings for Minneapolis. His name was Charles Coburn. She found three Charles Coburns. Did she have the nerve to just call him? What would she say?

"Glynis, you're just not a phone person," Kim used to say, laughing. And it was true. Glynis didn't like talking on the phone. She preferred e-mail. And if it had to be the phone, she preferred leaving messages on people's answering machines. She never minded a bit what people called "the talk mail jail." When they were young teenagers, it was Kim who felt no compunction about phoning the cute boys in their class and just gabbing away for no reason. Not Glynis.

Tentatively, tentatively, she dialed the first Charles Coburn. An elderly woman's voice answered a faltering but pleasant hello. She hung up. That couldn't be Chasco. Or could it? Did he live with his mother? There was so much she didn't know about him. Might that have been his mother?

Feeling braver, she dialed the next. A young woman answered. Glynis hung up, feeling foolish.

She dialed the third one. What was she expecting? To instantly recognize his voice?

Hi, you've reached Charles and Amelia. We're not able to take your call right now. You know what to do after the beep. And if this is Larry? No, Charlie's not going to the hockey game with you.

Glynis didn't wait for the beep.

Seconds after she hung up, the phone rang.

"Hello," Glynis said.

"Who do you wish to speak to?"

"What?"

"You just called here. Who did you wish to speak to?"

"What?"

"Your number was on my caller ID. You just called."

"Oh, uh, I was looking for someone named Chasco. I think it was a wrong number."

"Jazz co? Jazz? Jazz company?"

"Sorry. I knew it was wrong the moment I got your answering machine. That's why I hung up. Sorry to have bothered you."

Glynis activated her modem again, and there, finally, an e-mail from Chasco! Sorry, he said. A long staff meeting at church. I wanted to get here quicker. It was all I thought about, getting home and e-mailing you. It was a long e-mail and filled with his day's activities, from taking his car in to be serviced—big bills there, trusting God—to a new series of sermons he was working on. She e-mailed right back and they went into chat.

She wrote to him all about her day. He seemed very interested that she'd heard from her missing friend. He also seemed intensely interested in "L."

> *Chasco:* Who is this L your friend refers to? I'd like to pray for her. If you could tell me a little more about her, I could pray for her more intelligently.

> *Gwyneth88:* I don't know who "L" is. My friend Kim helped a lot of street kids. Also, her parents took in a lot of foster kids. L could have been one of them. Why are you so interested in this?

> *Chasco:* Just want to pray more intelligently.

> *Gwyneth88:* I have a question, do you, by any chance, live with your mother? (The reason I ask is that you seem like the kind of thoughtful person who would take care of an elderly mother.) Or do you live alone? Or with a roommate?

Chasco: My, you're curious, aren't you! The truth of the matter is, I do live with my mother. She's elderly and needs someone to care for her. I thought I probably told you about her already.

Gwyneth88: Maybe you did. I don't remember.

Chasco: I have a special surprise for you.

Gwyneth88: You have a surprise for me?

Chasco: I made you a video! Especially for you! I'll send it as an attachment after we say good-bye. That's why it took so long for me to get on-line. I was getting it ready to send.

Gwyneth88: I thought you said it was a church meeting.

Chasco: That too. Do you have a video camera or access to one? I'd love to see a video of you.

Gwyneth88: Oh, Chasco, you don't want to see a video of me! That picture I sent to you was a fluke. I'm not really much to look at.

Chasco: I DISAGREE! Of course I would love to see you. In a video. And in person. I sometimes think about meeting you in person.

Gwyneth88: I'll see what I can do, but I can't promise anything. Maybe someone at church has a camera.

Chasco: Don't tell me you're still going to that church?

Gwyneth88: Yes, not a lot. I don't get a lot out of it most of the time.

Chasco: That's the story I hear all over. There's something else I keep meaning to ask you—Melissa's been talking a lot

about finding her biological mother. I know you said you were
pretty happy with the detective you hired. Could you give me
her name and phone? I might contact her regarding Melissa.

Without hesitation Glynis gave him Teri's website and address
and phone number. After a half hour more of chatting, they said
good-bye. She clicked on Chasco's video. He was sitting on a green
couch wearing a denim shirt. It was a head and shoulders shot. His
hair was redder than his picture. And even though she knew he was
thirty-six, he looked somehow younger, cuter. He leaned forward,
smiled a cute smirky sort of smile, and then with a wink and a wave,
he said, "This is for you!" and he blew her a kiss. She watched it again
and again and again until her computer alarm rang.

She got into her valentine pajamas and climbed into bed. *This is
for you.* Maybe the elderly woman on the phone *was* Chasco's mother.
Glynis should have said something.

She and Chasco had a lot in common. Chasco lived with his
mother and took care of her, and she had lived with her mother until
she died. As sleep took over, she tried to imagine what Mrs. Coburn
looked like. A sweet little old lady with snowy hair. Someone who
would be like a real mother to her. She imagined the two of them sipping tea in a kitchen filled with flowers, while outside Chasco would
be setting the sprinklers around. Through the window he would wave
at her, throw her a kiss. *This is for you.*

33

Glynis was waiting for her when Teri arrived, late and apologizing for traffic. She was sitting at a little table at Borders bookstore, a cup of tea in front of her, and flipping through a *Victoria* magazine.

"It's okay," Glynis said. "It's nice here."

Teri dropped her jacket and satchel on a chair beside them and got herself a coffee.

"I have a few pictures I'd like you to have a look at," Teri said when she sat down.

Glynis looked different today. Her puffy hair was sleekly brushed back off her face and secured in a tiny bun at the back of her head. It made Glynis look striking. Teri had never noticed how dark her eyes were. And her eyebrows, bushy before, were plucked high and arching. The effect was so startling that Teri almost blurted out, "What happened to you?"

Instead she spread out the photos she'd printed off her PI listserv, pictures of people that other detectives were looking for. Shared information.

"Tell me if any of these men look like Gil."

Glynis was looking through them, and Teri noticed that her fingernails were expertly manicured. Glynis picked up one photo and studied it. "This one looks a little like Gil, but the hair is wrong. Gil's hair isn't black and curly. And Gil's not so dark complected."

The name on that one was Julius Dumain.

She picked up a few others. "And not these two, but this one is Gil," she said, pointing with a deep red nail.

"That's Gil?"

"No. Wait. I'm not sure now." She picked up the photo and spent a few seconds looking at it. She laid it down and tapped it with a red fingernail. "I'm not sure. It looks a little like him, but the jaw is different, the teeth."

The name on the back of that one was Troy Duncan, LKA Las Cruces, New Mexico.

Several patrons in Borders were stealing glances at Glynis, who looked like a runway model on her coffee break.

"Who are these men?" she asked.

"Various people who may or may not know where Gil is."

Teri had checked her map and knew that Las Cruces was less than an hour's drive from El Paso, which just so happened to be the place Kim had gone to with Gil Williamson. Presumably. Yet in her search she had found nothing on a Troy Duncan. When she called her old police partner Bill, he hadn't been able to help her.

"We don't have a Troy Duncan fitting that description in any of the data banks," he told her. "If you have any kind of hard evidence that this Kim person is in danger, we'll take a look at it."

"The guy's name is Troy Duncan," Teri said to Glynis. "Does that name ring any bells?"

She shook her head.

"With your permission," Teri said, "I'd like to take a short trip down to El Paso. That's where Kim and Gil went. Plus this Troy Duncan lives near there. Also, a woman who was once engaged to Gil lives there, too. Her name is June Redfeather, and she apparently runs an art gallery. Have you heard that name?"

Glynis looked up. "Someone was engaged to Gil before Kim?"

"It appears so. Did you know if Gil was at all interested in art?"

"Art? I don't think so."

"Do you happen to remember someone named Lanny Boucher?"

"A little. I believe she stayed with the Shocks for a while." She opened her eyes wide. "Is that the L who's writing to Kim?"

"I'm not sure. I think so. Susan Shock thinks so."

"I remember a whole group of them always in the Shocks' back-yard. Kim, too. But my mother was so sick then that I didn't pay too much attention to anything else at the time." She looked up. "I'm sorry I can't be of more help. When would you be leaving?"

"As soon as I can get a flight out. Maybe tomorrow. I've got my travel agent booking me a car for when I get there and finding me a cheap hotel."

"It doesn't have to be cheap. When my father traveled he never stayed in the cheap places. He said they weren't worth it. When you're away from home, you should at least be comfortable. At least that's what my mother said he said. Don't stay in a cheap hotel."

They were quiet for a moment, each drinking from their mugs.

"I would also like very much to talk to people at your work," Teri said. "But I promise I won't mention your name."

"Okay then."

"Also, if you get any more e-mails from Kim, I want you to listen to what she says. Don't share that information with anyone. Just pass them on to me. I'm going to give you an e-mail account I don't normally use. It's a secure one. Pass them on to me there while I'm traveling. I'll keep you informed using this address." She scribbled onto the back of a business card and handed it to her.

"I understand. The only other person I've told this to is my...uh, my boyfriend."

Boyfriend. Well, that explains the new hairdo and manicure. "Your boyfriend?"

"He can be trusted. He's a minister."

"Local guy?"

"He lives in Minneapolis."

"I've heard long-distance romances can be tough," Teri said.

"They are."

"Still, I would feel much better if you kept her e-mails to yourself."

34

Texas, well," said Jack when she told him.

"Want to come?"

"Impossible this time of year."

"I was afraid of that."

"But think of it this way—you get to miss the garage sale."

The garage sale! "I totally forgot!" she said.

But maybe deep down she hadn't. So much of this house wasn't hers. It hadn't taken her long to pack up the few things she had brought into this relationship. Her stereo and her office furniture were already over at the log house. Maybe leaving the packing to Jack to get rid of more than twenty years of stuff was a good thing.

"I could wait and go after."

"No, you go. We can manage. People from church have offered to help. Verna Plant phoned. She'll be here."

"You'll be better off without me, then."

"I'm never better off without you, Teri."

Teri was pouring water into the coffeepot, one of their few appliances that hadn't been packed tightly into boxes.

"When will you be going?" he said.

"Tomorrow."

"There's that Bible study group thing tonight."

"We're meeting again? Since when? I thought no one could agree on a night."

"This is that other group."

She turned from her coffee making and said, "What other group?"

"Didn't I tell you about it? Someone named Mike Wordman from church phoned and invited us. Remember we talked about it?"

"Vaguely."

"You want to go? We don't have to." The smell of fresh coffee filled the echoey kitchen. "I'm not sure I qualify anyway. From what I understand it's mostly young couples."

She put her arms around him. "We—you and me—are an enigma for church planners. We don't easily fit into age groups that Christian education specialists are so eager to put everybody into. But I think we should go. Those people knew Kim, and I'm still on that case. So, technically, going would be working."

"And you're more comfortable in social situations where you're working?"

"You got it." She poured coffee into two mugs and then wondered aloud whether there was a way to geographically locate people when you only know their e-mail addresses.

"Cooper might know," Jack said.

"Do you think he would mind if I asked him?"

"I think he would be flattered."

It was a potluck supper, as most of the Bible studies in this group were, she learned. It had been Kim's idea. Since they had few pots left, and fewer utensils, she and Jack went to the Market and bought a bunch of gooey turnovers and put them in a box.

Every bit of countertop and table space in Mike Wordman's small apartment was laden with casseroles, salads, and desserts. "Enough to feed an army," said a spindly young woman named Mari Beth, who wore her jeans slung low and a short, tight T-shirt. She looked all of fourteen, but Teri knew she was single and twenty-six and a physiotherapist at the hospital. Marcie was there, too. Teri heard her before she saw her. Matt, her husband, stood beside her, his huge frame encased in a red and yellow Hawaiian shirt, a can of Vanilla Coke in his hand. They were talking about the bullying that Madison was continually enduring in school these days, and how no teachers were doing anything about it.

"I say zero tolerance," Marcie was booming. "I don't care. You want this to be another Columbine? That's what's going to happen."

"Marcie, you're exaggerating," Matt said.

"No, I'm not, Matt. You heard what Madison said——"

And then another person with a softer voice said something, and the knot of conversation became quieter.

Teri was handed a glass of punch and stood beside the table eyeing the various groups that had formed. Glynis wasn't there, but Teri hadn't expected her to be. Jack seemed to be enjoying himself, though, talking to two young men who were grad students in mathematics. If they were wondering how an old, bald professor got invited to a young person's potluck, they weren't giving any indication. And Jack certainly seemed comfortable enough.

"It's the same thing as those King James Murders." Someone else was talking, and Teri inched closer to hear.

"That was Kim's brother you know," Marcie said.

"Adopted brother," said another. "And I heard he was bullied."

"And look what happened to him. Snapped." Marcie snapped her fingers.

"There were other factors in that one," someone else said. "They said he had that postadoptive stress disorder."

"Yeah," said Mike Wordman, joining the group. "But it was brought on by bullying."

"The same thing could happen here if we don't do something. I know it's only elementary school, but still. I was in talking to Madison's teacher and..."

More conversation, more talk about bullying, about the tremendous hardship Madison had endured at the hands of her tormentors.

"She comes home crying," Marcie bellowed. "The kids make fun of her, call her fat, and I have to sit her down and tell her she's beautiful."

"She is beautiful," said another.

At a break in the conversation, Teri said, "Did any of you know Barry Shock personally?"

"I remember him," said a voice from the side, and a hand raised. "We were in the same homeroom."

"You were, Marguerite?" boomed out Marcie.

"What was he like?" Teri asked.

"I remember he was Hamlet in the production the drama club put on."

"Your school put on *Hamlet*?" someone asked. "Who does *Hamlet*? People do modern plays now. Who actually does *Hamlet* in high school?"

"Our school did *Grease* when I was there," someone said. "I was in it."

"We did *Les Mis*."

"So, he was good?" Teri asked. "As Hamlet?"

"Everyone seemed to think so, but the one thing I don't remember is him being all that religious. The fact that he would get mixed up in a weirdo skinhead religious cult was strange."

"No one ever said it was skinhead," someone else said.

"People *do* go over the deep end," said Mari Beth of the bare midriff. "Especially if they've been bullied. It happens. Any of you see *Bowling for Columbine*? That movie makes you stop and think if nothing does." She rolled her eyes and downed more of her diet Sprite.

"I think it's guns," Marguerite said. "We're too gun crazy in this country. To me, that's the whole problem."

"Did Barry go to church?" Teri wanted to know.

"He used to come with Kim."

"I heard it was Glynis's aunt who took everyone to church," Teri said.

"Ida, the do-gooder," Marcie added.

"Ida?"

"Glynis's aunt. Aunt Ida. As formidable as it sounds."

Marcie snorted, yelled to the kitchen, "Hey you guys! Mike! Matt! Anybody getting the food out? We're starving out here! We can't last much longer!" And then to Teri, "It's the guys' turn to get the food out. We take turns."

Mari Beth said, "Did you know Glynis was the one who found her mother when she died? Kim told me that. Said it was horrible." She shivered.

"She overdosed on her medication," Marcie said loudly. "Suicide.

Because of the pain. And Glynis was the one who had to clean it up. Apparently Ida, the do-gooder, was no place to be found. When people die of an overdose, they throw up all over the place before they finally die. Kim and Kim's mother had to go over there and help Glynis clean up."

"Marcie, gross!" someone else said. "Not while we're eating."

"I'm not eating yet, are you? Not until the *men* get their act together and get some plates out!" she yelled into the kitchen, and then back to the group. "No, that's what happens. Really."

Mari Beth said, "That Glynis, she's another one who's sort of strange. She used to be bullied a lot, too. Because of her height, I guess."

"She could snap at any moment, too."

"And when she snaps, get out of the way folks, because she's huge!"

A few light snorts of laughter. The girl who said this covered her mouth with her hand and said gleefully, "Oh, that wasn't nice." Then she looked heavenward, pressed her palms together and said, "Please God, forgive me." But she was still grinning.

"Oh, you are so bad, Jen. *So* bad," said Marguerite, swatting her friend and laughing. "Isn't she bad!"

"You know who was asking about her?" This came from another young woman. "Martin Monday! I happened to bump into him in Bar Harbor, and he asked if I'd seen her. He wanted to know if she was seeing someone."

"You mean seeing someone like a psychiatrist? Or seeing someone like a boyfriend?"

"Martin Monday is adorable," Jen said. "What could he want with Glynis?"

"Probably he wants to know where Kim is."

"Zero tolerance," said Marcie, who was joining the group again after getting herself some punch. "That's what I say about this whole bullying thing."

"It's such a mystery why kids are so cruel to each other."

35

Chasco: I'm so tired, so exhausted. I'm feeling so lonely, too.

Gwyneth88: Lonely? Why are you lonely, Chasco? You seem to have so many friends. Everyone looks up to you!

Chasco: Not friends so much as people who rely on me to be the strong one. But I've no one, not one person that I can just unwind with. Put my feet up and unwind around. Chatting to you this way is the closest thing I have to unwinding and relaxing.

Gwyneth88: What about other ministers in Minneapolis?

Chasco: None of them face the same challenges I do. I have a peculiar, specific on-line ministry that they don't fully understand or appreciate. You've no idea the e-mails I get, the heartaches, the needs out there. In this anonymous setting people feel so much more comfortable unloading their personal problems. Plus, I've just come from the hospital. That's why I'm so weary.

Gwyneth88: What were you doing at the hospital? Is something wrong? You're not sick are you?

Chasco: No. I'm not sick. It's not for me. It's clearing up this business with Melissa's bill. I don't know why people can't be more understanding.

Gwyneth88: I thought Melissa was home.

Chasco: Oh, she is. I was trying to argue some sense into them there, trying to straighten out the mess that is Melissa's bill. I don't know why people can't be more understanding.

Gwyneth88: What's the matter?

Chasco: I promised myself that today I would not burden you with this. So, I'm not going to write anymore about this. God knows all about this. And that's all that matters.

Gwyneth88: I want you to be comfortable sharing everything with me, all your problems and difficulties. That's what I'm here for.

Chasco: You're right and I'm sorry for not sharing.

Gwyneth88: How much does she owe?

Chasco: More than $10,000.

Gwyneth88: That's a lot of money.

Chasco: It is. But that includes a number of MRIs, and they're quite expensive. Those machines aren't cheap.

Gwyneth88: I'll send you some money.

Chasco: And I'll send it right back. I can't accept any more money from you. I've prayed. God will supply. I'm not asking you.

Gwyneth88: Maybe me helping out is God's way of answering your prayer. Did you ever think of that?

Chasco: You are very perceptive, Gwyneth88, always setting me on the right track.

Gwyneth88: I'll send another check for five hundred dollars. That's what I have ready on hand. If I send more I'll have to go into my savings.

Chasco: I don't want to leave you short.

Gwyneth88: If you need it I can get more.

36

For three years the money lay buried underneath the house, the bricks and cement slab on top of it. About every two months I'd go downstairs and check on it, just to make sure it was still there. It always was. I never spent a penny of it. You would've thought that I would've kept out a fifty or two for myself, but I never did. Not one penny.

The money did a funny thing to me, though. It was almost like it made me work harder. Like it had been given to me for some purpose and I had to live up to it. I enrolled in college and started attending classes part-time. Between working at Zoles Café and going to school, there wasn't a lot of time left over to get into trouble. I was saving up to buy a computer. It's funny, but I never even thought of using the money for that, even though I could've bought ten computers. Heck, I could've bought the computer store, probably!

A lot of my school friends were on e-mail. I had my own Hotmail account, but I could get my e-mail only at school or at an Internet café. For a while Zoles had a computer, so that was nice. I could get my e-mail right after work. But Gerry, my boss, took it out. He said it just wasn't paying for itself, so there I was, back at square one without a way to check my e-mail.

"What's wrong with old-fashioned letters?" Gerry asked me.

Part of the reason that I didn't spend any money was that even after three years, I still had the nightmares. The fear was always with me. I was afraid that His Highness would find me, even though I'd cut my hair short and dyed it black.

Three years after it happened I was working my shift at Zoles, and my old friend came in, the woman that I looked up to more than anyone in the world! And there she was, her briefcase beside her on the little table. When she saw me she said, "Lanny?" Her eyes were wide and she stood up, knocking her briefcase and all her papers to the floor. I rushed over, knelt down, and began scooping them up for her. I needed to talk to her.

"You can't know me. It's not safe."

She grabbed my face and looked right into my eyes. I was shaking by this time. And seeing her reminded me of Coach and how much I missed him. How horribly much I missed him. I closed my eyes. I was going to faint.

"What's the problem here?" It was my boss.

"She's okay. Just tripped."

We didn't talk then. We didn't try. Too many people around, and I didn't trust anybody. She placed a business card in my hand, closed her hand around mine, and told me to call her or write to her or e-mail her any time.

Without e-mail, I started writing letters.

37

Glynis reluctantly said good-night to Chasco after chatting for another hour. She thought about him and his impossibly red hair as she stood at the window and looked out at Kim's old backyard. Bikes leaned up against the porch, but the swing set and the little wading pool and the wooden stage and all of Kim's mother's gardens were gone, trampled over by the new people who lived there.

A long time ago Glynis used to sit upstairs at her window in the dark and wish she lived at the Shocks' house. Late at night she would sometimes see Kim sitting on her back porch, her knees drawn up, her latest boyfriend sitting beside her. Low murmurs of conversation carried on the night air, but as much as Glynis leaned out of the window and listened, she couldn't make out what they were saying. Occasionally they would laugh. Sometimes they would kiss. She watched that, too.

Sometimes Kim's parents would be out there talking in the darkness, the tip of Glen's cigarette a tiny red dot like a firefly. Kim's mother would be in her bright, flouncy skirts and bare feet. Always bare feet. Glynis would watch them and wonder what it was like to have a regular family.

When she could, she escaped to the Shocks. She and Kim would sprawl on the living room floor and work on their language notebook. There was a rough messiness about the place that both appealed to Glynis and repelled her: the shouting, the stains in the couch, the puddles of Kool-Aid on the kitchen floor, the cookie crumbs on the rug, the children. So different from her own place, where her aunt ruled with an iron fist, doling out medicine to Glynis's mother at precise times.

She looked at Kim's backyard and wished she could walk over there right now and talk to her friend. How would Kim advise her? Continue with her relationship with Chasco? Or retreat. She prayed for guidance.

Back in her dining room, she watched Chasco's video a few times until the phone rang. Chasco? Did he know her number? She raced for it.

"Glynis?"

"Yes?" It was a male voice. Dare she hope? Dare she?

"This is Martin. Martin Monday."

"Oh. Hello." She relaxed her grip and tried to hide the profound disappointment from her voice.

"Did you get my message?"

"Yes."

"I've been thinking about you lately. Wondering how you're doing."

"I'm okay."

"I was wondering if you'd like to get together for coffee maybe sometime. Maybe dinner?"

What did he want? Information on Kim? Information on Gil? They'd been friends once, but it was a long time ago, and it was all about Kim then, too. "What for?" she asked.

There was silence for a moment. "I don't know. No specific reason. I just thought dinner might be nice. If you're not busy. If you're not seeing someone. I should've asked that first, I suppose."

"Oh." She put a hand to her neck. Martin Monday?

"I'm sorry, you are seeing someone, right? And I've made a complete fool of myself."

"As a matter of fact, I am seeing someone. I'm terribly sorry."

"Oh. Well. You be happy now. You deserve it, Glynis."

"Good-bye."

38

It's pretty impossible," Cooper was saying, "to figure out where a message originates, especially if it's from a Hotmail account like this one. Now, your personal e-mail, Teri, that would be easy, because it's got *ME* right in it, so I know it's from someone who lives in Maine. But Hotmail? You can be from anywhere."

"So it can't be done?"

"The only way is, maybe, try to trace it back to a specific computer's ISP. But, of course, if the person sent it from an Internet café or a library, you'd trace it back to that, but no further. And that's only if you happen to be on-line at the same time the message comes through, and only if you have special tracking software on the computer you received it on."

"So, it can't be done."

"Technically, yes, it can be. But practically, no."

"Thanks anyway, Cooper."

"Anytime. Any wife of my father's is a friend of mine."

Cooper was surprisingly upbeat today. Perhaps talking about something dear to his heart, like computers, helped. Cooper wasn't often upbeat, but always seemed to think that disaster was right around the corner for him. His glass was always half-empty. In his final year at university in Pennsylvania, he was living with an aunt, one of Jenny's sisters. Teri didn't know Jack's children well, but of the two, she knew Cooper the best. She had met Lily only once, and that was at the wedding where she'd breezed in with her girlfriends the morning of, and by the time she and Jack were home from their honeymoon, Lily was back in Boston in the apartment she shared with three friends. For a wedding gift, she'd given them pairs of matching socks, three pounds of Jamaica Blue coffee, and a bamboo steamer.

Since the wedding, Cooper had spent one weekend with Jack and Teri. He was quiet, polite, but plainly didn't know how to relate to his father's new and much younger wife.

Teri had several hours before she caught the flight west. She added that last bit of information to her database: Kim can't be traced through her e-mails.

Teri had one more stop to make. Glynis's office was on the way to the airport, so she had her cab drop her there.

The offices of Smith and Egan were on the third floor of a square office building near the river. She made her way up the stairs to the third floor and pushed open the door to the law firm. Glynis knew she was coming, and in fact had set up the appointment and said it was okay. Just as long as her work colleagues didn't know it was Glynis who had hired her. That was fine with Teri.

"She said you can go right in," Glynis told her.

Clara looked up from her large desk and smiled broadly. "Come in, sit down. I don't know if I can be much help. Actually, to tell you the truth, I never actually met Kim."

The buttons of her pink cotton blouse strained across her ample chest as she reached for a file. Teri thought of Lou's Ally McBeal description of Kim. This woman was anything but. Her black, elastic-waist full skirt was wrinkled, and there were something like mustard stains on the front.

"I understand you took over her cases," Teri said.

"Most of those I've finished by now—a couple of wills, a few other equally earth-shattering items, but nothing that would put her in any danger. You said on the phone she's missing?"

"It appears so."

"You might check with the others here. They all knew her. I just know her work. You also might have a talk with Glynis. I understand the two of them were good friends."

"I've been told that she was very interested in people who'd been scammed."

Clara took off her glasses and nodded. "Yes, she'd built up quite a case file."

"Is this normal practice?"

"I don't know what you mean by normal practice."

"Was she going to defend these scammers?"

"You know, I really have no idea what she planned to do. When I first came, I asked Tom what I was supposed to do with these, and he said that this was Kim's obsession. I didn't ask."

"Did you ever contact any of these people?"

Clara shook her head. "A woman phoned shortly after I came here. She was looking for Kim. When I told her that Kim was no longer here, she asked if I was going to take on her case then. She had turned over her life savings to some sort of faith healer in Florida."

"What did you tell her?"

"I didn't know how to get in touch with Kim. I thought it was odd that no one in this office knew how to contact her. Glynis had her e-mail, but that was all."

Barton Smith wasn't in, so Teri spoke briefly to John Egan, a wrinkled old man who looked like he should have retired long ago. He had no idea what Kim was working on.

"Don't you work together on things?"

"Of course. But if Kim was working on something on her own, I wouldn't be privy to that."

"So this might've been something she was working on by herself."

"Presumably."

Tom Rose was young, wide faced, and jovial and said he knew Kim really well, knew that she was working on scams and cons, but as for a place she might go when in trouble, he drew a blank.

"Was she planning on defending these scammers?"

"What?"

"You're not prosecutors, are you?"

He shifted in his chair. "To tell you the honest truth, I have no idea what Kim was up to."

"That's just what Clara said. Can you tell me something else, I'd like to know what Kim was like in the weeks leading up to her leaving."

He sighed, ran a hand through his hair. "Before she left she seemed anxious, somehow. Every little thing was bothering her. I just chalked it up to nerves."

"How were you notified that Kim had decided to stay?"

"An e-mail. The famous e-mail. Not a letter, not a phone call, but a blasted e-mail is all."

"Do you still have that e-mail?"

"Oh, probably." He hit a few keys and stood up. "I'll print if for you. Printer's out in the reception area next to the photocopier."

Teri followed him.

The e-mail was three lines long.

> Dear Tom, John, Barton, and Glynis,
>
> I've decided to stay here. I was offered a job in a prestigious law firm. Sorry to put you in a bind like this, but it can't be helped.
>
> Kim

"This was all she sent?" Teri asked.

"That was all she wrote."

39

Teri kept her face pressed to the window all the way into El Paso. Growing up in New England she thought she had seen every color God had created. Not so. The huge sun on the brown earth created a peculiar golden blood-rust that was not in her conscious memory. Every so often brown mountains appeared on the flat landscape, outcroppings which looked as though they'd been scooped up and molded by a child's hand.

When she arrived in El Paso, the first thing she noticed was an oppressive, saunalike heat. Almost before she was off the plane she had unzipped the bottom half of her pant legs and stuffed them in her backpack. Now clad in comfortable shorts, she picked up her rental car. Outside there was no cool edge to the breeze as there always is in Maine, fingers of cool just beneath the heat. Here it was just plain hot. She wasn't going to need the jacket she had brought. In Maine you always kept a jacket in your car, tied around your waist or strapped to your bicycle "just in case."

Her hotel advertised a view of the Rio Grande, and she drove to it down streets lined with bizarre looking plants that seemed to belong in a Dr. Seuss book.

"So where's the Rio Grande?" she asked the hotel proprietor after signing her name. "Is it on the other side of that culvert thingy out there?"

"No," he said, handing her room card. "It's not."

"Okay, so then where is it?"

"That culvert thingy. That *is* the Rio Grande."

Having never seen the Rio Grande before except in old western movies, she had a picture of it in her mind. Somehow she had expected Maine with palm trees. She raised her eyebrows. Anything she could have said now would only be impolite, so she said nothing.

"Dry summer," he said, as if that explained it.

Her room faced away from the mighty Rio Grande anyway, and looked out onto a parking lot with a lit billboard advertising Jones and Ortega Real Estate.

She decided to go for a walk and get some supper. She put her notebook and camera in her backpack, and without grabbing her jacket, she took off.

It was a delightful place, really, where tiny cactuses grew between the cracks in the pavement as if they were weeds. But they weren't real weeds. Weeds were dandelions and crabgrass and devil's club; these were tiny, charming plants that people in Maine would put in little pots in their windows.

The cement culvert of water that separated Mexico from the United States was fenced high on both sides with prison fencing, so she couldn't have walked the river bank even if she'd wanted to. She walked for more than half an hour, then had beans and rice and burritos in a little Mexican restaurant where she got to practice her Spanish.

Back at the hotel she hooked her computer up to the Internet. All the rooms had Internet access. That was one of her requirements. She followed the instructions printed on the card that leaned against the phone, and everything worked the first time. She checked her e-mail and sent a quick one to Jack and another to Glynis.

She got herself comfortable on the queen-size bed, got out her computer and the local phone book, and made a list of churches. They had to be big churches. In her e-mail to Glynis, Kim had said it was a big church. She also made a list of law firms and engineering companies, even though she had gotten a pretty good list from the Internet during the weeks previous. She got out her Triple A map of the southwestern states and figured out the best way to get to Las Cruces—get on the interstate and go north. Tomorrow she'd do El Paso, the day after she'd go into Las Cruces and visit June Redfeather's gallery and Davis Electronics. From the airport, finally, she had gotten through to June and told her she was coming.

"I'd love to talk to you about Gil. I'd like to help all I can. I'll be expecting you."

The list of churches she ended up with wasn't as formidable as she thought it might be. With a highlighter pen, she mapped her route from church to church on a city map of El Paso they'd given her at the main desk. There was nothing else to do this evening, so she called Jack and they talked for twenty minutes. He missed her. She missed him. Her flight was fine. The new house was almost finished. Can't wait to see you again. Love you.

40

When he was in jail, Snare used to wake up and hear his mother's accordion. He'd put his head under the blanket, his hands clamped on his ears, but still he heard it, including all the wrong notes that everybody noticed but didn't say anything about. "The Old Rugged Cross," "What a Friend We Have in Jesus," she played them all, and sang, too. He could see her, the way she used to sit: her thick legs spread, her cotton skirt washed too many times and faded to gray, the accordion balanced between her knees, one ample foot pounding the floor, her jello-y fingers searching for the keys.

If there could be a thing worse than her accordion playing it was her singing; screechy and loud and straining on the high notes that she was convinced she could reach. *You ask me how I know He lives, He lives within my heart...*

In jail he convinced himself it was the furnace coming on at night that was making that noise. It only reminded him of his mother. It wasn't his mother. She was long dead. He'd made sure of that. But the noise made his head hurt, regardless of where it came from. And sometimes he would sit on the edge of his bunk and groan and groan.

When he got out of jail the sound was gone. He could concentrate on his disguises, on his computer skills, on finding his money. On making Beamish pay for putting him there. He'd worked hard, too, and just by chance lucked into a fountain of money in the form of a lovely young lady lawyer.

But since last week, since he'd left Beamish faceless and bleeding on the floor, his mother was coming back to him.

"Stop it!" he screamed, clutching his ears. They were hurting, earaches that seemed to start from somewhere in the center of his skull. And it was his mother's voice he heard from the inside of his head. He rubbed the flesh around his ears, willing it to stop. Willing himself to remain in control. His vision clouded, and there not only was his mother, but his father holding his big Bible and from the pulpit calling him stupid. A disgrace to the family. Not worthy of the name.

"LEAVE ME ALONE!"

He reached for his bottle of Tylenol, dumped three in his hand, and swallowed them without water.

41

The first church Teri visited was one she'd heard about. Her pastor Ken had talked about an innovative Sunday school program that Second Church of El Paso had pioneered. She found the place easily enough and at nine in the morning there were a number of cars already in the lot. The church looked like an old brick grammar school circa 1970 instead of a modern church with a renowned program. Teri wasn't quite sure which door was the main entrance, so she picked one at random, parked beside it, and went inside. Door #2 turned out be the wrong choice because she had to follow blue arrows on a wall down a long corridor, past closed doors and up a steep stairwell and then down another long hall before she found anything resembling offices.

And in the end it was a wasted effort anyway because the minister looked down at the pictures of Kim and Gil and shook his head. No, he didn't recall ever seeing them.

"Please take a good look," Teri said. "Might you have seen them even once? Could they have come in and sat in the back? Left early, maybe?"

He frowned. "Come with me, let's ask some of the others."

She followed him down a narrow hall where they stopped one by one at offices where a variety of ministers and secretaries smiled and wished they could be more helpful, but none of them recognized Gil and Kim.

"He's supposed to be an ordained minister," Teri said. "Are you sure you've never heard of him?"

They shook their heads.

"How about the name Lanny Boucher? Is that name familiar to any of you?"

More *nos*.

There were thirteen churches on her list, and in every one she got a similar response. No one had heard the names Gil Williamson or Kim Shock or Lanny Boucher. But she diligently handed out her business card on which she scribbled the name and number of her hotel and encouraged them to leave a message if they remembered anything.

Her morning took her to old churches, new churches, large churches, and superlarge churches. "Old churches, new churches, red churches, blue churches," she chorused to herself as she would go out into yet another church parking lot to check her map for the next one.

She visited one that was a perfect circle, and a female minister looked down at the picture of Gil and Kim and said, "Maybe. I'm not sure." Then, "Can you leave this picture with me?"

Teri dug in her satchel for one of the dozens of photocopies she had made for this express purpose.

She visited a huge church that had bought an old hotel for its building; a husband and wife team of ministers shook their heads. She visited a church that had its own radio station and had a satellite dish hanging off the building instead of a cross, but they too had never seen nor heard of the couple.

For lunch she grabbed two tacos at Taco Bell and realized too late that they had Taco Bell in Maine, and what was she thinking? She sat inside and read the local paper placed conveniently for patrons. She wasn't interested in the headlines of war, crime, and terrorism. Like Taco Bell, she could get that at home. She turned to the local news: business, obituaries, who married whom, plus her personal favorite—the local court news. She finished her tacos and got herself another coffee, which she took with her. Nothing of interest in the paper. She left it for the next person.

She'd left her rental in the full sun and the seat was hot to the touch. She opened all the windows and turned the AC on high. Several miles later she was finally able to shut the windows and enjoy the cool. It was a nice rental. It had a CD player, a place to put your coffee cup and spare change, all the important things in a car. She didn't have any CDs with her, so she listened to Spanish radio trying to figure out what they were talking about. She caught bits and pieces, but not enough to call herself bilingual.

After visiting more churches, she stopped at the public library and sat in a comfortable chair and scanned through back issues of *El Paso Times*. Looking for what, she wasn't quite sure. After a little while she left. Whatever it was she was looking for, she didn't find it.

It was back out into the heat and more driving through blinding sun, feeling guilty that she was wasting Glynis's money on this wild-goose chase. They probably weren't here anyway. Hadn't Kim talked about a nonexistent flash flood? She obviously made that up. They could be in Alaska. They could be in Idaho.

She parked downtown and threw some money in the meter. The first law office, which was the biggest in El Paso (or at least they had the biggest ad in the yellow pages), had never heard of Kim Shock and didn't recognize her picture. They also did not know anyone named Gil Williamson. She left her card and a picture of Kim.

"Don't leave a picture," the secretary told her. "It'll just get thrown out. We get so much junk."

The second was more helpful. They didn't know Kim, nor had they hired anyone new in a while, but they had a list of a lot of the law firms in El Paso that included a few she hadn't found in the yellow pages.

"I need prestigious ones," she said. "I'm told it's a prestigious firm."

They gave her more names. She sat in their cool waiting room and added them to her map.

By seven she was tired, hungry, and hot, and the cool hotel room, her freshly made bed, and a new package of coffee next to the machine made her feel welcomed and almost cherished.

She called Jack, who told her that everything was fine and that Shauna and Stephan had been over helping him pack.

Shauna? Oh, great. "Be careful, Jack."

"Careful of what?"

"Never mind. I'll see you in a couple of days."

42

The next morning in Las Cruces she asked Mark Byers why no one at Davis Electronics seemed to check their references.

"What do you mean?"

"Every one of Gil Williamson's references is bogus. Every one. I checked them all."

He swiveled his chair away from an oversized, flat computer screen and said quietly, "It all makes sense then."

"What do you mean?"

"When you first called, I thought, yes, Gil worked out well here and we had no problems with him. But it got me thinking. There *was* something odd about him."

"Tell me about that."

"I checked through some of the projects Gil worked on. He finished none of them. When I looked over what he did for us here, after you called, I have to say I wasn't too impressed with his record."

"Would it surprise you if I told you that he probably wasn't any kind of engineer at all?"

He sighed. "No, it would not surprise me. He was always more interested in his art, anyway."

Teri raised her eyebrows.

"He was an art collector, which is why he and June were so perfect together. His heart just wasn't into all of this." He indicated the room with a whirl of his hand. "He was often late, came in apologizing. Plus, he had a few personal problems. We tried to give him the benefit of the doubt."

"What kind of personal problems?"

"He had a sister that required hospitalization. The bills were enormous."

She handed him a few photographs. "I just want to make sure. This is the man you hired? This is Gil Williamson?"

He picked up the photo, looked at it, then put it down next to his computer. "Yes. This is Gil."

"How about this woman? Do you know her?"

He looked at the picture of Kim. "No. I don't know her. Should I?"

"Her name is Kim Shock. She came out here to see Gil. She's missing, too."

She put the pictures back in her satchel. "Do you know June well?" she asked.

"I've been in her gallery a few times is all. Art like that is not really my thing. It seemed to be Gil's though. He was always off on art trips."

Before she left, Teri gave him her business card.

Next door, Teri stood for a moment in the quiet gallery and looked at paintings, baskets, wall hangings, and sculptures on podiums until a woman with black hair and dangling feather earrings asked if she could be of any help.

"Are you June?"

"Yes, I am. And you're Teri?" She glided forward and shook Teri's hand.

"Teri Blake-Addison. Nice to meet you." The name Redfeather seemed American Indian, and although the woman in front of her was certainly raven-haired and her clothes were Native American, her features were too thin, her nose too narrow, her lips too thin, her skin too fair.

"Let's go to my office," June said.

She flipped the Closed sign on the front door and led Teri past a display case of silver and turquoise jewelry and a collection of dream catchers to a small room in the back cluttered with paper, a computer, books, and file folders. On her desk, framed photographs of family members were randomly arranged. June took the chair behind the desk, whirled it around, and told Teri to sit on the one next to the wall.

She asked, "Do you know where Gil is? Can you tell me?"

"Does the name Kim Shock mean anything to you?"

She raised her high arched eyebrows. "Should it?"

"How about Lanny Boucher?"

She shook her head. Her feather earrings brushed her shoulder when she leaned her head to the side.

"I'm going to show you a few photos," Teri said. "First of all, is this a picture of Gil Williamson?"

She said yes.

"How about this woman. Have you ever seen her?"

"That's this Kim you're asking me about?"

"Yes. This is Kim."

June smoothed the picture on the desk. "I don't know. I'm not sure. She may have been in. What does she have to do with Gil?"

"You mean here? In your gallery?"

"Yes. I don't know. Maybe it's her. She was looking at my display of dream catchers. I remember walking over, if she's the one in this picture, and asking if she was looking for something in particular. She said she just wanted to look, and so I left her alone. She picked up several brochures and left."

"And she was here just the once?"

June nodded. "I'm sorry I can't be more help. It may not have even been her." She went through the photos of Kim fanning them out like playing cards, and then said, "What does this have to do with Gil?"

"She may know where Gil is. That's why it's important for you to tell me anything you know about this woman."

"Okay."

"How did you and Gil meet?"

June crossed her legs and retied the leather thongs of her sandals up her calves as she talked. "Gil worked right next door at Davis Electronics. One day as I was running out of the gallery with a bunch of papers, we bumped square into each other. I was late as usual and not looking where I was going, and before we knew it, both of us were sprawled on the pavement."

Teri raised her eyebrows.

"I know it sounds rather stereotypical, but that's how it was."

After they brushed themselves off, Gil told her that he had long been an admirer of the items in the gallery, had wanted to meet her for a long time, and if it wasn't too much trouble, could he have a look through the gallery now? Was she open? Art and in particular art of this region had always been of interest to him.

"So I took him on a tour of the gallery, and then we went out to dinner. It went on from there. We hit it off."

"Did Gil ever tell you that he was an ordained minister?"

June snorted, pushed her hair behind her ears. "No, because it's not true. That would be the last thing Gil would be. Neither one of us has any use for organized religion."

"So he wasn't an ordained minister?"

"I don't know where you got that information, but it's wrong. He was an engineer with a special interest in North American Indian art."

"And he lived here in Las Cruces?"

"All of his life. He grew up in this area. When we met he had an apartment in El Paso, then he moved in with me at my house."

"I'm just curious...did you ever lend Gil money? Let him use your credit cards?"

"I loaned him some money, yes. He had a sister in New Hampshire who was taken to the hospital rather suddenly with an aneurysm. She was on welfare and her bills were very high. MRIs are very expensive."

"And she couldn't get on Medicaid? Anything?"

"According to Gil, she was one of those people who fell through the cracks."

"Did he ever pay you back?"

"Of course."

"All of it?"

"Not all. Not yet. Why are you asking these questions? It sounds like you're accusing Gil of something. We were going to be married, so of course we would share our finances. This shop does well. Of course I would want to share with him."

Teri didn't know how to tell her, so she decided just to begin at the beginning. When she finished, June said, "You have it wrong. That's not Gil. You must have him mixed up with someone else," but her finger with the turquoise ring was trembling.

And suddenly, she looked out of place in her dress-up Indian clothes: her vest with the beadwork, her sandals, her bracelets and rings, the too-black hair for the color of her skin.

"I'm sorry," Teri said, "to be the one to tell you this. But I think people could be in danger. Kim and possibly Lanny."

"I don't believe you. I don't believe that about Gil. Gil would never hurt anyone. A few years ago I went through a terrible time. My sister died. And then my parents disowned me, and Gil, he was so understanding. If it hadn't been for Gil..."

June had picked up the framed photo and was looking down at it. "Your sister?"

June nodded and put it down. "Gil helped me through this really hard time."

Teri looked at the photo. Two teenage girls in wool hats and ski jackets against a backdrop of snow. They were smiling. The one on the left was undoubtedly a younger June. The one on the right made Teri go suddenly very cold. She reached out and touched the picture, not breathing.

"My sister," June said.

"How..." Teri choked on her words. "How did she die?"

"She was part of a religious cult in Maine."

Teri said slowly, "I don't remember the name Redfeather."

"My name is Johnson. My sister's name was Breanne. I changed my last name to Redfeather. We grew up in Connecticut. After it happened, I left. My parents and I, well, they blamed me. Still blame me."

"Why do they blame you?"

"I was the one who found the drama camp for Breanne. My parents were against her going so far away, but I persuaded them. I told my sister to follow her dream of being an actor. I don't know how she left it to get hooked up with this King James cult thing. After it happened, I left. I couldn't face my parents. Couldn't face the loss. My first morning in Las Cruces, I got up and there on my windowsill was a beautiful red feather. I took that as a sign, that things were going to be okay. I decided to change my name to Redfeather. And then I met Gil and it looked like I had a chance to be happy again."

Teri was still looking at the picture. She remembered Breanne Johnson. She remembered the names of all the girls who were murdered: Breanne Johnson, Charissa York, Jo Braslo, and Deirdre Maxwell. She had talked to Breanne's parents, who said they were not surprised that their daughter had gotten herself mixed up with the King James cult. Breanne was always a bit impulsive, they said.

Teri had never met the sister, didn't know there was a sister.

"You said drama camp? Tell me about that."

"I found it on the web for Breanne. Maine summer acting dot com, or there might be an underscore in there somewhere. In any case, it's not there anymore...the website, I mean."

"You don't have any brochures from this camp, do you?"

"No. It was all on the web."

Driving back to El Paso, Teri thought about something her commanding officer had once told her a long, long time ago: There is no such thing as coincidence.

The message light in her room was flashing when she got there.

43

It was quiet and restful in Andrea Silver's studio where Glynis stood for fittings. There was something soft in the background, maybe Enya. Glynis liked it here.

"I was thinking about a different sleeve," Glynis was saying. "Something more flouncy, maybe three-quarter."

"You could pull it off," Andrea said as she pinned the hem of Glynis's slacks. Getting long enough pants was always a challenge. "I don't know why you just don't make your own clothes, Glynis. You certainly have the talent. Where did you train?"

"Train?"

Andrea nodded.

"My mother taught me to sew," Glynis said.

"Why don't you come work for me, or with me?"

"Are you serious?"

"I'm serious."

Glynis looked around her. "I could never..."

"Why not? Why ever not?"

"I have a job."

Andrea sighed.

Not a job I like particularly, thought Glynis. And it wasn't as if she hadn't thought about quitting. And to get right down to it, she really didn't need the money. But what would she do? Sit at home all day? It was something she couldn't explain, this need to make her own way in the world, to prove herself. She had basically followed Kim into law school and then followed her into Smith and Egan. Always Kim, always wanting to be like Kim. And not going into fashion design because Kim proclaimed it silly. "Being a lawyer, that's where it's at," Kim said to her once.

"I think the two of us could work well together," Andrea was saying. "We could have a dynamite company, with my designs and your skills as a seamstress, plus your fashion sense. Just think about it Glynis. That's all I ask, think about it."

"I don't know. I'd have to think, and pray about it, too. Plus, there's this chance, this tiny chance that I might be moving."

Andrea backed away. "Really!"

"I have a boyfriend. Well, we're getting more and more serious. He's a minister at a church in Minneapolis."

"Oh, my! Well that's good. Congratulations! Or are congratulations in order yet?"

"Not yet. Maybe soon."

"A minister! That's great, Glynis. I always wondered when some great guy would snap you up."

Glynis felt her face reddening.

"I wish you all the happiness," Andrea was saying. "You deserve it."

It was the second time someone had said that to her.

44

Teri entered the appropriate sequence on the keypad and listened to the message.

"Hello, this is Rev. Nancy Curtain. We met yesterday. I'm the minister at Circle Church. After you left I looked at the picture again. Something about the face was familiar, so I went through the visitors' cards. We had one from Kim Shock and Gil Williamson. There was an address but no phone number."

At the front desk Teri spread out her map to get directions for the best way to get to the address Rev. Nancy had given in the message.

"That's the west side," the girl at the desk said. "There are some nice homes out there. You going out there now?"

"I was thinking of it, yeah."

"Well, here," she said, running a dark red fingernail along a series of roads. "The best way to get there from here is to take this road straight out as far as it goes, then hang a right here." And she pointed.

It was still light when Teri found herself driving through a residential area of white stucco homes with red-tiled roofs. The houses were large and looked expensive. Instead of green grass lawns like people had in Maine, these yards were groupings of white stones, thick succulent plants and cactuses, along with clumps of tall grass. No one was outside anywhere—no one watering plants or playing catch with kids in the backyard. Too hot? Maybe.

The address Teri drove to was a huge, sprawling home at the end of a street of huge, sprawling homes. Rich people houses. Engineering or art dealing or whatever Gil was doing must be a profitable business.

Next to the front door, a huge potted desert plant lay on its side, its tubular roots exposed, dirt strewn on the welcome mat. An animal? The wind? She stood at the double door and rang the bell, which wasn't a bell at all but chimes. No answer. She rang again and looked around. The whole area seemed deserted; no lights flickered in the neighboring homes. Maybe like the house Martin Monday was working on, these were lived in only one week a year. There was no nameplate on the front door. She looked for a mailbox, but the house had one of those mail chutes in the door. No help there.

The front window drape was drawn, but in a half-inch space between shade and window, Teri cupped her hands around her face and peered inside. She couldn't see much, but what she did see was messy. A couch cushion lay on the floor and several overturned cups on the carpet. She tried to see more, but the drape narrowed her field of vision to just a few inches.

Around the side of the house was an opened stone gate. She walked through. And recognized the smell. There is nothing on earth quite like the smell of decomposing human flesh. She put her hand to her nose and stood at the gate, wondering whether to go in or not. Ahead of her thousands of bugs skittered across a scummy kidney-shaped swimming pool. A fountain at one end was dry and filled with plant parts.

She inched into the yard and saw a few more plants in huge pots overturned near the back door. Wooden lawn chairs were upside down. Through the scum at the bottom of the pool, she saw another chair. Tentatively, tentatively, and against her better judgment as a cop, she made her way onto the patio and toward the open back door.

The kitchen had been torn apart. Dishes, pots, and broken jars of food lay on the floor, the fridge door swinging open. She tiptoed through the debris, aware that she was contaminating a crime scene, but she had to find out if this was Kim.

The smell was stronger. She choked and mouth-breathed her way into the living room where she saw it, the body, slumped on the floor and surrounded by dried brown blood. She thought of the farmhouse. Quickly, she left. In her car, she locked her doors and dialed 911.

It wasn't Kim. It was a man's body. Not Kim. Thankfully not Kim.

"I'd like to report a death," she said as calmly as she could. "And make sure you bring your Vicks. It's an old one."

Two police cars arrived promptly, and she told the officers she had touched the doorbell, the window, and had tiptoed through the kitchen but didn't touch anything. She told them she was a private investigator licensed in the state of Maine and why she was there.

An officer, who introduced himself as Walt, leaned in her car window and asked her if she had any idea who it was.

"No. The person I'm looking for is female. That's a male in there."

"Wait here," he told her.

So she sat in her car and watched the sun set, trying not to think about another old crime scene. Five bodies crusted with blood, four of them laid out in the shape of a cross. She closed her eyes. After what seemed like hours but was probably only fifteen minutes, Walt returned. He went to his police cruiser first, sat in his car for a long time talking on the radio, then came to her car where he leaned against her open window.

"When did you get here?"

"Maybe forty-five minutes ago now," Teri said. "It was still light."

"And why did you come here?"

"I was looking for Kim Shock or Gil Williamson. This is the address I was given. I have no way of knowing whether it's correct or not."

"Who gave you this address?"

"They wrote it on a church visitor's card."

"A what?"

"When you visit churches sometimes they have you fill out cards so they can keep track of visitors. The minister gave me this address."

"I'm going to want the name and address of this minister."

"No problem, I'll get that for you now." She reached into her satchel, brought out the phone information, and jotted down the particulars on a piece of paper. "Who is it in there?" she said.

"We don't know yet. There's no face."

"Ouch. Who owns the house?"

"I was just checking on that. Someone named Max Beamish. Name ring a bell?"

She puzzled on that one. Where had she heard the name before? "I'm not sure," she said tentatively.

"You'd recognize it if you're into finance. Guy's worth millions. Billions, maybe, I don't know. I can't count that high."

She blinked. The house Martin Monday was working on. That belonged to someone named Beamish.

Later, she followed them to the police station where she went through her story half a dozen more times, until they were satisfied she hadn't seen anything, didn't know anything. But by the time she left, they were fairly certain that the body did, indeed, belong to industrialist and venture capitalist Max Beamish. She didn't tell them about the house in Maine.

That night she dreamed about her mother. She dreamed they came to her and told her that her mother's body had been found at the bottom of a dirty swimming pool. When they brought her up, she was wearing the striped sweater she wore on the day she disappeared, but when Teri tried to touch her, her bones were sharp like the points of a cactus.

45

Little hints. All along Kim had been leaving little hints, praying, praying, that sooner or later someone would pick up on them. After his visit to Maine she was fairly certain. But not totally certain. She had tried in her own way to get the information out of him. Little pointed questions. So, you've never been to Maine before? No. Let's go for a drive out toward Exeter Corners. Don't know where that is. How about Belfast? You'll have to help me, I don't know where that is.

He'd passed the verbal test. He'd convinced her that he'd never been here before. Still, there was something wrong, something about the way his eyes darted, the way he would look beyond her, the way his fists clenched and unclenched at his side. She could almost watch him practicing his deep breathing. And the way he smashed that camera? That wasn't normal. She knew he was capable of great rage. And when she'd told him about her brother, hadn't there been a flash of recognition? And the way he seemed so intensely interested in her rich friend, Glynis.

But both of them kept up the act. She knew he was acting, and she supposed he knew she was, on some level. But why was he acting? What was he hiding? She still wasn't sure. So she made plans to go out there. She needed to know for sure. And if what she thought was true, he needed to pay for everything he'd done to her.

It's funny how you can look back on a thing and see all the times when you could've made the right decision, yet you made the wrong one. Why hadn't she called the police? At the first sign of this, why hadn't she? In Maine, why hadn't she? And why had she left the money at Glynis's? All done in innocence, thinking, I can do this on my own. Glynis's is the perfect place with her security system like Fort Knox.

Plus, I can be the hero. I can be the one who breaks this whole thing right open. I'll prove that the police were wrong all along. Stupid.

Stupid. Stupid! And telling him everything! How could she have possibly done that? What had possessed her? That really took the cake.

Right up until he had locked her in this basement she thought she could handle it. Not only could handle it, but was on top of it. Her game. Yes, he was monitoring her every move. Yes, he stuck by her with that gun in her back, even when they went to church. But it was still her game.

"What're you doing?" he had whispered to her that day in church.

"I'm filling out a visitor card. It'll look suspicious if we don't."

He scowled and she wrote Max Beamish's address. They'd been there the evening before. Max hadn't, and so Gil was full of curses and anger. "He's supposed to be here!" And he threw what looked like an expensive vase across the room. Then he sat on the couch, his pistol between his knees, and put his head in his hands.

"You should really see a doctor about your head," she said.

"Shut up!"

"He's not here."

"I can see that!" And then more quietly, "He has something that belongs to me."

"Well, you can stay. I'm leaving," and she made for the door. He shot at it with his pistol. "You walk out of here and both your mother and Glynis die."

He was crazy, but she believed him.

But she was memorizing things for when the police finally caught up with them. She memorized Beamish's address and wrote it on the visitor card. She and Gil were moving too often—a hotel room here, a hotel room there. Gil was rubbing his eyes and blinking when she placed the card in the offering plate. Fine. He didn't see what she wrote.

There were so many times she could've left. Even then. She could've stood up in church and yelled that she was being held hostage by this man. But was she? If she had stood up, if she had yelled that, Gil would have merely laughed. "She's not being held hostage. How absurd! We're in church, aren't we? She's free to come and go as she pleases. Aren't you, darling?" And what would she have said? That it was just a feeling? Just a horrible, hideous feeling that something was wrong? But she kept waiting until she had the information she needed. She was still in control after all.

But there was one thing she didn't count on, and that was that he would throw her down into this basement apartment with concrete walls and no windows and lock her in. She leaned against the wall and with the dull kitchen knife began picking away at the cement like she'd been doing now for many days.

46

Teri knew she wasn't going to sleep anymore. Finding the body plus the dream about her mother had taken care of that. At five she rose and made coffee in the little motel coffeepot. She stretched and in the bathroom splashed cold water on her face.

The man who died, Max Beamish, venture capitalist millionaire. Why was that the address given on Kim and Gil's visitor card? How did he fit into all of this? She turned on the desk lamp, opened her computer, dumped her notes onto the desk, and rubbed her eyes.

Her coffee ready, she poured it into the white motel mug, added a packet of Coffee-mate and a packet of Sweet'N Low, and took her mug of hot chemicals to her computer and began an Extreme Search on Max Beamish. A Google search yielded pages and pages of hits: *Forbes, Time, Financial Times, Financial Post.* She organized her search by date and skimmed the articles. It looked as if he owned several computer companies, had bought and sold a few dot-coms, and bought and sold real estate and hotels like he was playing Monopoly. There were a few pictures of him, and she had to admit he didn't look like much. Tall, scrawny with big ears that she bet were the brunt of many a childhood barb. Yet there was a keenness in his eyes. This guy was smart. He was forty-two, had never married, and as much as she searched, there was surprisingly little about his private life. His money was doing a fine job of keeping him out of the public eye, she thought.

No mention of any scandals in his life, but there was also nothing about his childhood—parents, schooling, degrees, not even a pet dog. Max Beamish appeared fully formed and rich around ten years ago. And his was not a household name, not like Bill Gates. "Now why is that?" Teri said out loud. "Now, just why is that?"

She also did a search for Mainesummeracting.com and was rewarded with a pop-up menu advertising this domain for sale. A search for Maine summer acting camps yielded nothing, either.

An hour later she called Jack at his office. She told him about the murder, and he told her to be careful. She told him she had a couple more things she had to do today and then she was coming home. She was beginning to formulate a kind of theory and needed some thinking time.

"Can you share it with me?"

"I only have odd thoughts. Nothing in any kind of order yet."

"Be careful."

"I will."

"I miss you. I'm just about to take Kelly for a jog down by the river."

"You do that."

When they hung up, she went down two flights of stairs to the exercise room. There were two people there, a well-muscled woman on a treadmill and a man lying on a bench lifting some free weights. It wasn't as good as a run down by the river with her dog, but it would have to do. She smiled when she thought of her couch-potato husband jogging with Kelly. She had surprised a lot of people when she decided to marry him.

"You're going to marry a professor from the university?" her police friend Bill had asked.

"Yup."

"Well."

"Yeah, well."

They met three years ago. She'd been out of police work for a year and had taken a job at the university doing grunt work for a conference hosted by the English faculty. It was her job to collate the registration packets, making sure each delegate got copies of the proceedings as well as a name tag in a clear plastic badge.

"I have a feeling this is not the type of work you normally do."

Teri had jumped and turned to see Dr. James Addison standing in the doorway.

"Does it show that much?"

"I came to help. I'm Jack."

"I've seen you. At meetings. I'm Teri."

"Nice to meet you." They shook hands. "Now, what needs doing?" he said, rubbing his hands together.

"I was just going to stuff those letters from the chancellor into the packages. They arrived late."

"Figures."

He took off his sweater, laid it on the back of a chair, and said, "I'll get this stack of folders and you get those."

"Fair enough. But you don't have to help, you know. It's what I get paid the big bucks for."

They worked across from each other for a few minutes, and then he asked her how long she'd been with the university.

"Not long."

"Nothing like a straight answer."

"Actually, I used to be a cop." Her telling him surprised her. This was not something she usually went around telling people.

"You used to be a cop?"

"Yeah." They talked. And stuffed. And talked some more. Teri didn't remember what they talked about, just that they talked and that she felt comfortable with him. He was miles older than she was, probably married (she thought), so talking to him was safe.

When the packets were ready, the speakers' gifts enclosed and labeled, he said, "I think we could both use a cup of coffee."

"Coffee," she said. "A man after my own heart."

They were friends for a long time before their relationship moved on to anything more.

Now, as she watched CNN on the television high on the wall, she thought about Jack and missed Jack and wished he were here. The woman on the treadmill next to hers said, "Sometimes I think I should give this all up and go sit on my couch and watch television for the rest of my life."

"Me, too," Teri said.

"You here on vacation?" she asked.

"Business." Teri slowed down the pace on her treadmill. Her twenty-five minutes were nearly finished. Funny, she could run with

Kelly beside the river for an hour, but twenty-five minutes on a tread-mill was all she could manage, given the inherent boredom factor. "How about you?"

"Conference. I'm in insurance. Look at that." She pointed to the television. "Look at that. Another murder. And right here."

The local news was reporting that the body of an unidentified man had been found in this western El Paso home last night. The home belonged to industrialist Max Beamish. It was not known, at this time, if that was the man found dead at that location.

"Where's the remote?" Teri asked.

"I don't know," the woman answered. "The TV was on when I got here."

"It's over there," the man with the weights said. "On the window ledge."

Teri reached for the remote and turned up the volume. She leaned against the treadmill while she looked at the house she had visited the evening before.

"Probably drug related," said the woman still on the treadmill. "They all are these days."

Teri waited until the newscast moved to the next item—a fire in a restaurant—before she went back to her room.

47

S nare was arguing with a pimply-faced kid in RadioShack when he saw the news on a bank of televisions against the wall. "The body of an unidentified male was found murdered in this west El Paso home late last night. Police were responding to a 911 call about a possible burglary. His name is being withheld pending notification of family members."

Notification of family members. Snare almost chuckled out loud ("Good luck with that one!") while the kid was going on about the wonders of this new gadget that was a phone, a date book, organizer, plus you could send e-mail on it. That's what he wanted it for, the e-mail. He didn't want to always have to be sitting at his computer to get his e-mail. He'd gotten quite good at this whole e-mail website stuff while in prison. Great courses you can take in prison. Really quite helpful. But while the kid was going on and on, Snare was listening to every word coming from the television, while he turned the cell phone over and over in his hand.

When the kid looked at him questioningly, he forced himself to still his hands. He could picture this kid saying to the police later. "Yes, he appeared quite nervous. He kept turning the phone over and over. I knew the minute I saw him that there was something wrong."

Control. It was all about control. But lately he felt like he was coming apart. The thing he had practiced so well and so often, he was losing. Maybe his old man was right all along when he called him weak and a girl.

"Sir, did you want that cell phone then, with the entire package?"

The boy had moved close enough that Snare could smell his bad breath. He backed away. Snare always required more personal space than most people. "I'm sorry, what package?"

"The whole package? The warranty? The immediate hookup with the sixty free minutes of long distance?"

"Oh yes, of course. I'll need the e-mail right away, too."

"No problem."

While the boy rang up his order, Snare watched the television. It had already moved on to the next item, a fire in a Greek restaurant somewhere.

"Your name and address?"

"Excuse me?"

"For the warranty."

"Oh yes. Of course." And he reeled off the phony name and address he had memorized from one of his many driver's licenses. "Tony King, 45 Pleasant View Drive, Las Cruces, New Mexico."

If anyone would have taken the time to look, they would have discovered that there was no Tony King at 45 Pleasant View Drive in Las Cruces. In fact there wasn't even an Pleasant View Drive in Las Cruces.

"There, it's in. Now, if you have any trouble, you can go to any RadioShack in the country and they'll have your information."

"How convenient."

As soon as he got into his car, he'd destroy that license and strip his computers of that name. No more Tony King.

48

Glynis was going to spend the entire day chatting with Chasco. She had written "Chat with Chasco" on her computer calendar. She even took a vacation day from work. (She had lots saved up and didn't often take them.)

Before she had gone to bed the night before, she had looked at his video over and over and over again, the way he waved to her, the way he smiled, that little lifting of his chin. "This is for you," and the kiss, for her.

She was up early even though it would be hours before he was on because of the time difference. She logged on to her computer and answered a few e-mails left over from Sewinglady, Lark7, and KarenP. She was surprised there was nothing from Melissa, but Melissa was healthy now, and perhaps she had her own friends and what did she want with an old lady like Glynis? Nevertheless, she sent a message to her with a verse for the day.

Then she read through her listservs and sent messages when appropriate. With nothing else to do, and still hours before it was morning in Minneapolis, she went into her mailbox named "Chasco" and read every message he'd ever sent to her. She'd gotten involved with Chasco's church at about the same time Kim left for Texas. He was a minister, and she would e-mail him with various questions about her Christian faith. He would answer with a clarity that surprised her. Then they began e-mailing once or twice a week. She learned all about a pet dog who'd died suddenly when Chasco was little, and his parents who had died in a house fire when he was ten. She dug out the very first e-mail he had ever sent to her. It was dated six months ago.

Dear Gwyneth88,

Thank you for your encouraging e-mail. I'm glad you are
enjoying the Bible studies. As you know, this on-line church
is very new to me. Sometimes I feel like I'm going out on a
limb with God in this whole venture, but I believe I'm doing
what he wants me to do. Because this ministry is so new, I'm
putting together a group of prayer partners. Let me know if
you would like to be involved in this important part of the
ministry.

God bless,
Chasco

She flipped through and read random e-mails.

Dear Gwyneth88,

You are so faithful to the Bible studies. I was telling my
roommate about you, how faithful you are. I really appreciate
all your prayers. Let me know if you want to be involved
even more in the ministry, on the ground floor.

Chasco

Dear Gwyneth88,

I'm glad you liked that study on redemption. God gave
me that one in a dream. It's true! No, I'm not crazy, and I
wouldn't tell too many people about my dreams. Most
people look at me funny when I tell them that sometimes
God speaks to me in dreams. I hope you don't think I'm
crazy!

Sincerely,
Chasco

Dear Gwyneth88,

I can't tell you how MUCH I appreciate the cash gift you just sent! It's really being used in the furtherance of God's kingdom. If it weren't for faithful people like you, the Christian witness would surely die! I so appreciate your putting me on your gift-giving list. I wanted to tell you that personally.

Sincerely,
Chasco

Dear Gwyneth88,

I really appreciate your friendship, Gwyneth88. You are truly a special person. You have been such an encouragement to me. I just wanted you to know that.

Chasco

Glynis read through those early messages and felt her first pinprick of unease. Chasco told her he lived with his mother, yet here was an e-mail talking about a roommate. It could be nothing. Feeling a sudden chill, she retied her terry cloth robe tightly around her waist. She would ask Chasco about that. That would be one of her first questions.

49

O n the morning of her flight home, Teri called Rev. Nancy Curtain, filling her in on what had transpired and warning her that the police might call.

"They already have," she said. "Do they know the name of the person who died? Was it that Max Beamish that they're talking about?"

"I'm not sure. I haven't heard."

"I wonder why that address was on the card?"

"A mystery," Teri said.

"I've been doing a lot of thinking about this since you came. I do remember that couple. Or at least I think I do. If it's who I'm thinking about, they sat very close to each other, and she did not seem happy. That's all I remember."

"Thanks, Rev. Curtain, for your help."

"Nancy's my name." She laughed. "And now I get to go back to another battle we're facing."

"Oh yeah?"

"A number of my parishioners have donated money to a bogus faith healer out of Florida. Scam's been around for a while. Don't know why people don't clue in."

Teri frowned. "Tell me about this."

"One of my parishioners received a spam e-mail. It was finally brought to my attention after a number of people had already sent in money. She brought the e-mail in to me."

"Do you still have that e-mail, by any chance?"

"Sorry, that's not something I would keep. Are you interested in this?"

"I may be. What about the name of your parishioner who received the e-mail?"

"I'll get that for you. If you hold the line I could look right now."

"Thank you."

Later, from the airport, Teri called the woman in Nancy's church who had received the spam e-mail from Julius Dumain. She told Teri she had never met him in person. All she did was print off the e-mail and show it to her minister.

"Would you still have that e-mail somewhere?"

"No. I got a new computer since then. All that old stuff's gone."

The two elderly women who'd sent money to Julius Dumain didn't want to talk with her.

50

It was noon and still Chasco had not signed on. Several times Glynis had sent him messages: Chasco, where are you? Chasco, it's now an hour later and still you're not there. Chasco, I took the day off from work just to spend it with you, and you're not here.

Glynis answered all her other e-mails and more, and still nothing from Chasco. For the dozenth time that morning, she downloaded his video and watched him blow her a kiss. She liked the way his voice sounded. Gentle. There were probably lots of explanations about the roommate thing. Maybe he and his roommate lived with Chasco's mother. Maybe he had had a roommate, but no longer.

She logged on to his website and downloaded his recent Bible study, a thought-provoking one on grace. Since this topic was of so much interest to her, and since she had nothing but time while she waited for him, she decided to do a little study of her own.

She opened up her word processing program and created a new file and labeled it "Grace." Then she began a Google search on grace. Using her on-line Bible and concordance, she began compiling thoughts and Scripture references. She was surprised at the number of Bible studies and sermon notes she found on the subject. Getting into a routine now, she was writing, reading, looking up Bible passages, and writing some more. And then something stopped her and made her gasp and made her stop breathing for an instant. The prick of unease turned into a shudder, and she hugged herself and stared at what she was seeing.

The words on this website, which featured the works of Charles Stanley, were very familiar. Too familiar. She flipped over to Chasco's website. What Chasco had written was exactly what she had read on Charles Stanley's website. She kept reading, going back and forth. They had used the same Bible references, the same progression of thoughts, even the same anecdotes! She looked for any reference, any reference at all on Chasco's website to Charles Stanley, but found none.

How could this be? These Bible studies that Glynis had found so helpful, so profound, that had meant so much to her? This one that she wrote to Chasco about saying how much it helped her, and he had written back and said that God had given him these words. The one that got her thinking that this man of God, this special man of God could be somehow special *to her?* Plus others, many others, copied. Word for word.

She pushed herself away from her computer, choking, gasping. She needed to get away. She heated some chicken noodle soup in the microwave and put the kettle on. When the soup was heated through, she tried eating it, but it hit her stomach like lead. She dumped the rest down the sink and went into the bathroom and threw up. Then she wiped her mouth and brushed her teeth and walked past her computer without looking at it.

In her bedroom, roughly, gruffly, she made her bed like a hospital bed, her mother's hospital bed with corners all correct and even, the way her aunt demanded, sheets tight, not the hint of a blanket showing from underneath the spread. She took the braided rug outside and hung it on the back railing and beat it with a broom and watched the dust fly off. But no matter how much she did this, there was always more dust. Nothing was ever clean enough.

She left the rug there in the sun and went back inside where she got down on her knees and scrubbed the kitchen floor with a bucket and brush until it gleamed. She did two loads of laundry. She turned on her stereo and put in classical music CDs and sat in her mother's chair and rocked back and forth and back and forth until they ran out.

At four she checked her e-mail. Still nothing from Chasco.

She cleaned, she scrubbed, she washed, until by early evening she fell on her bed exhausted and stared at the ceiling. She had lived in this house for thirty-two years—all her life—and how was it that she'd never noticed how old and worn-out it was? How was it that she had never noticed how the ceilings were stained and discolored? How had she never seen those mildew stains on the wallpaper? The frayed edges, the bits of pieces coming off?

She grabbed at a tiny edge of frayed wall paper and pulled. It came away easily in her hands. She tore it all the way down to the floor. Then she grabbed another edge and ripped it down. And another. And then another.

This ripping of frayed edges was nothing new to her. When she was little she used to tear the plastic off the covers of library books. Her mother was sick and her aunt would be yelling at her and she would be in her room sitting on the edge of her bed and tearing the plastic covers off library books.

It was late evening when she left her wrecked bedroom and went back to her computer. She opened up a new word processing document and titled it "Chasco's Bible studies." And then she searched and surfed. She went to his website and into his archived sermons. An ordinary Google search, nothing special really, and she found that all of Chasco's sermons and Bible studies, ALL of them, had been taken from other sources: James Dobson, Charles Swindoll, Charles Stanley, some minister in South Africa she had never heard of, a study on worship from a church in Australia, something from a ministry to street people in Toronto. He had even stolen a message from Billy Graham!

He seemed to favor an on-line sermon preparation site called sermonon-line, a service, she supposed, for ministers too busy to come up with their own. Log on on a Saturday night, and in five minutes, voila, you have your Sunday morning sermon. That these places even existed astonished her.

By the time her bedtime alarm rang, she had a long documented list of Chasco's plagiarized works.

51

Y ou're going to be amazed at the house," Jack said to Teri at the airport.

"Which house? Old or new?"

"Both."

Jack looked happy. This made her glad. His arm was around her as they made their way out of the airport on a warm, end-of-summer day.

"You're happy," Teri said.

"The garage sale raised more than two thousand dollars."

"Good."

The money was going into the Jenny Addison bursary, a scholarship set up shortly after her death and given to a high school graduate going into either early childhood education or family studies. Jack had been one of the major supporters, with various other monies raised through church functions. A year ago, when he and Teri had married, he had given the scholarship to a board to manage. He would still donate funds each year, but that was his only involvement now.

"Having you back makes me happy." He let go of her and said, "The people who came to the garage sale were an interesting sort. There were people there the night before scoping out the place—"

"Ah, surveillance. Been there. Done that. Got the T-shirt to prove it."

"And people were there at six in the morning. And I couldn't believe the junk they bought. You know all those mismatched and misshapen Tupperware lids? I was ready to throw them out, and Verna said to put a twenty-five cent price tag on them. People actually bought them! One lady bought ten. I have no idea what she'll use them for. What would you use a bagful of old Tupperware lids for?" He fiddled with his keys.

"Maybe she's building a bomb."

"That's what I get for asking a former cop!" He grinned and

pulled her into a sudden embrace, which caught her off guard and she tripped on the pavement. He held her firm.

"Two more nights."

"Two more nights?"

"Till we're in our new place."

"Why can't we go in sooner?"

"It's not quite ready. It's not quite perfect. It's got to be perfect."

They stopped for a quick supper at a restaurant, where she told him all about her three days in Texas, including the finding of the body of Max Beamish and the suspected link between Gil and the King James Murders.

Back at their old home, Teri couldn't believe the place. It was so empty. She walked into the echoey living room and stared. Instead of the stained bricks and mantel, the wall was flush and tiled in a kind of burnished green.

"Wow," Teri said. "I take back all my complaints about the Renali brothers and the Millers. This looks great."

"That's what I said. I never knew this place could look so modern."

"Nuevo-old," Teri said.

"What?"

"Never mind. But where will they hang their stockings at Christmas?"

"Something tells me the Millers don't have any kids to hang stockings for."

The kitchen was empty, devoid of boxes and clean, just a small stack of paper plates on the counter and a bag of plastic utensils. "I thought we'd eat out for the next couple days."

"Where's all the stuff?"

"New house. But you see how empty this place is? The new house is just the opposite."

"No coffeepot?"

"For two days we can buy coffee."

52

In the morning, Glynis lay in bed. She had taken another vacation day from work, but it could well have been a sick day. Her nose was running and her throat was dry. Maybe she was coming down with something. Maybe that's why her emotions felt so out of kilter and disordered. The faded paisley wallpaper lay in shreds covering her floor, and all she could do was stare at it.

She was not Gwyneth88, the romantic heroine of a romance novel with the long blond hair riding a horse, but Glynis. She was not five foot seven, Kim's height, the *perfect* height, but six foot one, taller than any woman should be, according to her aunt. She'd never finished university and all she was was a secretary in a law office. And she didn't love her work. She hated it and would rather be working with Andrea making clothes.

Her hair was not pixie-cute like Kim's, but frizzy and uncontrollable. Even the picture she had sent to Chasco was false because now, only a week later, her bushy eyebrows were growing back and her hair was sproinging out of its gel and her fingernail polish was chipping off. Maybe she and Chasco deserved each other. Both frauds. The sermon stealer and the Amazon crazy lady.

Maybe she could stay in bed all day. Maybe if she just slept. The funny thing was that if she never woke up, if she just stayed here and stayed here and stayed here, no one would miss her. It would be a long time before anyone would even realize she was gone. She would have no one, like her mother did, to find her body. She turned onto her side, hugged her knees, and stared at the little square light coming through the window and reflected on the wall.

She was like this house, old and frayed and falling apart. Peeled down, exposed, the covering all torn off and smelling of dust and mildew.

She should have gone to work today. At least at work there would be things to do: coffee to make, letters to type and send, phone calls to answer, and ways to forget. She wondered if her mother's pills were upstairs anywhere. She could go up and get them. She could do what her mother did when the pain became too great. The coward's way out. The shameful way out. Why shouldn't she do it? Like mother, like daughter.

At noon the phone rang, and she reluctantly got out of bed to answer it. It was Teri, back from the southwest.

"Do you know the name Max Beamish?"

"No. I don't recognize that name. Sorry."

The detective was telling her then about a rich businessman named Max Beamish and how Kim had somehow written down his address on a church visitor card, and also that Gil might somehow be involved or know something about the King James Murders because of a picture she saw in June Redfeather's office, while Glynis blinked her eyes and tried to pretend she cared.

53

I wrote letters. I told my good friend all about the money. I had never told anyone about the money. For four years the money had sat inside of the army backpack buried in Georgina's basement, and now, all of a sudden, I'm telling my friend all about it in a letter. I don't know, but maybe I was beginning to think I needed to do something about the money.

Seeing my friend, bumping into her out of the blue like that, that surely was a sign. It solidified something I'd been thinking about for a while—that I was supposed to take care of the money and give it to charity, maybe.

It's funny, but I think that was in my mind from the minute I took it out of the well, that somehow God had given this money to me as a sacred trust, and I was supposed to give it away. But it was becoming a burden. I thought about dropping the backpack off at social services with an anonymous note to divide it up and give it to foster parents. I'd lived with foster parents my whole growing up years, and most of my experiences had been good ones, a darn sight better than living with my prostitute mother. I knew they could use the money.

But I knew if I did that they wouldn't get the money even if I did leave a note. A backpack full of fifty-dollar bills? That's not how donations are made. They're made by checks from rich people. No, they'd decide that a sack full of money looked suspicious and they'd report it to the police. The police would come and take the money, and who knows what would become of it then?

I thought of leaving it at a church, any church, with a note. But it would be the same. Any honest church would call the police before they even so much as counted it.

I thought of randomly distributing fifty-dollars bills to the homeless people I knew on the street. But that would probably engender some sort of frenzy, and maybe even an increase in the drug trade.

Do you see what I mean about the money being a burden? So I didn't do anything with it, which is in a way worse. I was sitting on a sacred trust, and no matter how much I prayed, I didn't seem to get an answer about the money.

That's why bumping into my old friend like that seemed like a sign. She was someone I could trust. She would know all about what to do with it.

54

Dear Gwyneth88 (or Glynis),

I'm so used to calling you Gwyneth88, I may find it weird to think of you as Glynis88! But that's okay. First of all, when you write about being a phony and finally wanting to "come clean" as you say, I don't see that at all! I think you are a nice genuine person! So your name isn't Gwyneth, so what? And I don't care that you're six foot one! I think that's cool. It doesn't change anything, as far as I'm concerned. That's the neat thing about e-mail, what people look like doesn't matter. None of this really matters.

But Chasco's Bible studies are another matter! I couldn't believe it! I asked my pastor about this and he said that it might have been okay if Chasco had mentioned where they came from, like adding something like, "This Bible study comes from James Dobson," or something like that. Can't a person get into a lot of trouble doing that??

I haven't heard from Chasco recently either. I noticed that his website hasn't been updated since last week. I also haven't heard from Melissa.

Your friend,
Lark7

Dear Glynis88,

What Chasco has done is against the law. I'm furious! Should we report him? I went to the website for Charles Stanley and there's this place where you can send an e-mail to his ministry. I had an e-mail all written out to send him, but didn't. But we need to do something!

Love,
KarenP

Dear Glynis88:

I don't care that you're not Gwyneth88. That's absolutely no big deal as far as I'm concerned. You're one of the sweetest people that I know. But plagiarism is against the law. And we need to take steps. I've written a long e-mail to Chasco and I've copied it to you at the bottom here. I, personally, will have nothing more to do with him or his Bible studies. The only good thing is that it was through his Bible studies that we connected.

Blessings,
Sewinglady

Forwarded message:

Chasco (of the so-called Chascoministries.com),

What you did is against the law! Glynis (and yes, I guess her name is Glynis, but what she did, giving us the wrong name, is nothing compared to what you did!) told me all about it. She has pages and pages of documented notes that she sent to me as an attachment. When I began going through it I couldn't believe it! Just to double-check I went over the URLs listed in her document and compared them to your archived sermons. I was appalled! I just want you to know that I've decided to report you. We have a man in our church who's a police officer, and just as soon as I send this to you, I'm going to phone him to find out what he suggests. What you did wasn't right!

Sewinglady

Sweet Glynis88,

I feel the total fool. When I got your e-mail I immediately got down on my knees and cried and cried before God, and like David, I asked for forgiveness. I've lied and defrauded you and so many others. I've hurt my best friend (you), and the woman I find myself falling in love with (you), because yes, I guess I did borrow a few sermons and claim them as my own.

A lot of people don't understand the pressure I'm under. (I thought you would have!) The demands of the ministry are so great, there are temptations that ministers face that are unknown to the laity.

First of all, you are correct. It is common practice for ministers to glean thoughts and sermon illustrations from the Internet. Before the Internet there were books of sermons and sermon illustrations. It was no secret. What I did that was wrong was to forget to give proper credit to these fine men. I plan to do that in the future. And if you go to my website today you will be visiting a very different place. I have credited these fine men who have leant their expertise to my Bible studies and sermons. As for Sewinglady's threats to contact the police—well, so be it. If she does, she does, and there's nothing I can do about that, but I would like to ask Sewinglady if she has prayed about this first? And has she removed the log from her own eye before she attempts to remove the sliver from mine? Has she looked carefully at her own life before she casts the first stone? But, I guess that's between her and her God.

My only wrong, Glynis, was in being perhaps a bit too zealous for the Lord.

I am not the least upset by the fact that you are Glynis and not Gwyneth. What that does is tell me that we're both human. Maybe we can both start afresh with each other. ☺ I hope you will see fit in time to forgive me.

All my love,
Chasco

PS: I'm sorry about the other day. I found myself busy all day with an unexpected hospital emergency. I DO hope you understand. These kinds of things happen sometimes in the ministry. I hope you're not too upset about that, and I'm hoping that some of the anger that you exhibited toward me in regard to my website is really anger because I wasn't there for you.

Dear Chasco,

Now I don't know what to think! Perhaps I have been a bit too hasty in judging you. I went to your website and I admit it IS different. I'm glad you did the right thing. I just have one question. You say that Sewinglady should pull the log out of her own eye. I guess it's my experience working all these years for lawyers, but if everyone took that advice we would get no justice for anyone. Because how would we convict anyone of any crime if we all had to be perfect first?

Love,
Glynis88

Dear Sewinglady,

I hope you haven't contacted that police officer in your church yet. I admit, I was too hasty about condemning Chasco outright. Have you been to his website? He's added credits to all of his Bible studies and Sunday morning sermons. He really apologized to me. He said he felt God rebuking him for that, and has totally changed. If you did already contact the police, I doubt there would be much they could do now, since his website is all changed and he's publicly asked for forgiveness. That's right on his website, too. It's called *An Open Letter to my Faithful Supporters*. I'm writing to Lark7 and KarenP about it. I think we need to give him another chance.

Your friend,
Glynis88

Dearest Glynis88,

How pleased I was that you signed your e-mail *Love,* Glynis.
That shows me that maybe you have forgiven me just a little
bit(?). You are correct, of course, in your interpretation of
that passage in Matthew. Sometimes I just write the first
thing that pops into my head. I wrote this without praying
first. Please forgive me, dear Glynis. I feel you are the one
person I can be totally honest with, that I can say the first
thing that pops into my head without being judged for it. Are
you there? Do you want to go to private chat?

All my love,
Chasco

Chasco: I wanted to go to chat because I have something
really important to tell you.

Glynis88: What is it?

Chasco: I'm coming to Maine! I'll be attending a worship
conference in Portland in a week! It would mean so much
to me if we could finally meet! I would love to straighten
out this whole mess with a face-to-face chat.

Glynis88: How did you know I live in Maine?

Chasco: That's very simple—you told me.

Glynis88: I don't remember telling you.

Chasco: I'm sure you must have.

Glynis88: A few days ago I went through all the e-mails we
ever sent to each other, and I know I never told you that.
Because I remember thinking, I know he lives in Minneapolis,
but he doesn't even know where I live.

Chasco: I guess because the address of the detective you hired is in Maine, so maybe I just assumed from that that you live there, too. Can we meet?

Glynis88: I don't know. I'm kind of nervous about this. I don't know why. I'm just nervous.

Chasco: That's understandable. I feel the same way.

Glynis88: How about if I come to that worship conference?

Chasco: Unfortunately the conference is full. If you'd told me, I could have booked a space for you! How about if we meet after the conference?

Glynis88: Okay.

Chasco: That's my girl.

55

S nare sat on a park bench and drank a can of orange juice and ate a muffin. On the sidewalk in front of him two spindly girls on in-line skates glided past him, deep in conversation. They came so close that he could have reached out and tripped them. It was breezy, and red leaves fell onto his lap as he ate his muffin and worked away on his e-mails on his little handheld.

His knees hurt him this morning, and despite the end-of-summer warmth, he kept a jacket over them while he sat there. His left leg had refused to hold his weight when he had stepped out of bed that morning. He'd fallen on the floor, flat on his face. He cursed the floor. He cursed his legs. He was several minutes rubbing the circulation back into them before he could get up. Not good when you're work-ing construction, he thought, to be stumbling all over the place, not able to hold a hammer or carry a can of paint. There was also a film of something over his eyes, and when he got his legs working, he stood in the bathroom splashing water into his eyes until his vision cleared.

But he was fine now, except for chilly knees and a tiny black dot in his field of vision. That was new. He forced himself to look around it and beyond it. It was all a matter of control. And he had lots. Just a little pressure, a few questions, and his little lawyer girlfriend had told him everything. Everything. Even where the money was. And now all that remained was for him to pick it up.

"Sir, is this yours?" A woman was standing in front of him hold-ing his wallet.

"Uh, yes." He grabbed it out of her hand. All his driver's licenses, all his passports, his money.

"It was lying right there," and she pointed.

"I must've...uh, fallen asleep."

"Well, it's a beautiful day. We're not going to get too many of these before the snow comes."

"Right. Yeah." He shoved the wallet in his jacket. He couldn't afford mistakes like that anymore. Control. Control. He clenched his fists. By now everyone knew that rich Max Beamish was dead. And of course, it was all over the news, how many companies he owned and what he was worth. And also how private he liked to keep his private life. A recluse, people were calling him. A rich recluse.

And of course, the police, in their stupidity, were clueless when it came to figuring out who killed him. They were looking at business partners, old lovers. Wouldn't they be surprised to find out that it was the one called *stupid* by his father, *not a brain in his skull* by his mother. He who was already here!

His fingers were twitching and he watched them as if watching something not related to him. He laid his hand on his lap and watched the little finger move all on its own. Twitch. Twitch. He touched it with his other hand. Still, it twitched.

He clenched his fist and relaxed. Control, he told himself. He kept his fists clenched until his finger stopped its movement. There. You're fine, now. Soon, they would be writing about him like they were writing about Beamish. He was on his way.

56

"How're you doing, Teri?" Bill said. "I don't think we've seen each other since...when, the wedding?"

"Too long. We should keep in touch. When we're settled, Jack and I will have you and Fran up for a meal."

"It'll just be me."

She looked at him.

"Fran and I separated six months ago."

"Oh, man! I'm so sorry to hear that."

He shrugged. "It happens. We tried to work it out. But when all was said and done, Fran just didn't like being married to a cop. Never did. It finally got too much for her."

They were sitting across from each other at a picnic table in the park near the police station. Wind blew leaves on their table, and Teri pulled her sweatshirt hood up over her head and thought about Bill and Fran. If there was ever a marriage that seemed stable, it was Bill and Fran's. What did that say for everybody? That any marriage can shift sideways?

"It's cold," Bill said. "We could go inside somewhere."

"No, it's nice out here."

"So, you and Jack happy?"

"So far."

"That's nice. That's good."

They were both quiet for a while, then Teri said, "I want to have another look at the King James Murders."

"Why?"

"In my current investigation I keep bumping into it."

"How so?"

She told him. She told him about Breanne Johnson, Lanny Boucher, Kim Shock, Barry Shock. "I know the King James Murder case is officially closed, but we both know that you and I were never totally satisfied with it. There were too many things that didn't add up."

"The bottle of shampoo for one."

"Conditioner," Teri corrected him. "A brand-new never opened bottle of Pantene conditioner."

"Someone came in later and put it there."

"But we never found out who that woman was."

"Woman?"

"Woman. It's usually women who use hair conditioner. There were other things, too, Bill. There was no evidence that those girls were tortured, yet that little piece of news was everywhere—CNN, Fox News. And they all told us they had to protect their *sources.*"

"It was a media frenzy. Things got out of hand."

"There was no evidence of any ritual torture or even any sexual abuse, and one of them, Jo Braslo, was even a virgin when she died. And the neighbor, our main witness, reported five girls out on the farm. Yet there were four bodies found."

"He said he made a mistake, remember? All the other neighbors saw four. We never found any evidence there were five girls."

"Except for the fact that the neighbor reported seeing that fifth girl stabbed through the heart."

"We never found any evidence there was a stabbing there. No residual bloodstains, nothing on that porch."

Teri looked down at her hands. "I think there was a fifth girl."

"You do."

"And her name was Lanny Boucher."

"Lanny Boucher?"

"She was a foster child of Shocks, and Barry Shock's girlfriend."

"Do you think she was there?"

"I think so, and I think she escaped. She sought out Kim, wrote letters to her. I'd like to have a look at the police report again."

"They're police property now, Teri."

"I know, but I'd like to have a look at them anyway."

"You know I can't do that."

"I also need a copy of the social service documents and any

information about Lanny Boucher."

"Now that's something that I definitely can't do. Social Service documents are locked up tighter than a drum. I'd need twenty-five court orders and an equal number of warrants."

"I'm not saying I want you to get it for me. I'm just saying that this is my wish list." She paused. "The whole thing is like a math puzzle."

"I hate math."

"I love math. It was the only subject I was good at. I love puzzles. And in this math puzzle, the one common denominator is Barry Shock."

"I'll see what I can do about some, emphasis on *some,* of the report."

"Thanks, Bill."

57

On the last day in their old house, Teri and Jack sat on lawn chairs beside the new fireplace working on the *New York Times* crossword puzzle together. They had spent the morning finishing up the cleaning and were spending one last day in this place.

"Why don't we just go to the new house now?" Teri had suggested.

"No," Jack said. "I have my reasons."

Teri understood that these reasons probably had to do with Jack's long history in this house. She understood that he needed to say good-bye. She'd allow him that.

Teri had spent the better part of yesterday at the library at the microfiche and the Internet, reading all the old articles about the King James Murders. The farmhouse, the quotes in the papers, the pictures of the four girls and Barry brought back memories: the rain, the blood on the floor, the smell of the place. The newspapers didn't show those kinds of pictures, just long shots of the farmhouse strung with yellow tape and serious-faced police officers standing about. Or they showed insets of the girls, high school graduation pictures of them, their smiles showing so much hope and promise.

The farm had belonged to someone in North Carolina who'd been given it in a will. He hadn't been there in some time, and in fact was trying to sell it, but while it was unoccupied, Barry and his girls squatted. The closest neighbors didn't immediately report them as squatters because the girls tended the garden, mowed the lawns, and waved hello to passing cars.

"You okay?" Jack said now. "You seem quiet."

She put her hands on her knees. "Did I ever tell you why I quit the force? I mean *really* why I quit the force?"

Jack put the crossword puzzle down. "No."

Outside, the late summer sun shone vertically into their room, leaving icicles of yellow light on the new tiles. "I'd been to traffic accidents, gunshots, fires. But never anything like...like that."

"The King James Murders."

She nodded. Tiger came into the room, his claws clacking on the new tiles, and jumped into Jack's arms.

"Did you know that the human body contains six quarts of blood? Multiply that by five bodies and that's thirty quarts. If you had thirty quarts of paint, do you know how much that is? You could paint this room with thirty quarts of paint. By the time we got there, they'd been dead for a while. Seeing those bodies, the way they were laid out in a circle, their hands out like they were on a cross..."

Jack rubbed Tiger's ears.

"I knew I didn't want to face this kind of death anymore. I didn't want to be the one to accidentally come across my mother's body. I didn't want to know what she suffered. I used to dream about the sweater she wore when she disappeared. It was striped and ugly. Before she left I said to her, 'Mom, you're not really going to wear that, are you?' And that's haunted me too, that my last words to my mother were *'Mom, you're not really going to wear that, are you?'* I used to dream about that sweater. I used to dream that I saw it hanging in my locker at school. I dreamed that I would come to my car and it would be folded on the passenger seat, or I'd see it hanging in my closet."

"I didn't realize your life was so filled with angst and sorrow, Teri."

They both looked up suddenly. Shauna was there, standing in the doorway, a paper bag from the Market in her hand. She hurried over to where Teri was and knelt on the floor in front of her. "Teri, I didn't realize that about your mother. So much angst."

"How long have you been standing there?" Jack asked.

"The door was open. I knocked and knocked. You didn't hear me?"

Teri and Jack shook their heads.

Teri said, "I thought I locked the door. Maybe I didn't. Obviously I didn't."

Shauna emptied out her bag and began unwrapping sandwiches. "I know you guys have been so busy, and just this morning I was sitting in my little apartment and thinking about what I could do for the two of you. Both of you so busy—Teri busy playing Miss Marple and Jack playing little teacher. So I thought, what can I do? I thought you might like something to eat. When do you move in?"

"Tomorrow," Jack answered.

"What's this 'playing Miss Marple' thing all about?" Teri asked Jack after Shauna left.

"She means well," Jack said.

"No, she doesn't. She does not mean well. She's after you, Jack, and you just can't see it. Did you see how close she was sitting to you there? Practically at your knees!"

"She's not after me, Teri. If anything, she's after you."

"Me?"

"She likes you, Teri. She's always asking about you."

"She's only asking about me so she can goad me with references to Miss Marple and Hercule Poirot."

"Stephan calls you Sherlock."

"That's different. I *like* Stephan."

58

ear Glynis88,

I still think you shouldn't trust Chasco the way you seem to. If the guy lied about his sermons, what else is he keeping from you? If I were you, Glynis, I would be a little leery. KarenP agrees with me.

Blessings,
Sewinglady

Dear Sewinglady,

You should see Chasco's website now. It's completely redone. He said he has repented of putting sermons on his website without giving proper credit. That's all over. I've forgiven him for that.

Do you know what he wants to do? He wants to buy Bibles for every teenager in the city of Minneapolis! We're planning on meeting. He'll be in Portland for a worship conference. I can drive down, or he'll drive up.

I think despite everything, I'm falling in love with him. His little video is so cute! If it weren't such a personal message I'd send it to you so you could download it and see just how cute he is.

Love,
Glynis88

Dear Glynis88,

You have a friend who ran off with someone she met on the
Internet and who now is missing. Aren't you the least bit
concerned about this happening to you? You don't even
know what he's like.

Yours,
Lark7

Dear Lark7,

How can you say you don't know what he's like? We've been
e-mailing for a year. I know SO much about him. I've completely forgiven him for the sermon thing. To me, that just
shows me how vulnerable and human he is.

Glynis88

Dearest Glynis88,

I'm SO looking forward to meeting you. It's all I can think
about! I feel so cleansed, and so freed! I know God has forgiven me for taking others' sermons as my own. It was
wrong and I acknowledge that. See, that's why I need you.
You would not let that pass! You would not let me go on
being a phony! That's why I need you so much, Glynis. (And I
like the name Glynis. It's far more feminine than Gwyneth.)

What you wrote to me about Kim was quite interesting. You
mean she just took off like that with someone she met on
the Internet? I wonder what would make her do something
like that? How close were you two, anyway?

All my love forever and ever,
Chasco

P.S. Thanks for the donation for the Bibles for Minneapolis program. It's going well, and thanks for your promise to send more money. It's being put to good use.

Dear Chasco,

Kim and I were very close. We've been best friends since we were both seven. I was even planning her wedding. Now I don't know where she even is!

Love,
Glynis88

Dear Glynis88,

It must be nice to have such a close friend, someone that you trust and that she trusts. I imagine she left lots of things in your care when she left—like taking care of her mail and all that, plus if she's anything like the friends I've had down through the years, she probably left you a basement full of her stuff, too! I remember when my friend left. I even had to do his banking! Are you saddled with that responsibility too?

Love forever,
Chasco

Dear Melissa,

I wondered where you had gone when I hadn't heard from you for a few days there. I'm so glad you're doing so well. Chasco tells me you're back at school and everything. That's wonderful! Are you still doing plays? I hope you're reading the Bible faithfully each day. I know a couple websites where you can get a devotional a day. And of course, there's Chasco's site. He does that, too. That's the first thing I do every morning, I go onto his website and read my devotional for the day.

Take care,
Glynis88

P.S. As you can see, I've changed my handle to Glynis88.
I'm not Gwyneth anymore. I graduated from high school
in 1988. It's a long story that I won't bore you with. I was
just fortunate, I think, that the username Glynis88 wasn't
already taken. Chasco says that was the providence of
God—that I got the username I wanted.

59

Moving day, Teri and Jack were awakened at seven by a loud knock on the front door. Teri looked out the window and saw a white van in the driveway with *KJ's Kleaning Service* along the side.

"Someone's here," she told Jack. "KJ's Kleaning Service, whatever that is."

Jack, hair still askew from sleep, threw on his bathrobe and bounded down the stairs, the cats and dog following. Teri threw water on her face in the bathroom. When Jack came back upstairs, she was in the shower.

"What do they want? Don't tell me, they're in the neighborhood and want to give us an estimate?" she said, peeking around the shower curtain.

"No, they've come to clean the place."

"What do you mean they've come to clean the place? The place is clean."

"I know. But they've come to clean it, anyway."

"Did you send them away?"

"No, they're downstairs. Getting out their mops."

"We better not be getting the bill for this, that's all I can say," said Teri, tromping out of the shower and wrapping a towel around her.

"Teri, we're moving into our new place today. Let's make it a good day."

She smiled. "Thanks, Jack. I just get mad sometimes. At unfairness."

"I know. You have a highly developed sense of justice."

"Comes with the territory," she said, drying her hair.

The two of them took their time, however, packing their suitcases, gathering the animals, taking the garbage out, stripping the bed. Teri told the two men—Renali brothers knockoffs, who stood with their mops and buckets—that they would be out in an hour or so, as soon as their friends came with a truck to load their bed and a few more boxes.

"Millers told us they wouldn't be in until tomorrow," Teri said.

"I don't know anything about that. All we know are our instructions," said the one.

They started in the basement. At ten, when they were finished recleaning what Teri and Jack had spent hours cleaning the day previous, Stephan and Peter arrived in Harvey's son's truck to load the last remaining bits of furniture and boxes. Shauna was there, too, and sat between Stephan and Peter on the bench seat. Her long hair, usually tied back, fell around her shoulders.

Teri thought it would take Jack longer to say good-bye to his house, but he seemed positively jovial as they drove off following the truck without a backward glance. Teri decided not to comment on it.

In the kitchen of their new place, boxes were piled up three and four high, but if you squinted just right, you could imagine the hardwood flooring in the kitchen and entryway, and the deep blue carpeting that would soon cover the living room floor. And if you had a really good imagination, you could picture the new living room couch and chairs that would soon be arranged in a conversation circle around the fireplace. You could see already the plants hanging in the bay window, and Gilligan taking up a perch there. Teri noticed the walls.

"It's painted!"

"I was busy when you were gone. The kids helped. Stephan and Peter and even Shauna pitched in. I wanted to have it done when you got back."

"I want to see the loft. Our bedroom."

"Wait," he whispered, his finger to his lips. "Until the kids go."

An hour later, they had wiggled the old bed into the downstairs guest room and the boxes and odd bits of things into their proper places: coat hangers into closets, bars of soap onto their appropriate sinks, rolls of toilet paper conveniently placed in new toilet paper holders.

"It's beginning to look like home," Teri said after the kids left.

"Come," Jack said, taking Teri's hand and leading her up the stairs to their loft.

At the top Teri grinned. It was completely finished and furnished right down to the crisp, colorful woven spread on their brand-new bed. Clothes were hung in the walk-in closet, and her favorite shampoo was already in their en suite.

"Jack, you did all this? This is so great!"

"I had fun."

Teri flopped down on her back on top of the bed. "This is excellent!" she said. "Look, Jack, come here."

He lay beside her and looked straight up to where she was pointing.

"Up there, through the skylight. At night we could see the moon through here, and stars. Won't that be great?"

"Yeah. All we have to do is wear our glasses all night."

"My grandmother used to tell me that if I wore my glasses at night, I'd see my dreams better." She smoothed her hand over the plaid bedspread. "And this. You picked this out all by yourself?"

"I had help."

"Help?"

"Peter has a friend who's a weaver. And that photo on the wall, do you like it?"

"I love it!" It was an underwater shot of some bright blue fish. "Let me guess. Stephan."

"Right."

Their conversation was interrupted by a loud HELLOOOO from downstairs. Jack and Teri jumped up from the bed.

Irving and Elizabeth were standing at the bottom of the stairs with two plastic shopping bags and a red plastic thermos. William and Harry stood beside them, and Tiger regarded them from high on a box, ears back, tail swishing.

"Welcome to the neighborhood," Irving said.

"We brought muffins," Elizabeth said. "I made these this morning. I knew you were moving in today, and we thought you might like something warm from the oven."

"Thank you," Jack said.

"Come in," Teri said, although they were very much in already. She wondered if she and Jack were going to have to lock their doors to have any privacy in this neighborhood.

"Your house is amazingly far along," Elizabeth said. "From the way you were talking, I thought it would be months before the Sheetrock was even up."

"It's up," Jack said.

"And painted," Irving added.

"It's basically finished," Jack said, "except for the offices downstairs. The Sheetrock's up in Teri's office, but not mudded and taped yet. The walls in my office aren't up yet. That room will be our junk room for a while. And of course, the basement will be hopeless for a long time."

Jack unfolded the lawn chairs they had brought over, and they sat in the living room drinking hot black tea and eating blueberry muffins.

"You know, Jack, if you ever need a hand with anything," Irving was saying, "just give me a call. Also in the winter? I've got a plow blade for my tractor. I'll be happy to plow you out."

"That'd be great. Thanks."

Before they left, Elizabeth said, "Just curious, but did that fellow ever connect with you?"

"What fellow?"

"There was a man who came by. I was down walking William and Harry and saw him looking in your windows. I called to him and walked up. But he saw me and scurried away."

"Did you get a good look at him?"

"Dark hair, I remember that. Curly, I think. Of course it could've been nobody. Could've been somebody just walking by. They see a new log house where there wasn't one before, of course they get nosy."

60

Are you sure you want to do this, Teri? Go back there?"

"I have to. There's a connection between the King James Murders and Kim. Maybe if I go out there, I'll be able to figure it out."

The last time Teri was out here, the sky was sleek with rain and the tires of her patrol car splashed mud on the roadside. Today birds sang and insects buzzed. The farmhouse looked tranquil now, the stuff of muted watercolor paintings, with its broken-down steps, the porch with weathered boards, the cracked window panes. They parked close and got out. It was warm. For a while they stood together and looked at the place.

"So, this is where it all happened," Jack said.

"This is where it all happened."

"I remember the news."

"The news went crazy. That was part of the problem."

"It's pretty," Jack said. "It would be a nice place to live. Way out here."

"People don't like to move into a house with a lot of bad history. Ghosts. Bad karma, or whatever they call it."

There were several rusted farm implements lying about, and along the side, the garden was overgrown. Only a tiny piece of yellow tape wedged in the door gave any indication that this had once been a major crime scene.

"How long has it been?" Jack asked.

"Five years. Almost to the day, five years."

"Who owns this place now?"

"Same guy, I think."

"So no one's here?"

"I don't think so."

In one of the windows a clay flowerpot was tangled with brittle

247

weeds. Teri touched a branch. It broke apart and fell to the porch.

The call had come from a neighbor who hadn't seen the girls in a while and had walked over to investigate. The door to the kitchen stood open and he saw the bodies.

"They're all dead," he told the 911 operator. "I've been warning and warning you guys about them, and now they're all dead."

His warnings had consisted of two or three 911 calls per week about "strange goings on" over there. He heard loud chanting, singing, reading from the Bible. The 911 calls had begun when he reported seeing one of the girls stabbed on the front porch, and then "the weasely little guy, their master, he raises up the sword and there's all this blood dripping and the girl's dead. Fallen right over. I about fainted dead away when I saw that."

The police responded immediately but found nothing, not a trace of blood.

"That proves it's from the devil. Being able to get rid of the blood like that," he said.

"It's just not natural," he said to the 911 operator on another occasion. "Them girls, I seen 'em digging in their garden in them long dresses they always wear, hiked up on their legs, digging. It's one of them religious cults, it is."

"You can see their back garden from your property?" the officer had asked incredulously.

"I can if I stand on the cab of my truck and use my binoculars."

After that he became known as the Peeping Tom Witness and not a lot of what he said was taken seriously. Teri knew all about this. Teri had read the reports.

Even his final 911 call was met with suspicion, and it took an hour before anyone was dispatched to investigate. That too was played up in the media, that it had taken the police an hour to respond to a 911 call of such a serious nature.

As Teri stood on the front porch, unwilling to go in, she wondered about the fifth girl. Was there another girl? And had she been the one to drop the bottle of conditioner? She held tightly to Jack's hand and looked at the closed door...

It was raining when they arrived, and water dripped off her glasses and she wiped it away with her hand. The smell of death was everywhere. Bill handed her a pair of latex gloves and a little bottle of Vicks. She rubbed a smudge under her nose and put the gloves on. Others, grim-faced, were already there, including members of the crime scene unit carrying their little black cases. No one talked, or if they did, their voices didn't carry through the rain. A television van had arrived and was parked some distance from the farmhouse. She had been told that there were five bodies inside in what looked like a ritual murder-suicide.

"Insane," said an officer she didn't know, walking past her and shaking his head.

On the porch, flowers bloomed in a dozen window boxes. The place looked neat, clean, not the stuff of such horror. Teri followed Bill inside. Four bodies, shot through the heart, lay on their backs, bare feet touching, hands spread out. It was thought that this was supposed to look like a crucifix. Their eyes were open and staring toward the ceiling. There were smudges of dirt on their foreheads. It was later determined that this was common ash from their wood stove.

They were wearing the long cotton dresses that neighbors had seen them in. The fifth body, that of Barry Shock, lay where it fell beside the stove. It was determined that after he had arranged the bodies in his horrible tableau, he turned the gun on himself.

The only thing out of place was a bottle of Pantene hair conditioner encrusted in the dried blood beside the legs of one of the victims. A photographer was standing over this, getting a shot from a variety of vantage points.

"Are you sure you want to do this?" Jack asked her now.

"I need to."

Today the kitchen smelled like earth and old rags. The linoleum was a pale brown, and there were still brown spatters on the walls. Even after five years. A Luma Lite would light this place up like a Christmas tree. A mouse scurried into the corner. Teri remembered a metal table against one wall covered in oil cloth, as well as canning jars full of wildflowers all over the place.

The only piece of furniture now was a lopsided couch that leaned against one wall, probably home to many families of mice through the years. She also remembered coats and jackets hanging from a bank of hooks on the wall. This too was empty, the hooks gone. The wood stove had been removed, and black mold grew in the place it had once been.

Teri opened a few of the kitchen cupboards. The dishes were gone, but there were several boxes of dried soup and a small box of tea bags and some crackers.

"Squatters," Teri said. "Thing is, this is a little off the beaten track for your basic downtown homeless city dweller." When she turned back, Jack was holding in front of him a small bouquet of flowers tied together with string.

"What are those?" she asked.

He pointed. Under the far window were dozens and dozens of dried flower bouquets. Some were brittle and brown, but others, like this one, were newer.

"People do this," Teri said, kneeling in front of the flowers. "At scenes of disaster."

"This one looks to be only a week or so old," he said.

He placed the bouquet back on the pile.

Teri rose. "I remember there were all these Bibles around. We took them all. Some of them had fire-and-brimstone notes in the margins, things like, 'America: pride goeth before a fall,' and 'America: sinners will not go unpunished,' or 'America: the immoral nation.' It was all written in this tiny, tiny handwriting and we couldn't find who wrote it. It didn't match Barry's or any of the girls'. That was one of the unanswered questions. And those front pages where people write down important dates like marriages and births? They were all torn out. Come on," she said. "Let's go upstairs."

The second floor contained several mostly empty rooms. In the room that faced the back, they made their most surprising discovery: a nest of blankets. Teri tentatively lifted a corner, and underneath was a small plastic GladWare box. Inside were a few Pop-Tarts and a bag of Oreo cookies.

"Because of the mice," Teri said. "That's why they're sealed in plastic."

"A smart squatter."

There was nothing much of interest in the other rooms, just more mouse droppings. Back outside it was hot as Teri and Jack walked around the place.

"It's pretty here," Jack said.

"It is."

"Where does that path go?" Jack pointed.

"Just to the top of the rise. It's quite a ways up. There are paths all over the place, and we scouted all around here. That ended up being my job. At least I didn't have to be in there with the bodies. We didn't find anything."

61

You think this guy still lives here?" Jack said. Teri was driving and instead of turning right at the end of the driveway and heading out to the road that eventually would lead to I-95 and home, she turned left and drove on a narrow road where long dry grass scraped under their car.

"We're about to find out."

They turned into a driveway, and Teri remembered this place with its pieces of car and machinery in the yard and bicycle parts and boards, and the famous truck where the man used to spy on his neighbors. The whole scene looked exactly as it had five years before.

Ty Forrest was his name, and Ty Forrest was sitting on his porch on an old bench seat from a truck in precisely the same place Teri and Bill had left him five years ago.

"Stay close to me, Jack," she said when they got out.

"Okay."

"This guy's a real sleaze."

Closer to the porch, Teri said, "Mr. Forrest?"

"That's me. Who's asking?"

"I'm Teri Blake-Addison. I talked to you five years ago about the King James Murders."

"Oh yeah?" He squinted up at her. "I told you guys they shoulda taken me more serious."

"Mr. Forrest, has anyone been at the farmhouse recently?"

"People come and people go all the time."

"Who have you seen recently?"

"How much is it worth to you?"

"What do you mean? You want me to pay you?"

"That'd be about right."

"I'm not with the police anymore, Mr. Forrest. I'm just asking you a simple question, have you noticed anyone over at the abandoned farmhouse?"

"And I'm telling you, what's it worth to you?"

"Let's go," Teri said to Jack. "Let's get out of here."

They walked away.

"Okay," Ty yelled. "A girl's been there."

Teri and Jack turned.

"What does she look like?" Teri asked. *I'm sure you know that little detail with great intimacy.*

A woman appeared in the doorway. "Ty?" she said. "What's going on?"

Ty turned. "Get inside, woman, this don't concern you." The woman went back inside.

Ty got off the bench seat and walked toward them. "Okay, she's about yay high," he gestured with his hand, "dark hair, carries a backpack. Rides a bike."

"Rides a *bike?*"Teri asked. "From where?"

He shrugged. "How should I know?"

"Any distinguishing marks, characteristics?"

"Nothing that I could see from here."

"How often have you seen this girl?"

"She comes and goes."

"When was the last time you saw her?"

"Couple weeks ago. Maybe."

On the way home, Jack said to Teri, "What's the story on the woman?"

"Common-law wife. He's not, shall we say, one of the greatest examples of husbandly love. When we were out five years ago, she was covered in bruises."

"You can't do anything?"

"Not then and not now. She flatly denies he hits her. She falls against the stove and breaks three teeth. She walks through panes of glass, she tumbles down the stairs and breaks her wrist, and we can't do anything. The problem is, she's not the sharpest tool in the shed, either. The pair of them." She shook her head.

"And he was the prosecution's chief witness?"

Teri smiled. "Sad, isn't it."

62

While Teri thought, pondered, wondered, and worked on a theory, she placed a couple of blooming African violets on the wide window ledge in her new office. When they first chose logs for their walls, she wondered whether it might be too dark, but they had put in enough large windows that their home was brighter than she imagined. Her office walls weren't ready, and most of her files still resided in boxes because the bookshelves she'd ordered from Ikea hadn't arrived.

As she watered her plants, she thought again about Ty Forrest. He had his moment of glory when for weeks on end he was in the news testifying in this high-profile case and became the expert on everything.

While she arranged plants her fax machine whirred on. Bill's report. Of the four, only Charissa York's mother mentioned acting. "All Charissa wanted to do was go to Hollywood and be an actress. I don't know how she got herself mixed up in this."

What did an acting camp have to do with a cult? Teri sat down and bent over the papers. Something was wrong. June Redfeather, Breanne's sister, thought that Breanne was attending a drama camp. Barry Shock loved doing plays. How did these two and the others get mixed up in a religious cult? What had gone wrong? Had Barry suddenly turned so crazy? What had gone so terribly wrong with him? With them?

Teri picked up the phone, and Charissa York's mother answered her call. As gently as she could, Teri introduced herself and asked about the acting camp. "I told the police everything then," she said. "Charissa would never have willingly been a part of a religious group. We didn't even know she was until we started getting the phone calls and the threats. I told the officers this at the time."

"And you sent them money?"

"Yes."

"How much would you say that you sent to them?"

"I think all told, about twenty thousand dollars."

Teri wrote *$20,000* on her paper.

In her next phone call, Teri learned that Jo Braslo's mother had died of cancer five months ago, and Jo Braslo's father said they had paid around fifty thousand dollars in ransom but never saw their daughter.

20,000 + 50,000 = 70,000

The only difference in Jo's story was that Jo was religious. She went to church and was active in youth group. The press had a field day with her church connection, interviewing so-called religious experts who as much as said, "See, proof once again that a strong religious faith can ultimately lead to all sorts of wacky weirdo behavior." They had sent another thirty thousand dollars.

30,000 + 70,000 = 100,000

She wasn't able to locate the parents of Deirdre Maxwell. They had moved since their daughter died, and as much as Teri looked for them on the Internet, she couldn't find them.

Her new desk phone rang.

"How's Jessica Fletcher today?"

"Who?"

"Murder, She Wrote."

"Hello, Shauna."

"I was wondering about something."

"Yes?"

"Do you ever come to the university?"

"Do I what?"

"I was wondering if you ever came to the university?"

"Well, yeah. To meet Jack. Sometimes for lunch."

"I was wondering, would you happen to be coming in today?"

"Hadn't planned on it, why?"

"Well, if you were coming, I was wondering if you could come and see me?"

"You want me to come and see you?"

"Well, yeah, if you're coming anyway. If it's no trouble."

Teri didn't know what possessed her to, but she said, yes, she could be there in an hour. Maybe she wanted to see how close Shauna's office was to Jack's. Maybe she wanted to figure out what made this girl tick. Or maybe she was just plain curious.

"Okay, I'll be waiting."

Not five minutes after she hung up with Shauna, the phone rang. It was Walt from the El Paso police department. They had found fingerprints on the scene belonging to someone named Mason Jordan.

"Now, who the heck is Mason Jordan?" Teri asked.

"Ex-con. Reason we have his prints is because the guy was in jail. Served less than two years for bank fraud. He was caught posing as a bank clerk—actually, the bank president, if you can believe that—and taking people's deposits they were going to make in an ATM he claimed was out of order. You ask me, the people who shoulda gone to jail are the people who handed him their money. Guy's got a string of aliases longer than my arm: Troy Duncan, Tony King, Henry Snare, Julius Dumain. There were bullet holes in the walls at Beamish's place, too. Don't know how they fit into the whole scheme of things."

"Did you say Julius Dumain?"

"Yeah."

"Wait a minute." She leafed through her notes. "He was a faith healer, a new age guru—give me money and I'll tell you that the power is within you—something like that. I don't know what he called himself, but he had some sort of religious group going, a cult—" Teri choked on her words.

"Teri?"

"I'm here."

But Teri's mind was going in a thousand directions. Cult group. There were too many connections. Too many coincidences. She doodled on the top of her paper. Wrote names. Drew arrows from one name to another.

But in the end, it still made no sense.

63

Teri, who prided herself on never being late for a meeting, was late for a meeting the second time in one week. She had been researching Mason Jordan on several data banks and was reluctant to leave. Her research was yielding some fascinating stuff. When she realized it was already five minutes after she was due to meet Shauna at the university, she grabbed her jacket and hurried to her car. There was a parking place next to Jack's car. She liked it when school wasn't in session. A month from now there would be cars crammed every which way, and the closest place to park would be clear across the lot, if she was lucky.

"Hey, Teri." It was Harvey Bestletter, and he was carrying a stack of books. "Jack's in a meeting with the dean."

"It's not Jack I want to see, it's Shauna."

"Shauna? Last I saw she was in the student lounge."

"Thanks, Harvey."

Shauna was on a couch facing away from the door when Teri entered. Her little black glasses were perched on the end of her nose, and she was reading through manuscript pages. Next to her on the arm of the couch was a cup of tea. The room smelled of old books and magazines.

"Sorry I'm late," Teri said, sitting down on a couch across from her.

"Life-and-death case?"

Teri nodded. "Still, I should've been here when I said I would be."

Shauna took off her glasses and looked at her. "I find you and Jack such fascinating people."

"You do?"

"I do."

Teri got up and poured herself coffee from a pot on the counter. She didn't know how fresh it was, but it was hot. Why was she here? She had crimes to solve, better things to do than to sit here with a lonely grad student.

"Coffee's terrible," Teri said, making a face.

"I never drink coffee, so I wouldn't know." Shauna paused. "Jack said I should talk to you."

"About what?"

Shauna brought one long leg up underneath her on the couch and sighed. She laid the manuscript pages on the cushion beside her. Teri could tell by the way the words were spaced on the page that it was poetry.

Shauna was quiet, so Teri said, "You're writing something? Poetry?"

"Oh no." She smiled. "This is Stephan's."

"Oh."

"What I was wondering...I was just wondering if there was a chance for us."

Teri choked. She and Jack? She comes to me asking if there's a chance for her and my husband?

"Jack says you have great insight."

"A chance for you?"

"For me and Stephan."

"Stephan and you?"

"Yeah, I know it's silly. But you know him a lot, and he respects you. Jack says Stephan confides in you more than he does with anybody. He respects you."

"Well, I don't know about that. He's a good kid and all..."

"I thought of asking him out. Do you think he would go out with me?"

"You and Stephan?"

"What's so funny? Do you think it's that stupid of an idea?"

"No, I think it's a great idea! And you want me to put in a good word for you with him?"

"If you would."

"I would be delighted."

Shauna relaxed and pulled both legs underneath her, yoga-style. "You know what I want to do more than anything?"

"What's that?"

"Write detective stories."

"Really?"

"I just think how serendipitous it is that the wife of the professor I work for just so happens to be a private eye, and I like to write classic detective stories."

"Yes. Serendipitous. Exactly how I would describe it."

Teri's cell phone rang just then, and she shuffled through her bag. "Excuse me, Shauna."

"Teri? This is Clara Winkel at Smith and Egan. I was doing some filing and found a couple papers of Kim's. They look like notes of some sort. Perhaps they might help you. They're here at the office, and I'm here until around five-thirty, six if you want to pick them up."

"I'll be there in a bit," Teri said.

But instead of running off like she normally would have, she stayed and talked with Shauna a bit. She asked her about her family. She asked her about her studies. She asked about her ambitions.

Maybe what Jack said about her was true. Maybe she was just lonely.

64

Dear KarenP,

I'm sharing this with you, KarenP, because I consider you one of my closest friends, even closer than Lark7 or Sewinglady. But I've discovered something *else* about Chasco and I don't know what to do. I really don't know what to do this time.

Chasco and I were becoming closer and closer. We were even going to meet. I'd forgiven him for not attributing his sermons. I'd gotten past that, because of all the other good things he was doing for people. Well, today I discovered something that has made me question absolutely everything about him. I was doing a little surfing around the web. And I don't know what made me do it, but I got into some of the singles dating websites. I guess I wanted to prove to myself that I was lucky, that Chasco was a real find. I went back to the one where Kim had found Gil.

Do you remember, KarenP, when I said Chasco sent me a personal video of him, and he's waving and winking? Well, to make a long story short, I found it. And it's not Chasco! It's not anybody named Charles Coburn. It's the dating video of someone named Philip Landover from Joliet, Illinois. I even e-mailed this Philip Landover and he said yes, it's him and did we want to e-mail! So, Chasco stole this video and pretended it was him! I don't know what to think! Oh, KarenP, what should I do? I feel so stupid! This was the video where Chasco says, 'This is for you' and he blows a kiss. I feel so foolish. I feel like crawling into my bed and not coming out!

Your friend,
Glynis88

65

I t was still early when Teri headed out on the highway to meet Clara Winkel. Who would have ever guessed that Shauna was not after Jack but was interested in Stephan the whole time? And in being friends with her?

"I hated for you to drive over here and this not be important," Clara said, handing Teri a file. "I was just looking through the file cabinet in the closet and found a file folder that looked like it belonged to Kim. It looks like some notes and a couple of news articles. Maybe it's important, maybe not."

Teri skimmed through the file. She was interested in the handwritten notes.

"Do you know if this is Kim's handwriting?" Teri asked.

"I think so. It looks like it."

"Glynis isn't here today?"

Clara shook her head. "She's taking some vacation days. Good for her, I say."

In her car, Teri looked over the file. On the top was a sheet of lined notebook paper on which Kim had written in ballpoint,

> Gil Williamson = Julius Dumain = Mason Jordan
> Breanne Johnson
> Jo Braslo
> Charissa York
> Dierdre Maxwell
> Lanny Boucher
> Barry Shock

There was another page of her neat handwriting that looked to be a list of con men and people who'd been conned. Teri recognized many of these names as people whose letters Glynis had given her. There were also a few yellowed news clippings and photocopies of news stories about the King James Murders. A printed e-mail caught her attention. It was from Bshock54@yahoomail.com to Jdumain@hotmail.com.

> Dear Mr. Dumain,
>
> I would be very interested in helping you with your drama camp. I've always loved Shakespeare. I know that not many kids my age do. It's interesting how you found me. I look forward to this summer.
>
> Barry

Another interesting item was a clipping from a denominational magazine dated June 1983.

TRAGEDY STRIKES MINISTER'S FAMILY

In March, tragedy struck the Jordan family. Former Assemblies of God pastor Clint Jordan and his wife, Betty Ann, lost their lives in a tragic fire that broke out in their mobile home near Minneapolis, MN. Their only son, Mason, twelve, was not at home at the time.

Clint Jordan broke away from the denomination six years ago citing doctrinal differences. Even so, our prayers are with Mason, and many will remember Clint and Betty Ann's popular, albeit unorthodox at times, traveling ministry.

It didn't take a genius to read between the lines and figure out that the good reverend had been royally kicked out of the Assemblies of God because of his "popular, albeit unorthodox at times, traveling ministry." She could only guess at what the doctrinal differences were. She would've loved to be a fly on the wall at that meeting.

There was a small black-and-white photo at the bottom of the article. Clint Jordan was a huge, imposing man who held a large black Bible with one hand, while the other rested on the shoulder of a plump woman in a shapeless cotton dress. In front of them was their tall blond son, Mason, in black pants and white shirt and tie and holding a Bible.

When Teri got home, she searched the Internet for any information about what happened to Mason after the fire. He didn't reappear until years later when he was arrested for a string of scams. She was aimlessly doodling names on a piece of paper—Julius Dumain, Tony King, Troy Duncan, Gil Williamson, arrows and pictures and more arrows—when Jack came in, a container of white flowering mums in his hand.

"For your new office," he said.

"Lovely."

"I thought you might like some flowers."

"Thank you."

"You haven't even looked at them."

"It's driving me crazy."

"What is?"

"This. This whole thing. This guy's fingerprints were all over the place where Max Beamish died. He was somehow involved in this. He grew up with religion. He would know that scene inside and out. I mean, this Clint Jordan, his father, was probably some sort of cult leader himself, or dangerously close to one. He might have had some really weird ideas, and that's why he would've been kicked out of the denomination. I'm trying to puzzle it together."

"I have no idea what you're talking about, but you've got a bit of a Shakespeare theme going here."

"Shakespeare theme?" She looked at him. "Only a professor of English literature would come into the office of a private investigator and say there's a bit of a Shakespeare theme going on here."

"No, I mean with those names."

"Names?"

"Julius, that's obviously from *Julius Caesar*. Duncan, from *Macbeth:*

Where is Duncan's body?
Carried to Colmekill,
The sacred storehouse of his predecessors,
And guardian of their bones.

And Dumain, he's a character in *All's Well That Ends Well:* 'We'll see what may be done, so you confess freely; therefore, once more to this Captain Dumain: you have answered to his reputation with the duke and to his valour: what is his honesty?' And Troy, that's from—"

"Jack, just curious...do you have the entire works of Shakespeare memorized?"

"I teach it, my dear, so some of it rubs off. Tony King, now that's an easy one. The King could be any king from *King Lear* to—"

"Gil Williamson?"

"That's easier still. That's the easiest one. Did you know that William Shakespeare had a brother named Gilbert? And Williamson, well, that's a derivative of William and..."

She looked at him for several seconds, then said, "Jack, could you recite more of Shakespeare for me?"

"What would you like? *Macbeth*? *Romeo and Juliet*?"

"It doesn't matter. Anything."

He did. In a loud, dramatic voice with all the flourishes.

"Do you have a complete works of Shakespeare anywhere?"

"Do I have the complete works of Shakespeare? Do *I* have the complete works of Shakespeare, Teri? Is the pope Catholic?"

"Are you doing anything right now? Can you come with me somewhere?"

"Your word is my command, my liege," and then he bowed low, theatrically.

66

After the fire, Mason lived with his grandparents for four months, but after he killed their poodle, they left him at a home, which he soon figured out was a jail for kids.

"Your parents would be happy you're here," they told him. "They would want you here. They would want us to try to help you."

"My parents..." He stopped talking then and didn't talk again for a year.

People smiled at him a lot there and tried to get him to tell them what was "troubling him" by leaning into him and touching his wrist. He always pulled away. He didn't like people touching him, breathing their breaths on him, getting so close he could smell their smells. When they came and sat in front of him, he would look at a point on their shirtfronts and concentrate until he blocked out everything they said. He got pretty good at that. Plus, he had the buttons of the police uniforms memorized, which helped in his later adult profession.

At the end of the year he was put in a room with an older boy named Max, who was "a heartbreak to his parents and a social misfit." Max would recite the litany of charges against him in a high singsong voice, which sounded just like Mrs. Bloom from the school. That got Mason laughing for the first time in years.

It was Max who taught Mason everything he needed to know to survive. He taught Mason how to be charming when needed, but most of all how to remain in control in every situation.

"It's a matter of concentration," Max said, swinging his wiry legs over the top bunk. "You already know a little about this. You don't talk to them. That's good. But take it one step further. Talk, but pretend in your mind that you're not talking. So, when they're asking you questions, all you do is concentrate, like you already know how to do, but then smile and tell them something *they* want to hear. Like how wonderful they are. And how happy you are here. You can get everything you want like that."

"They'll know I'm lying," Mason protested.

"No, they won't. Trust me. Not if you do it right. Here let's prac-tice." He jumped down from the bunk. "Okay, you're you, and I'll be the social worker..."

Max said he learned these things from an uncle who was a Shakespearian actor. And he dubbed his young charge Snare, telling him Snare was a character in a Shakespeare play.

"You will be Snare, and henceforth, I will be British!" And he grinned and began speaking in an English accent. Forever after that, he spoke with that accent. He even looked British with his big ears and long face.

It worked. Six months later Snare was released, fully rehabilitated, into foster care and stayed with a family named Smith. When he killed their German shepherd, he was sent away again. It was an acci-dent, he told everyone, practicing the techniques Max had taught him. "I was playing around with that .22 rifle. How was I to know it was going to go off like that?"

But they didn't believe him. He still had a long way to go to be both charming and believable. The truth was, he shot the dog because he wanted to see what would happen.

He grew. He perfected his techniques. He perfected his acting skills. He learned how to be charming.

67

But screw your courage to the sticking-place,
And we'll not fail. When Duncan is asleep—
Whereto the rather shall his day's hard journey
Soundly invite him—his two chamberlains
Will I with wine and wassail so convince
That memory, the warder of the brain."

Jack was reading random pages from *The Complete Works of William Shakespeare* while Teri drove. "I like your voice when you read that," she said. "It's like a preacher's. You know how they always speak in different voices from normal life? That's what you're doing now."

He chuckled. "You want more?"

"Sure."

"But, soft! what light through yonder window breaks?
It is the east, and Juliet is the sun.
Arise, fair sun, and kill the envious moon,
Who is already sick and pale with grief..."

"Even I know that's *Romeo and Juliet*!"

"Bravo, bravo! But would anyone mind telling whence this trip to the backcountry, my lady?"

"I need you to come and read Shakespeare for me."

When they got to the Forrest farm, Ty was still sitting on the front porch on the truck bench seat.

"You again," he said when he saw them. "I don't have the time to talk to you today."

"I'm sorry we're intruding on your full social calendar, but we have a few more questions," Teri said.

"So?"

"I want to talk to you again about what you saw, about what you heard five years ago."

"Yeah?"

"You say you saw a woman being stabbed."

"That's right."

"What did you do then?"

"Like I said, I saw that numskull kid raise this sword thing, dripping with blood, and he's reciting some Bible thing, and so I hightailed it down off my truck and called the cops."

"Did you see them clean up the body?"

"After I called the cops, I climbed back up and the body was gone."

"Kind of quick, weren't they? Moving it that fast? A body with all that blood?"

He shrugged. "Thems were Satan worshippers. They can get rid of bodies fast. That's what I told the police."

"Jack, would you read, please?"

He opened the book and began in his dramatic voice:

> *"Against acquaintance, kindred and allies:*
> *The edge of war, like an ill-sheathed knife,*
> *No more shall cut his master. Therefore, friends,*
> *As far as to the sepulcher of Christ,*
> *Whose soldier now, under whose blessed cross*
> *We are impressed and engaged to fight."*

Jack closed the book.

"Is this the sort of thing you used to hear?" Teri asked.

Ty nodded. "Yeah, they were reading the Bible. I know what the Bible sounds like."

"Mr. Forrest, that wasn't the Bible. My husband was reading from *The Complete Works of William Shakespeare*. And that woman who was being stabbed? They were acting a scene from Shakespeare.

If you'd stayed and watched, you probably would've seen her get up and walk away."

"But they wore all them Bible dresses."

"Method acting," Jack said. "Getting into the part. They do that at these summer acting camps sometimes."

Ty looked at them, chewed the insides of his mouth and said after a while, "Well, the cop who came out? After I called that time about the stabbing? He said it was a religious group. He's the one paid me to keep my eye on 'em. Told me it was a cult."

"Someone paid you?" Teri asked.

"That cop did."

"To keep an *eye* on them?"

"Yep."

"A cop?"

"Yep. A cop. He wanted me to keep an eye on 'em. Paid me and told me they use informants all the time. Said it was a place filled with religious wackos."

"Why didn't you say this before? Like to all the million people at the inquest?"

"He told me not to, the cop did. Said it was against policy for them to pay informants. So I had to be quiet now."

"So you lied while under oath."

"That cop said people do it all the time, that it's just a formality."

"But you feel no compunction about telling us now?" Jack asked.

"Guy never paid me the last installment. Figure he owes me."

Teri was shaking her head. "What did this so-called cop look like?"

"Can't remember."

"Tall? Short? Dark? Blond?"

"Tall. Dark hair. Curly, I think."

"You know what, Mr. Forrest? If I were you I wouldn't go any-where. There are a whole lot of people who are going to be interested in what you have to say."

"I get to go to court again?"

"You get to go to court again."

"And be on television?"

Teri walked away. On the way home she said, "We had it wrong, Jack. We were so convinced it was a religious cult, another Waco, that we didn't even want to see the truth. Especially when the media got a hold of it. They loved the King James Murders. Their ratings soared. Plus they got to interview every person in the country with an opinion on religion. And yes, I admit, there have been a few cult group murders, but this wasn't one of them. It was set up to look like a ritual killing, but what it was really about was good old-fashioned money. It was nothing other than an acting school, a summer drama camp, like they all thought it was—at the beginning anyway. It's my opinion that the girls were kept against their will, but maybe didn't even know it. They probably wrote letters home that were never delivered. It was all about money."

"So where's that money now?"

"I think I know where it is."

"You do?"

"I think Kim had it. I think she gave it to Glynis. Plus, I don't think Barry killed them. I think he was murdered by whoever murdered those girls."

68

Their Bible study friends, Andrea and Ben Silver and their daughter, came by that evening with a tin of fudge and a plant.

"A housewarming gift," Andrea said, handing it to Teri.

"Thank you. I love plants."

Teri closed the top of her computer and pressed her palms against her temples. Although she had a working theory, she was still no closer to finding Kim. Plus, she wanted to have all her facts in order before she went to the police.

"Fudge," Jack said. "We both love fudge."

"Everybody loves fudge," Andrea said.

"What a great place." Ben stood in the middle of the living room.

"We like it here," Teri said.

"I don't blame you," Andrea said.

"And it came together amazingly easy," said Jack. "Once we got the land and the plans, it just built itself."

Teri groaned. "Not really! How about some coffee?"

Their living room furniture hadn't arrived, so they sat on lawn chairs on the unfinished floor and talked while the daughter did pirouettes in the corner.

In a weird kind of way, Teri felt funny about Andrea. So she wasn't Andrea's best friend? So Andrea already had a best friend? So what? Big deal. Get over it, Teri, she kept saying to herself. But then why did she feel like she was in the fourth grade and asking Lisa Fenyo over and over again, Will you be my friend? Will you be my best friend?

"This is going to be a beautiful place," Andrea said. "I love the location, the open loft. And that's your bedroom up there?"

"You want a tour?"

"We'd love a tour."

It *was* a great place, Teri thought as they wandered from room to room. The plants, the skylight, the windows, the view. All wonderful.

Jack and Ben were in the kitchen pouring the coffees, the little girl danced in the hallway with the cats, and Andrea and Teri stood beside the window looking down at the river.

Andrea said wistfully, "I was thinking about it, and I hope we don't have to cancel the Bible study."

"Really? I thought you guys were the ones who couldn't make it?"

"I'm realizing, both Ben and I are realizing more and more, that this is something we need. Even if it's just a few couples."

"Well, Jack and I are interested. We were really going to miss it. We feel like there's not a lot of places where we belong. You know?"

"I know exactly what you're talking about. Have you found a church that you're comfortable in?"

"We think so. We've been going to the one in Coffins Reach."

"Do you like it?"

Teri shrugged. "So far. But it's so hard to break into a new place, a new church. It can get so lonely."

"Everybody's lonely. I've come to the conclusion that there are times when everybody feels lonely, times when everybody feels like they don't belong anywhere. Because if you're looking for friendships or people to make you whole, it won't work. It has to come from within a person, and that inner peace won't be satisfied until that person puts God into that place."

"How come you're so wise?"

"I'm not wise. I'm not old enough to be wise. I have the sort of occupation where I get to talk to a lot of people. That bit of advice comes from an eighty-five-year-old, wonderful, saintly woman that I call my best friend. I make all her clothes for her. She's a delight. One day I was complaining that I didn't fit in anywhere. I was too artsy for most Christians and too Christiany for the arts community. And that's when she put her hand on my shoulder and said, 'Dear, there's not a person in the world who feels like they fit in. All of us struggle at times, with feeling like we don't belong.'"

Before they left, Andrea asked Teri if she'd come any closer to finding Kim.

"I'm working on it. I've been working all day on it."

"You have it figured out?"

"I have a theory."

69

Dear Glynis88,

I was shocked when you wrote to me about Chasco's picture! Does that mean the picture on his website isn't really him? What a scandal! I'm beginning to think both of us should steer clear of him and his on-line church. If he lied about this, plus his sermons, what else is he lying about? My boyfriend had a funny feeling about him from the beginning. I should've listened. And if I were you I would NOT go meet him in Portland! Why not hire that detective friend of yours to find out about Chasco, AKA Charles Coburn from Minneapolis. What could it hurt? Plus, it might put your mind at ease about him. If he turns out to be a great guy and the video was all a big misunderstanding, then you certainly haven't wasted any money.

Your friend,
KarenP

My sweet Glynis88,

You caught me. The video. You are right about the video. It isn't me. Why did I do it? What can I say that will make you possibly understand? Words fail me at this point. I am open. I am caught in a multitude of lies. The reason is—and it's not a good reason—in actual fact I'm not all that much to look at. And I wanted you to like me. So, I cheated. I downloaded a video of someone that I thought you would like. I found him and pretended it was me. But, Glynis, surely you of all people understand this! You had the name and persona of your romantic heroine Gwyneth for so long. Surely you understand that all I wanted to do was to make a good impression! It was the same with my sermons and Bible studies. God knows my motives were pure! I'm still looking forward to meeting. I hope that's not off. How can I possibly convince you that despite everything, my heart is in the right place.

Always,
Chasco

Chasco,

I find it difficult to believe that you would use not only another person's sermons and Bible studies, but another person's picture, another person's identity! I have to admit, I just don't know what to think.

And one other thing before I say good-bye (and this IS good-bye, Chasco), me taking the name of Gwyneth88 as a handle is nothing compared to what you have done!

Glynis88

My dearest Glynis88,

I am weeping. I am weeping before the Lord because of the awful sin and fraud I have perpetrated on you. I know you're there. Do you want to go to chat?

Chasco

Dear Glynis88,

Glynis, Glynis, Glynis, why aren't you answering me??? I am just wracked with pain. You were the only bright light in a horrible sea of darkness for me. What am I going to do?

I love you, Chasco

Dear Glynis88,

I have your phone number. I'm going to call you. I know
we've never spoken, but I feel I know you better than I have
ever known anyone in my life. I will miss you if we don't talk.
There is no reason for me to go on living if you reject me
like this. All my life people have been rejecting me. If you
reject me, I will die. I mean it.

I love you,

Chasco

Dear Glynis88,

I am not a strong person. People think I'm strong, but I'm
weak, and I'm nothing without you. I need you. I may as well
take my father's gun and put it to my head and pull the trigger.

I will love you forever,
Chasco

Glynis88,

Why are you doing this to me? You can't do this to me!
I keep phoning and phoning you and you don't answer!
I know you're there. I can feel it. When I come to Maine for
that conference, I will come to your house and we'll talk
together like adults. I said I was sorry. I said I was stupid.
What more do you want? We used to be so close. What
happened?

Chasco

Chasco,

When the phone rang just now, I knew it was you and I didn't answer it. I just don't know what to write to you and wouldn't know what to say on the phone. But PLEASE, don't do anything harmful to yourself. So many people depend on you, people like Melissa. I guess what I'm saying is that I need time to think about all of this. You lied twice. And that makes me wonder, what other things are you lying about?

Glynis88

Dearest Glynis88,

When we meet we'll talk. My life then will be an open book. I'm hoping we can start over. Because I've never felt about anyone the way I feel about you. And I'm not lying about anything else. I promise you that.

Chasco

Dear Teri,

I'm wondering if we could meet. I appreciate what you're doing for me so far in trying to find Kim. I have something else I need to ask you to do and so I was wondering if you might be able to come over to my place on Saturday afternoon. If this isn't good for you, e-mail me back and we can change the date or time. I'll have another check for you then.

Glynis

70

Their first scam occurred while they were still in reform school. Max Beamish and Snare made a thousand dollars by selling phony raffle tickets in the mall.

"See," Beamish said. "See how easy this is? I'm going to make a million dollars this way. You wait. I've already been in touch with a guy about a phony diamond mine in South America."

When they left reform school, Beamish kept in touch with Snare. It wasn't the other way around. Beamish never told Snare about the diamond mine nor, Snare suspected, about a multitude of other scams and investments. But when Beamish wanted something, when he needed Snare, he always found him. He would simply show up in Snare's life, give him a job to do, pay him some money, and then leave again.

It wasn't until later, much later, that Snare realized why Beamish needed him. It wasn't that he needed Snare's expertise, even his computer expertise; Beamish had plenty of his own people he could hire. No, he needed Snare to be the fall guy while Beamish walked away with the bulk of the money and with his reputation unsullied.

The whole ATM fraud thing was Beamish's idea. And while Snare sat in jail, he realized that the whole thing was a setup to get him out of the way for a while. And he, stupidly, fell for it. But it was while in jail that Snare dreamed up the King James Cult. He liked the fact that Beamish had given him a name from Shakespeare. He'd lie awake at night, his hands behind his head, looking at the ceiling and making his plans. And they were flawless plans. They were faultless. They were perfect. He'd thought of everything, right down to paying the slimy idiot next door to "keep an eye" on them, planting the idea of a religious cult. He'd trolled the Internet until he'd found the perfect "leader," a young Shakespeare fanatic named Barry Shock.

When Beamish showed up at his apartment one day, Snare

couldn't help but brag. But Beamish had laughed out loud, whooping his way around Snare's small kitchen. That's when he'd taken Snare's curly black wig, swung it around on the end of his finger, and crooned *amateur*.

Even though Beamish said the plan was amateur and reckless and stupid and wouldn't work, Snare could tell he wanted in, and Snare needed his expertise. The two forged an uneasy alliance once again.

But when it was over, Snare worried. He had to find out what the parents suspected. He'd tracked down and spoken with some of the parents. No one knew. No one suspected a thing. He even got to know June Redfeather. He had to find out how much she knew, how much she suspected. But if she suspected anything, she didn't let on. But Beamish said that following her out there was a stupid, foolish, asinine idea. "You just don't know how to leave well enough alone, do you?"

"She doesn't know anything."

"And you're sure of that?"

"I'm sure of that."

But Beamish bought a house in El Paso, and Snare suspected he did it just to keep an eye on him.

Snare woke with a start. The motel room was dark. He glanced at the beside clock. Still two hours until he needed to drive out to Mount Desert Island and work on that house. Excuse me, *guest* house. Plus, he had to check out that gumshoe, find out what she knew.

He lay back down on the bed. His hands were shaking, his head hurt, and he was sweating profusely. He grabbed two Tylenol and sat by the window shaking and shivering until morning.

71

I see you're doing some renovating," Teri said to Glynis.

"Oh, well, working on it. This old house is so worn-out. I have to do something. The place needs a whole new look."

"My husband and I just moved into a new house, so I notice things like cans of paint."

"I just picked those up. Plus some magazines." Paint color charts and several interior design magazines were on her table, along with more dress pattern magazines.

"Do you sew?" Teri asked.

"I used to. I should get back to it. Maybe when the house is done. Would you like some tea? I've made a pot."

"That would be nice."

She poured two teas, and they took them to the living room, where they sat on brocade chairs opposite each other. Glynis looked around and tried to see this old room from Teri's eyes and was suddenly embarrassed. It looked like a tired old woman, from the floral drapes to the faded pink textured wallpaper. The chairs were Victorian and old, and there were a lot of dusty ballerina statues around that belonged to her aunt. She should bag them up and take them to a secondhand store.

"You probably want to know how the investigation is going," Teri said, opening her satchel and pulling out some papers. "I've found out some interesting things."

And Glynis smiled. Yes, that would be nice to know, but what she really wanted was to find out about Chasco. She didn't want to tell her that Chasco was the boyfriend she had talked about, or that she had been a regular supporter of his ministry.

"I have a theory that I'm working on," Teri was saying.

Glynis put her hand up. "Actually, I'm sure you're doing a fine job, but I wanted to see you because I have another person I'd like you to check for me."

"Another missing person?"

"No. Not exactly. I just want you to check out this person. He
has an on-line church, and I want to know if his ministry's on the up-
and-up."

"My specialty is finding missing people."

"But you have more resources than I do. And it is a missing person. Sort of. I can't find his church on the Internet, and I've looked in
a lot of those business websites. I'm thinking of...um...supporting his
ministry, yet I can't find out anything about it. Or him." Then she
told Teri about his website and Bible studies. She also told her about
the plagiarized sermons and false video, but she left out her romantic
involvement.

"Glynis," Teri said gently, "it seems to me you already have your
answer. If he plagiarized sermons, I'd give him a wide berth."

Glynis kept her face a mask. "He apologized for that, plus he's
done a lot of good things. A girl in his youth group was rushed to the
hospital, and he took care of the whole thing."

Teri shrugged.

"He e-mailed me that he's coming to a worship conference in
Portland this weekend and wants to meet me...a potential supporter."

"You've been in e-mail correspondence?"

"Oh yes, we're..." But she didn't finish the sentence.

"Where does this guy live?"

"Minneapolis."

Teri looked at her. Had Glynis mentioned Minneapolis before?
Yes. Oh dear, what Teri must think of her. "A friend, ah, my friend
has donated some money to his organization and wants to know if it's
on the up-and-up." She blinked. She was only making it worse.

"How much did your friend send to him?"

Glynis shrugged. "A little."

"How much is a little?"

"Just a couple hundred dollars. Maybe a bit more."

"You want me to find out everything I can about this guy?"

"Yes. Please."

"Okay, tell me everything you know about him."

Glynis had printed off the document noting all of his plagiarized messages and Bible studies, and she had printed off the home page of his website as well.

Teri leafed through it. "You've done a lot of work already."

Glynis nodded and looked down into her tea.

72

Hey Cooper,

How's it going? Can you do me a favor? What I need is to know who's behind the website www.Chascoministries.com and where this person lives, if possible. I've been hired to do this, so I'll pay you. I've been told that the guy who set it up is a youth pastor named Charles Coburn who lives in Minneapolis, but I've gone into every link on the site and I can't find any reference to Minneapolis, or the name of a real live church, other than this guy's on-line church. There's an address to send money to, but it's just a PO box in Minneapolis, so it could be just a drop box with a forwarding address. I've done some phoning to churches in Minneapolis, and no one has heard of him or his church.

Also, this guy's supposed to be coming to some sort of worship conference in Portland. And I phoned just about every church in Portland and no one knows of any conference. The only conference remotely having anything to do with church is a homeschooling one. I called them, but they'd never heard of the guy. So already, I don't think he's on the up-and-up, so anything you find out about him would be appreciated. Thanks a million, Cooper.

Your dad and I would love it if you could come up and spend a weekend one of these days. The new house is great and we have a guest room reserved just for you. The cats miss you and Kelly would like to get to know you better. She remembers the good time the two of you had the weekend of the wedding. :-)

Love,
Teri

73

W hat's your opinion of on-line churches?" It was Sunday, the service was over, and a few people were standing outside in the sunshine of an early fall, reluctant to leave.

"They're all right, I guess," Ken, their minister, said. "If you're living in Antarctica or some place where there is no real church, and I mean no real church, not one other living Christian person."

"What about these people who drop out of real church and attend an on-line church?" Teri said.

"Is it really possible to *attend* an on-line church?" he asked. "Isn't what you're doing merely observing? All of this technology is meant to enhance life, not replace it." He shaded his eyes. "Internet pornography has destroyed many marriages, but I wonder how many lives are destroyed by Internet churches."

"That's a pretty strong statement," Jack said.

"I mean it. People withdraw into a place where no one sees their faults, and they can be whoever they want. We lose sight of the Incarnation when we live on-line. And this is something that I'm battling in my own house. Nicole comes home from school and the first thing she does is go to MSN Chat. We time her when we're there— one hour. That's all. But when we're not there, I have a feeling she's on chat for hours. And these are people she doesn't even know. I've said why not go out with your friends? Go for a walk. Even go to the mall. Jesus came as a flesh and blood person. People could see His humanity. His flesh. He came two thousand years ago, and I think there was a good reason for that. Today, He would've been just another person with a website. But He came and walked dusty roads. There was no doubt that He was who He said He was. No hiding behind an on-line mask."

"So the church needs a place to be," Teri said, "and an on-line *place* is too nebulous."

Ken was shaking his head. "Not exactly. The church isn't a place at all. The church is people, real people with real flaws. On-line, nobody has any flaws. On-line, people can be who they want. They give themselves names, handles. That's why I think on-line churches are almost as dangerous as on-line pornography. You're believing in something that's not real. It's a fantasy."

"I'm doing some research on a specific on-line church," Teri said. "It looks like the minister, or whatever he calls himself, doesn't have an original thought in his head. His sermons and Bible studies are all recycled from other places. He gives them credit with statements like, 'the following comes from a January 5 Bible study by Charles Colson,' or whoever it happens to be. And I'm thinking, why wouldn't people just go to the original source to begin with?"

"What's the name of this ministry? I wonder if I've heard of it."

"Chasco Ministries dot com."

"Jazz Co? As in music?"

"Chasco. Short for Charles Coburn."

"Never heard of it or him."

"There's a picture of him on his website. It's kind of hard to make him out because it's a distance shot of him behind the pulpit at some youth rally, or supposed youth rally. Apparently he's the youth minister in some church in Minneapolis."

"What denomination?"

"Haven't a clue. And my client doesn't know either. I've called the offices of most of the major protestant denominations there, and no one knows him."

"Smells fishy."

"I'm going to tell my client to stay away from him."

"And I would tell her to go to a flesh and blood church."

74

Maine is a beautiful state, with all its green trees and lakes, not to mention the ocean right beside it. More colorful, for sure, than Texas and New Mexico, and way better than boring Minnesota. No comparison. When you get right down to it, Maine is probably the most beautiful state in the whole of these United States.

He breathed in the cool air laced with the scent of cleanness and trees. Even his head seemed to hurt less when he was outdoors doing a good day's work. He was smiling. Grinning, actually. What a stroke of genius working here, on Beamish's old place. During the time of the acting camp, Beamish had bought this mansion from a movie star.

"To be near my investment," he told Snare.

It wouldn't be long now before Snare had everything he wanted: his money back and revenge enacted.

He stood, stretched, and looked behind him. Out in the distance, the ocean gleamed in the sunlight. Maybe one day he'd just get enough money to buy himself one of those big boats and take off. Like Beamish suggested. Maybe he would do just that.

He was already making plans for when this was over. On-line, he had met a nice woman who lived in Kennan, Wisconsin. He was a dentist, a widower with two little kids, he told her. The lady in Wisconsin was impressed with that. She owned a real estate company in the area, but most of all she loved kids. He had no idea where Kennan, Wisconsin, was, even though he had recently told her he'd been through there when he was a boy and it made such an impression on him he vowed he'd go back some day. And wasn't this such a coincidence that he should meet her and she just *happened* to be from Kennan!

She was like putty in his hands. He had printed off a Yahoo! map of the area and was figuring out a way to get there when this was over.

But first he had work here. If he had learned anything from his father, it was don't give up. Don't let them get the upper hand. Don't ever let them win. He could still remember with vivid clarity the fight his father had had with those people from the denomination, the way he'd yelled at them, telling them they were all bound for hell for the heresies they preached. He and his mother had sat huddled and listening at the bedroom door of the trailer. They would hear the quiet murmurs of the other men, and then the fierce, loud rantings of his father.

"What's going on?" Mason had asked.

"Shh," his mother said, her finger to her mouth. "Your daddy's setting them straight on a few things."

It was a matter of honor. The money was his; he'd earned it. And he was going to get it back. Breathe in. Breathe out. Relax. There.

He went back to his hammering, laughing and joking with his construction buddies, all nice guys.

75

Hi Teri,

A whois search didn't yield a whole lot, but I didn't think it would. It did give me the name of the registrar, that is, who Chascoministries.com was registered to. So my friends and I did a bit more digging, spent the good part of last night trying to crack the passwords and codes to let us in, and here's what we found out: Chascoministries.com is registered to someone named Henry Snare. We don't have a street address, but only a post office box in Las Cruces, New Mexico, if that helps. The interesting thing is that the box number is the same as the Minneapolis box number on his website. We haven't been able to figure out how he routes his mail though. Do you want us to keep digging? This is fun!

Cooper

P.S. Thanks for the invite. I may take you up on it. The new house sounds nice. It'll be weird coming home and not going to the old place, though.

76

For the first time in many months, Glynis didn't sign into Chasco's on-line church on Sunday afternoon. She'd even swallowed her pride and gone to regular church in the morning. She'd sat where she always did, in the back row by herself. Ahead of her on the right were Marcie and Matt and their little girl, and on the left Mike Wordman and Michelle next to him, and next to her, Marguerite and then a skinny girl with black hair and lots of earrings that Glynis didn't know. There had been that potluck, a kind of beginning of the year thing, which Glynis hadn't gone to. She knew about it, of course. There had been an e-mail invitation from Michelle, one of those group e-mails that goes to everybody on a list. She was only on the list because of Kim.

Instead of leaving early after church the way she usually did, she'd left on time and shook Pastor Ken's hand and had even talked briefly with his wife, Cheryl, who asked how she was doing and said they should keep in touch. She was just walking away when Cheryl said, "Glynis, wait."

She turned.

"There's a group of women who get together on Tuesday nights for prayer and Bible study. It's just an informal sort of group. We've just started, and I was wondering if you'd like to come."

"Well. I don't know." Tuesday night was Chasco's Bible study for single adults. But would she be attending?

"We'd love to have you," Cheryl was saying. "I think you'd fit right in. There are some women your age, a few a little older. We're a mixed bag, but I think you'd like it."

"Okay then. Well, maybe. Thank you for thinking of me."

"I'll call you. I'll remind you."

At home she opened a can of chicken noodle soup, toasted a piece of wheat bread, and made herself a pot of Earl Grey. She put her food on her little tray and took it to her computer and sat down. She looked at the screen brightening in front of her, but instead of the happy expectation that watching her screen come alive usually engendered, it made her feel odd and a little lonely.

The day was sun-filled, and she looked longingly out her window. If there was just someone to go for a walk with, that would be nice. A nice walk beside the river. She also had several novels from the library to read. Wouldn't it be nice to take one of those and sit down by the river? Or would seeing everybody walking by in twos and threes and family groups make her feel even lonelier? She could even paint her bedroom. That task would have to be done sometime. She had chosen a peach color and planned to do the trim in a forest green. The living room needed doing, too. Maybe today she should tear the living room wallpaper down. That would guarantee that she'd have to redecorate it.

She'd do that, she decided. But first, she had some work on-line to finish. She logged on to the Internet and unsubscribed from all the listservs that Chasco moderated. Then she trashed the video of Philip Landover from Joliet, Illinois. No, she didn't want to meet him or exchange e-mails, even though there was another from him on her screen, a two-sentence one saying that he'd like to keep in touch and what was she looking for in a guy? Next she removed Chascoministires.com from her list of favorites. She emptied her trash. Then she e-mailed her three best friends, Lark7, Sewinglady, and KarenP, and told them what she'd done. They weren't on-line, because they didn't answer back. Well, of course not, she thought. Who spends their time on-line on a beautiful Sunday afternoon anyway? Only thirty-two-year-old women with no life.

She was in the middle of writing to Melissa (despite Chasco, she needed to keep in touch with this girl; it wasn't her fault that her youth leader was such a jerk!) when the doorbell rang. Her doorbell never rang, and it took several seconds for her to even figure out what the sound was.

Chasco! He said he was going to come see her! How did he know where she lived? Well, of course he would know where she lived, he'd gotten her phone number somehow, hadn't he?

Trembling, she went to the door, checking her appearance in the mirror on her way. No help there. If she'd known someone was coming, she would at least have gelled back her hair into barrettes. With all the security equipment she had installed, she really should have had one of those peepholes put in.

Tentatively she opened the door, keeping her hand on the edge of it.

It was Teri along with her husband, plus another man she didn't recognize.

"Yes?" she said, opening the door wider.

"Glynis, we need to talk," Teri said.

"Come in."

Teri was already through her kitchen and had pulled up a chair to the dining room table before the others, including Glynis, even got there. Glynis quickly moved her lunch remnants out of the way and offered chairs to the two men. She sat on her computer chair and swiveled it around to meet the table.

Teri moved Glynis's papers and books aside just like she lived there while Glynis tried to gather them up. Her offer to make tea was also met with silence. Teri dumped the contents of her satchel on the table.

"What's this about?" Glynis finally asked.

"Glynis, this is Bill, a police officer. We're worried. We think you could be in danger. Real danger."

"Danger?"

"This Chasco, or Charles Coburn, Chasco Ministries dot com? Glynis, what we need is for you to tell us everything, absolutely everything you know about this guy."

"I've never met him. I was just asking for a friend. I..." Glynis looked away from Teri down at her chipped nails.

Teri slammed her hand on the table. "Glynis! You could be in danger. Your life could be in danger. This guy has killed once and he'll kill again!"

Glynis touched her sweater at her neck, pulling it tighter. "I don't understand. I just..." There was a queasiness in her stomach she couldn't quell. Outside some children were talking.

"Glynis," the police officer was talking now. His voice was miles gentler than Teri's. "We're pretty sure that Chasco's not who he says he is."

"I already know that. That's not new to me. He plagiarized his sermons and used a video that wasn't his."

"There's more to it than that," he said.

Teri said, "Exactly what is your involvement with him?"

Glynis didn't say anything for a while. Was she supposed to tell the private investigator, her husband, and this strange police officer just what a stupid female she had been? How she had let herself fall in love with him? Just how lonely and miserable her little life was? She swallowed hard to quell a rising nausea. She felt suddenly so cold.

"Glynis, okay, listen," Teri said. "We need to know everything you know about his guy, beginning from when you met him and ending with every e-mail you two have ever exchanged."

"I can't do that."

"Yes, you can! Or we'll come back with a warrant."

"No, I can't because I trashed them all. And I emptied my trash."

"Can we untrash them?" the police officer asked Teri.

She nodded. "Jack's son can do that in about five minutes." She turned to Glynis, "We'll need your hard drive."

"Okay, but what's going on? You need to tell me." She could feel tears beginning at the edges of her eyes. She would not let them see her cry.

"He's killed people, starting with his own parents and ending with Max Beamish, whose body was found a few days ago in Texas," Teri said.

"We're also fairly certain that he is Gil Williamson."

Glynis gasped, her eyes wide. "But Kim..."

"We don't know where Kim is. We've alerted the police in New Mexico and Texas."

"I don't understand. Chasco?...How?"

Jack grabbed one of the sheets of paper that Teri had dumped on the table. "It has to do with Shakespeare," he said. "Chasco Ministries dot com is registered to someone named Henry Snare, who gives his address in Las Cruces, New Mexico."

"I don't know any Henry Snare."

"Bear with me." Jack showed her the names Gil Williamson, Troy Duncan, Julius Dumain, Henry Snare. She patiently listened while he explained that these were all derivatives of names in Shakespeare's plays. "Snare is a character in the Shakespearian play *King Henry IV*. Hence, Henry Snare."

"As soon as we saw that name, we knew," Teri said. "Kim knew this name."

"And Teri called me, and we came right over," Bill added.

"Everyone who ever met Kim's brother, Barry, said he was a great lover of all things Shakespeare," Teri said. "His parents, his teachers, all of them said he had long sections memorized and loved drama. He'd been to a bunch of Shakespeare festivals, and all he wanted to do was to spend his life acting in Shakespeare plays. We haven't worked out how this Chasco or Henry Snare or Gil Williamson met Barry, but we think it might've been on the Internet. He was scamming money from parents whose kids wanted to act in Shakespeare plays."

"But I thought Barry was involved with a religious cult," Glynis protested. It was all too much to make sense of. She kept shaking her head. She couldn't speak; her mouth felt as if it were filled with glue.

"That was set up to get the police scurrying off in the wrong direction. And it worked. Until now," Bill said.

"So that's why," Teri said, reaching across the table and touching Glynis's arm, "we need you to tell us everything you know about this guy."

Glynis told them and ended by saying that two thousand dollars of the money she had given to Chasco was for Melissa's hospital care.

"We don't think there is any Melissa with hospital bills," Teri said. "I checked with the hospital—you said she had e-mailed you from the hospital? Well, that's not a service many hospitals have."

"But Chasco seemed so genuine."

"Con men generally do."

"But he knew all the Christian terms, the Bible, everything."

"He grew up in a religious home," the police officer said. "He would have learned the terms."

"I'm supposed to be meeting him—" Glynis put her hand to her mouth. Pasted above her computer was Chasco's phony picture. She'd forgotten to tear it down. How embarrassed she felt when she saw it there, and saw them looking at it. What a fool she'd been!

The police officer turned to her and said gently, "This guy's a con man and he's good. He's conned a lot of women. It's nothing to be ashamed of. You're the victim of a crime, and you're not at fault."

She rose, sighed, and shut down her computer. "So, do you need my hard drive then?"

"We'll take it. We'll also take the money Kim left with you."

"Can you go someplace?" Bill asked. "A friend, perhaps?"

"No," Glynis said, looking down. *I don't have any friends.* "I'd prefer to stay here if that's okay."

Before they left, they promised to set up police surveillance around her house. Then Bill examined all her windows and proclaimed them sound. "You have a good security system here," he told her. "Make sure you arm it after we leave. We'll keep an eye on the place."

77

Please, someone help me! She called and called, but her voice seemed to echo back and mock her. Help! Help! she called. But nothing. But she hadn't expected an answer. She'd been screaming for a week, had screamed herself hoarse, and still no one had come.

She'd been a week in this funny little room. Maybe at one time it housed a college student or two. It had a little kitchenette with fridge and stove, a teensy bathroom that you had to back into, and a concrete shower that was up a couple of steps. There was no shower curtain, either, so when Kim showered, the entire tiny bathroom got soaked. But that was the least of her worries.

After the first few days, she realized that this little place was probably under the garage. She couldn't be sure. She was fairly certain she'd been drugged when he brought her here. All she remembered was waking up on that lumpy double bed on a gray-striped mattress with no blankets.

The place also had no windows. Well, if you wanted to call a narrow barred slit in the far wall a window, well, you could, she supposed. At least it let a bit of light in. And don't think she hadn't tried getting out that window. She'd poked sticks through the bars. She'd yelled until her voice was hoarse. She'd written notes and sent them sailing through the bars, well aware that if some kid picked up a note that read, *Help! I'm being held prisoner in the basement,* they would toss it aside thinking it was a joke. But she kept writing notes, folding them into airplanes, and sending them through. She hoped they were sailing into the sky, but probably they were piling up at the bottom of the window well. Someday, years from now, someone would find her dead body, and the window well next to the room would be filled with pages torn from paperback western novels pleading for help.

The room had a lumpy double bed, just a gray, stained mattress, no sheets and no pillows. Nothing resembling a blanket. A wobbly pine chest of drawers, empty. There was a bookshelf made of cinder blocks and boards loaded with books. So at least she had reading material. If you liked westerns. Every Louis L'Amour ever written, plus Zane Grey and a few others.

In the kitchen was a small stove, an apartment-sized fridge, a pot, a fork, a knife, a couple spoons, and in the back of a drawer, a black felt-tip marker. Under the sink was half a bottle of dish detergent and some bleach and half a roll of paper towels that had gotten wet, had dried, and were spotted with mildew.

After she had screamed her head off that first morning, she had taken inventory of her surroundings. She didn't have her purse, so no cell phone, no wallet. Not even a comb for her hair. The freezer compartment of the fridge held half a package of freezer-burned hot dogs and a few frozen peas. In the fridge was half an old pizza in a cardboard box, plus plastic jars of mustard, ketchup, and relish, and a tiny jar of ultra low-fat mayonnaise. The cupboards contained three cans of soup, a bag of puffed wheat, and a box of tea bags.

The hot dogs were now gone, even though she had rationed herself to only one a day. The peas were gone. And now she was eating a quarter can of soup a day. Soon she'd be eating nothing but condiments. Back at university she remembered a stand-up comedian talking about writing a cookbook that contained nothing but things made from condiments. Ketchup soup with a mustard base swirled through decoratively with a mayo garnish.

It wasn't funny. Soon she'd be eating ketchup soup.

That first day she'd turned the lights on and off, on and off in the SOS code—three short, three long, and three short—hoping that someone walking outside would see. But then she worried about lightbulbs. All that flicking would be sure to shorten their life. Without lightbulbs, the skinny shaft of light that came in through the window would not be enough. She knew she needed light to keep her sane.

She also worried about the felt-tip marker. Those things notoriously ran out just when you needed them most. The only writing she did, therefore, were paper airplane cries for help.

So far she'd taken two showers, washing her hair with the dish detergent. She rationed them, too, not knowing how long her hot water would last. It must be connected to a hot water tank in another part of the building, she thought, but if he truly was gone and no one paid the bill, that could be turned off. There were no towels, so she had to stand in the bathroom wiping off water until she was dry enough to put on her one set of clothes, a pair of jeans and a T-shirt. She combed her hair with the fork.

He would be back for her. That's what he told her when he locked her in—he would be back for her when he got his money. And if she had lied about the money, well, that would be too bad for her.

And so today, the seventh day in her prison, she sat on the bed below the shaft of light and worked on boring a hole through the concrete next to the window with the kitchen knife. She had been working on this for the past week. If she could just get it large enough, she could maybe slip something through. She thought of shoving all the Louis L'Amour paperbacks through. Surely someone seeing all those paperbacks littering the street (or whatever was outside that window) would be alerted to something. She didn't know what. If she were walking along the street and saw hundreds of Louis L'Amour paperbacks blowing down the street, what would she think? Probably not a lot. Still, she had to do something. But she was tired and dreadfully hungry. A quarter can of soup a day, even seasoned with mustard or mayonnaise, wasn't enough.

She picked up the pot of water and drank. She had water. At least she had water. With no glass, she drank it out of the kitchen pot. Whenever she felt hungry she drank another pot of water. Her one treat was a cup of tea per day.

She'd done a lot of stupid things in her life, but putting her best friend in danger was the worst. Dear sweet Glynis, not a mean bone in her body. So trusting, even after all she's been through, and always there for me. The money Lanny had given her should have gone right to the police.

Kim was openly crying now. And there was nothing to wipe her tears on, nothing to blow her nose into. *Oh, please God!* She scratched desperately with her raw fingernails at the concrete. *Oh, please God!*

78

S nare rented a car and drove back to the Motel 6 he was staying at as Julius Dumain. He was working with Martin Monday— good plan that...get a job with the old boyfriend, find out more about his little lawyer—and then, as soon as his business here was complete, he'd go and kill the lawyer in the basement and move to Kennan, Wisconsin, with a whole new identity. Maybe he'd even shave his head.

He'd forgotten about Lanny Boucher, the little girl who came and went out at the farm. It was his lawyer friend who reminded him— not in so many words, but she'd reminded him. They were in the living room in Beamish's house. He'd had his gun on her, and she told him he wasn't going to get away with it. Standard line.

"Of course I'll get away with this. I'm smart. I have it all figured out. I found you, didn't I? And your little friend Glynis?"

"So why isn't Glynis with you here instead of me?"

"Because you were so eager to come with me. I have that effect on women. I repeat, I found you, didn't I?"

"Don't flatter yourself. Did you ever think it was *me* who found *you?*"

He looked at her.

"Yes, I've been looking for you for a long time. You were the one who killed my brother. I don't know how you did it, but I know you did." She'd paused. "Mason Jordan."

He'd come at her then with a roar that began deep in his belly. How could she know this? She was making it up. He grabbed her wrists, nearly breaking them.

"I'm right, aren't I?" she said. "But you don't have your money from that little scam, do you? That little scam backfired when your money walked out the door."

He'd known then. Lanny, the little girl who'd come and gone. She had somehow taken the money. She had it all this time.

The murders were all her fault. Barry said he was going to the police with what he knew. He had to be gotten rid of. And then, of course, he had to kill the girls. And he'd taken his father's old King James Bibles, torn out the pages in front, and placed the Bibles around the farmhouse.

But then when he went to get his money, it was gone.

"We're going on a trip," he growled at her.

"Where?"

"Back to Maine. Back to get my money. And you're going to help me this time."

79

D ear Chasco,

Hi! Remember I said I needed time to think? Well,
I've done a lot of thinking and praying and I guess, yes, it
would be nice to meet and hash over everything. I still
have lots of questions for you, but like you said, maybe if
we met in person we could talk about this. And what you
say is right. I was a fraud, too, pretending to be some
heroine in a book.

So, let's plan to meet when you're out for the conference.
We probably have more in common that we know!

I also have some news! I heard from Kim! I got an e-mail
this morning. She said she didn't have time to talk, but that
she was on her way here. She said she had a whole lot to
tell me! She's had quite an adventure, she says. I can't wait to
see her!

You know my number, call me when you get to town.

Love,
Glynis88

80

A week before everybody died, Coach told me about the money. We were weeding in the garden, and Coach called me over. Breanne and the others looked up, but didn't follow us. They all knew that Coach and I had this special friendship. He was always telling me I should just call him Barry, and not Coach. But the others called him Coach, so I did too. I always thought that was the right thing to do.

I never wore the stupid dresses the others wore. I guess I just wasn't into it as much as the others. I didn't spend my entire day memorizing *Romeo and Juliet*. I'm not an actor and have no aspirations to be one. I was just there because Coach and I were friends.

"I want to show you something," Coach said to me when we were in the kitchen. And then he opened a wall safe hidden behind a picture, and pulled out a briefcase.

"How do you know the combination?" I asked.

"He trusts me," he said. "Actually, no, that's not the reason. The reason is he thinks I'm stupid. *Simple* is the word he uses."

"That's stupid. He's the stupid one. You're the smart one."

He opened the briefcase and I stared, just stared. I'd never seen so much money. "What *is* all that?" I asked.

"Money."

"Duh! I know it's money! Where did it come from?"

"From the stupid parents of these girls who keep sending it. Snare, as he likes to be called, demands it. I heard him on the phone, 'If you want to see your daughter alive again, you'll send twenty grand to this address.'"

"Are you *kidding* me?"

"I'm not kidding you. I heard them talking. He's planning on leaving. That's why the money is all in fifties like this. He gets the checks and then changes them into fifties. He's been doing it for a couple months now."

I still couldn't quite believe it. "You mean, he's actually phoning up, like, Breanne's mother, and telling her to send twenty thousand dollars or they'll never see her again?"

"Something like that."

"I'm going to tell Breanne. I'm going to tell the others. They could just walk out of here! What's this ransom business?"

"It's a scam kidnapping, not even a real one."

"But Breanne and Jo, they write letters home all the time."

"Think about it, Lanny, who takes those letters to the post office in Bangor? Snare."

I knew Snare was a slime weasel of the first order, but I never thought he could do something like this.

"What're you going to do?" I asked.

"Turn him in. Take the money to the police."

"Right now?"

"He's going to be back soon." While he talked, he stuffed all the bundles of money into an old army backpack that had been hanging on a nail in the kitchen from before we got here. "I'm gonna hide it. I have a good place." He closed the briefcase, locked it, put it back into the wall safe, and put the picture in front of it.

"Follow me," he said.

We stopped at the top of the rise. From where we stood you could see the whole farm, the neighboring farms, and then the woods. Coach moved a rock and revealed a kind of filled-in well. Then he pulled up the brick, which exposed a space big enough for the backpack. He shoved it down in and put the moss and rocks and brick on top.

"In a few days, as soon as I can get a ride, I'm going into town to tell the police."

"You can borrow my bike."

81

Glynis?" Snare asked.

"You must be Chasco." She smiled and extended her hand. "Or I should say Charles Coburn. It's nice to meet you."

He looked straight across at her eyes as they stood next to each other at the entrance to the restaurant in Bangor. "You look a little different than the picture you sent," he said. She was his height exactly.

She patted her curly hair. "Well, it's me. In the flesh. How's the conference?"

"Oh." He looked up. "Fine. It's good." He flexed his hands at this side. Nervous. Nervous. Did she recognize him? Did he look different enough from Gil? From the last time they met?

"You look different than I expected," she said. "Of course, I never saw a real picture of you." She laughed, and it unnerved him slightly.

Control, he told himself. He grinned. "Just old pride getting in the way. I wanted to make a good impression."

"I didn't think you'd have such dark hair. And it's curly like mine."

"Well, that's me." He patted his hair, hoping that the wig hadn't gone crooked on him. "Shall we sit down?" He offered his arm, and she took it.

"Tell me about Kim," he asked. "You said you heard from her?"

"Oh," she waved her hand. "Let's not talk about her now. Later."

She looked so self-assured. He was somehow expecting someone more sniveling and vulnerable, not this tall woman who moved with confidence through the restaurant. Already he'd taken more than seven thousand dollars from her, and he was about to get more, plus find out where his money was. Were her pockets limitless? They seemed to be so. Wouldn't his father like to see him now! His father took money from stupid people who gave it to him to be healed.

304

They were given menus, and she ordered lobster and he ordered a steak. She put her hand on the table; he covered it with his own. Charm, he thought. Act. He looked around him. A man at the table next to theirs was reading a newspaper. Up at the desk, a man and a woman were talking. Did they look too much in his direction? No, he thought, he was just jumpy. It was only his imagination.

They small-talked their way through dinner. She answered his questions. Maybe they really could get married. He'd play the devoted husband for a while, then get rid of her and get all her money. He would still talk to his friend in Kennan.

At one point in the meal she got up and went to the ladies' room. Still slightly suspicious, he followed her. But she made no other stops, never acknowledged anyone, just went into the ladies' room and a few moments later came out again.

Coffee came, and he ripped open a sugar packet and the contents sprayed all over the table and onto the floor. His hands were suddenly twitching and he couldn't stop them. He was also fairly certain that if he stood up, he would stumble.

"Are you okay?" Glynis asked.

"Fine. I'm fine," he said.

Trouble was, he wasn't fine. There was that darned black spot in his vision again. Not now, he thought, not now when he needed his wits about him. He rubbed it. Still there. Ignore it, he told himself. Control. He practiced his breathing and forced his facial muscles into a kind of repose.

Glynis was eyeing him oddly. This was not going well. He adjusted his glasses, which were just clear glass. Maybe it was the glasses that had the spot. He took them off, cleaned them on the cloth napkin, and put them back on. It was still there. Getting larger.

"Tell me about Melissa," Glynis said. "I haven't heard from her in a while."

"Oh, you know how these kids are."

"Did her hospital bill ever get straightened out?"

He smiled and leaned forward. Now here was a subject he was familiar with. "Those goons are still after me, those sons of Satan who have no heart. I still get regular bills from the hospital. I still owe more than five thousand dollars."

"You still owe? Why do you still owe?"

Control, he said to himself. Wrong choice of words. "We still owe. I guess I said *I* because the case was so close to me personally." He put his hand to his heart. "That's my problem; I take things too personally."

After he paid the bill, Glynis suggested that he come to see her house. "I'll make us some tea," she said.

"Tea." He felt gleeful. As soon as he wheedled his way into Glynis's life, he'd look for that little girl who'd stolen his money. Manny or Lanny.

He followed her car to an old house and pulled into the driveway behind her. Behind her, trap her in, he thought. He whistled as he followed her in the side door into the kitchen.

"Nice place," he said. What a dump, he thought. A person with her kind of money living here? "I would think," he said, sitting down in a terribly uncomfortable chair in the living room, "that with your mother gone and all, you'd want to move into a new place, maybe a small but nice apartment somewhere, a condo, a high-rise."

"I like it here. I grew up here. Don't mind the walls, I'm redoing the place. Let me get the kettle on."

The ends of his fingers tingled, but at least his head wasn't hurting so much. And the black spot seemed to have shifted to the upper right side of his vision. Good. At least he could see now.

When she came back, he asked about Kim again. "Any more word on your friend, Kim? I'm interested."

"Oh, Kim. She's fine," Glynis said. "I can't wait to see her. She's coming over later today. Here. You want to meet her?"

His hands trembled. "What?"

"She'll be here..." Glynis made a show of checking her watch. "In an hour. She said she has lots to tell me. Are you okay, Chasco? Oh, I mean Charles? You look a little pale."

"I'm fine."

"Something's wrong with your hair."

He touched the wig, arranged it slightly. Glynis moved toward him. Something was the matter with Glynis. He couldn't put his finger on it, but something was wrong. He didn't like the way she held her hands so still. Wasn't she nervous at all?

"Tell me about your parents, Charles."

"You want to know about my parents?"

"Tell me about the fire."

"How do you know about the fire?"

"You told me all about it. Remember? We shared so much in e-mails. So much."

"I never told you about my parents."

"Of course you did. Or else how would I know? You wrote to me that they died in a fire and that you escaped, and all about how your dad got kicked out of the denomination. You told me all about it."

"I never did. I don't remember." His fingers were tingling, and he rubbed and rubbed them trying to get some blood down there. Had he told her? What else had he told her? None of this was making any sense.

"Your father sounds like a really harsh person. No wonder you did that to the dog."

He wasn't saying anything, but he rose, knocking over the tea tray. He was conscious that his knee was twitching. He stilled it. "I should leave," he said.

"Why? Where are you going?"

"Back to the conference. I need to get back." He looked toward the door, wondering if his legs would carry him there. The black spot was moving.

"You weren't at a conference."

"What?"

"There was no worship conference in Portland. I checked."

He stared at her.

"Tell me about Max Beamish."

The room was spinning. Something was very wrong. "I need to leave. I don't feel so well."

"Why did you kill him?"

"I killed him because he didn't think I would. So I had to."

"Why did you kill those girls?"

"He was going to the police. I had to stop him." He put his hands to his eyes.

"You set up the whole thing."

"I had to make it look like a cult." He held his hand tightly against his eye. "Did you like the ash on their foreheads? I got that idea from the Catholics. My father hated the Catholics."

Suddenly there were people, lots of people. And then there was another Glynis. And the Glynis he'd been with all night tore off a wig and was rubbing her head. Both tall women. And seeing them together, standing next to each other, they looked nothing alike. He realized that now.

They were grabbing his hands. He was falling, falling...

"You have the right to remain silent. Anything you say..."

It wasn't Glynis. Of course it wasn't Glynis. And if he hadn't spent so much time worrying that she would recognize him as the man she'd met before, as Gil Williamson, he would have noticed.

And his last conscious thought was, they've shot me. They've shot me through the head.

Epilogue

I'm moving," Glynis said.

"You're moving?" Teri asked.

Glynis nodded. "Thought it was about time. Too many bad memories in that place."

"Where are you moving to?"

"A place on Mount Desert."

Teri raised her eyebrows. It had been two months since Mason Jordan had fallen dead from a brain tumor–induced seizure on Glynis's living room rug. Since his death, law enforcement, with the help of Teri and Glynis and Kim and Lanny, had pieced together what happened. In total, Mason Jordan had murdered eight people and killed two dogs. As before, the news media had descended on Bangor with a fury. After it was over, Teri retreated to her new log house and didn't answer the phone for a month.

But in that time, Glynis had been seen in the company of Martin Monday on more than one occasion. And they looked stunning together, both tall and beautiful people.

"Some special reason for that location?"

Teri and Glynis were sitting on wooden chairs on the front porch of Teri's new log house. It was a rare warm day for October.

"I've quit the law firm and I'm going to work for Andrea," she said.

"That's great, Glynis."

"We're opening a shop in Bar Harbor for the summer tourists."

"And any other reason for moving there, may I ask?"

Glynis blushed and pushed back her hair with her hand. She'd gotten it cut quite short in a curly style that flattered her. Also, the gray was gone. She looked years younger, although that could have been the light in her eyes.

"I'm glad you're happy," Teri said. "You deserve it. And it's so great that Kim is back."

"Yes, it is."

After Mason died, the problem of where Kim was still remained. Some thought she was still in Texas. Others thought she might be anywhere in the southwest. The items in the box of money were tested for her fingerprints, and when they were determined to match ones found at Max Beamish's house, police concentrated their efforts in Texas. But they couldn't find her.

It was a Maine lobsterman who eventually reported seeing an SOS signal. He noticed it one night when he was late getting home with his traps. It looked high, and on land, and for several minutes he peered at it before calling the Coast Guard. The Coast Guard called the police, and Kim was found in the basement of a mansion belonging to murdered industrialist Max Beamish.

Kim was reunited with Glynis and with Lanny, who also became a part of the story. She'd been living at a rooming house in Bangor, but when she could, rode her bike out to the farmhouse and paid tribute to her friends who'd died there. As for the money, it was divided equally between the families of Mason's King James Murder victims, including Barry Shock. Susan was going to build a new greenhouse.

Kim was able to clear up a lot of questions. No, she told the police adamantly, she had not written those e-mails. "I never use that many exclamation points!"

"So, where on Mount Desert are you going?" Teri asked. Down below by the river, Elizabeth and Irving were walking their dogs.

"I've bought the place that used to belong to Max Beamish."

Teri choked on her iced tea, opened her eyes wide, and stared. *"That* place? You bought *that* place?"

"For a while. Until I can get something smaller."

Teri's eyes were wide as saucers. "What do you mean, until you can get something smaller?"

"When the guest house is ready, I'm going to live there. Marty says it'll be ready soon. He's building a beautiful studio facing the water, where I'll sew. The apartment Kim was kept in for so long? It's going to become a storage place. Marty already tore out the door."

Then she paused and leaned back. "And then I want to turn the big house into a hospice care center, a place where people can go to die with dignity and love and care. Instead of having to..." Her eyes clouded. She blinked a few times. "And not cost a bundle, either. Especially that. Kim is drawing up papers and helping me plan it. Those are my dreams, Teri. There they are. That's what I'm planning."

Discussion Guide

1. Which character in *Chat Room* did you most closely identify with? Why? Which character did you least identify with? Why?

2. Do you ever feel lonely in church? Explain the circumstances. What did you do about it? What could you have done differently?

3. Are there people in your church that you know are lonely? Is there something you can do for them?

4. Near the end of the book, Pastor Ken says that Internet churches are as harmful as Internet pornography. What do you suppose made him make such a statement? Do you agree or disagree? Why?

5. How much time would you say you spend on the Internet? Do you have Internet friends that you have never met? Where do you have more people that you dialogue daily with, on the Internet or in person?

6. When Glynis's e-mail is down for an evening, she doesn't know what to do. How do you (would you) feel when (if) your e-mail is (were) down for an evening? A day? A whole week?

7. Do you find yourself relying on television, movies, or the Internet for your entertainment? Glynis turns on the television automatically each evening just for company. Do you ever find yourself doing this?

8. Daniel 12:4 says, "But you, Daniel, close up and seal the words of the scroll until the time of the end. Many will go here and there to increase knowledge." This could refer to activities such as our use of Google and other search engines to get "knowledge." What are some advantages of this? What are some disadvantages?

9. How do you vet or confirm the information you get from the web? How do you know if what you see is true?
10. *Chat Room* looks at Internet dating. How do you feel this affects people around you?

THE COLD ATLANTIC OCEAN SWALLOWS OLD SECRETS

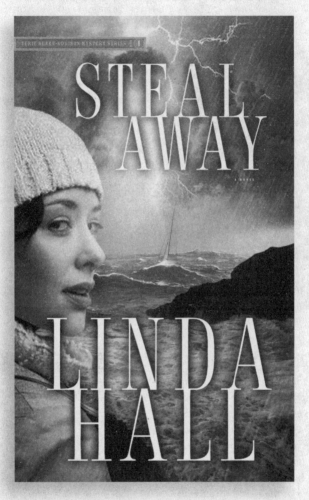

Dr. Carl Houseman, celebrated minister and speaker, is determined to find out what really happened to his wife, declared dead five years ago after her sailboat washed ashore on a coastal island of Maine. Private investigator Teri Blake-Addison must piece together the life of this woman who felt she didn't know or understand the God that her husband so faithfully served. Did Ellen really die in those cold Atlantic waters? When a murder rocks the island, Teri knows more is at stake than just the puzzling life of an unhappy minister's wife.

ISBN 1-59052-072-6

MORE GREAT FICTION FROM LINDA HALL

SADIE'S SONG

Children are disappearing in a New England fishing village, and a wife suspects her abusive husband may know why. Are her own children safe? Should she tell her pastor of her fear?

ISBN 1-57673-659-8

ISLAND OF REFUGE

Naomi and Zoe are distraught as police begin an extensive investigation of a friend's death. In a different state, Margot begins her own investigation. What she discovers shatters her to her core and intertwines the lives of the island dwellers as they seek to make peace with themselves, their lives, and God.

ISBN 1-57673-397-1

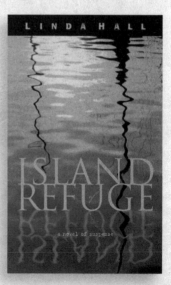

KATHERYN'S SECRET

While investigating a long-unsolved murder, mystery writer Sharon Colebrook and her husband, Jeff, find unexpected secrets, startling revelations, and dangerous truths within her own family tree.

ISBN 1-57673-614-8

MARGARET'S PEACE

Margaret returns to her family home on the Maine coast in hopes of finding peace and the God she has lost. Instead, she must relive the death of her sister and face long-buried secrets.

ISBN 1-57673-216-9

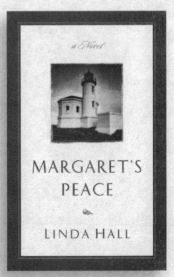

www.letstalkfiction.com